Roundabout
Revenge

Robert Archibald

Cactus Mystery Press
An imprint of Blue Fortune Enterprises, LLC

ROUNDABOUT REVENGE
Copyright © 2019 by Robert Archibald.

All rights reserved. Printed in the United States of America. No part of this book may be used or reproduced in any manner whatsoever without written permission except in the case of brief quotations embodied in critical articles or reviews.

This book is a work of fiction. Names, characters, businesses, organizations, places, events and incidents either are the product of the author's imagination or are used fictitiously. Any resemblance to actual persons, living or dead, events, or locales is entirely coincidental.

For information contact :
Blue Fortune Enterprises, LLC
Cactus Mystery Press
P.O. Box 554
Yorktown, VA 23690
http://blue-fortune.com

Book and Cover design by Wesley Miller, WAMCreate, wamcreate.co

ISBN: 978-1-948979-21-4

First Edition: August 2019

Acknowledgements

Roundabout Revenge is a work of fiction. Any resemblance between the characters in the book and anyone I've known or met is a complete coincidence.

The book benefited from the efforts of many friends who read drafts and gave useful comments. The list is long. In alphabetical order, I would like to thank: Brian Archibald (my son), David Archibald (my brother), Emily Archibald (my daughter), Fred Lederer, Kirk Lovenberry, Peter Stipe, James Thompson, and Rich Watkins.

Special thanks should go to Narielle Living, who gave the book a deft final edit.

Finally, I would like to thank my wife Nancy, for editing, for love, and for support. I couldn't have accomplished anything without her.

Dedication

This book is dedicated to my newly arrived granddaughter Elizabeth Rose Archibald.

~ *1* ~

MARY JANE PHILEMON MADE THE right turn off Main Street onto 76 and headed out of town. She was anxious to get to the airport in Henderson. She always looked forward to her husband Phil's return from his conferences. Mary Jane could cope without Phil, but life was so much better when she was with her true love. She thought it was Dr. Brown's car a couple of blocks ahead of her. She wondered how long the 75-year-old would continue working at the hospital. He was already almost deaf. His car weaved over the center lane. *It might be time for him to stop driving*, she thought. She was behind Dr. Brown when the light turned green, and he made the right turn onto Anderson Road. As Mary Jane entered the intersection, she slowed. *Just check to make sure he made the turn okay.* When she glanced back to her left, a giant truck barreled down on her.

~~~

Phil Philemon waited patiently as the passengers seated ahead of him shuffled off the plane. The puddle jumper from Pittsburgh to Henderson was small. Even at a half inch under six feet, he had to duck as he went down the aisle. Phil waited at the bottom of the stairs to retrieve his carry-on, then made his way across the tarmac to the terminal.

His wife, Mary Jane, wasn't there to greet him, which surprised him.

In the past, she'd always been on time. Phil looked around the small newsstand—no Mary Jane. He wasn't too concerned. Lots of things could have held her up. As an operating room nurse, there could have been an emergency surgery. Also, the road between Lackey and Henderson, though only twenty miles long, was narrow and winding. She could easily be stuck behind a slow truck. He sat down and decided to read one of the papers he'd picked up at the conference.

He finished the paper and put it in his briefcase. He didn't like it. It had nothing original to say. He glanced at his watch. *Twenty minutes late. This isn't like her at all.*

While he wasn't a complete Luddite, Phil had resisted getting a cell phone, although one would have come in handy in this situation. He suspected the airport still had a pay phone somewhere, so he set off to find one. The pay phone wasn't too difficult to locate. When he stood in front of the thing, he discovered he didn't have any change. He always got rid of change before going through airport security.

A trek back to the newsstand and one candy bar later, he dialed the hospital. "No, Mary Jane isn't here." The operator remembered saying goodbye to her about two hours ago. Next, he dialed his home. The phone rang until the voice mail picked up. He left a short message.

Phil began to worry. Mary Jane had been late on other occasions. Once a short shopping trip had taken much longer than expected. He'd been extremely worried by the time she'd returned three hours late. After that episode, they'd vowed to always phone if they were going to be late. Since he didn't have a cell phone, there was no way for her to follow through now. He checked his watch again. *Thirty-five minutes late.* He began to tense. He decided to sit and try to calm down. Airports were good places to people watch.

It didn't work. The Henderson airport seemed almost deserted. He checked. There were no more departures and only one other arrival coming from Philly and scheduled an hour after his plane. Too nervous to sit, he took a tour of the terminal and even went outside.

After five minutes outside, he went back in and flopped down in a chair. What now? She was now forty-five minutes late. *Where is she?*

He got up and went to the restroom. Nervous energy he expected. As he washed his hands, he looked at himself in the mirror. His blue eyes looked back at him. He didn't like the way his hair looked. The race between balding and graying made it look funny. At least he'd been able to keep his weight down. Getting this close to sixty with the associated sagging did not look good if you were overweight.

He didn't see Mary Jane after he emerged from the restroom, so Phil decided to call his best friend Jeremy Terrell. Jeremy might be able to find Mary Jane. Phil needed more coins. This time he only asked for change; one candy bar was enough.

He got Jeremy on the phone and explained his predicament. Jeremy said he'd see what he could find out. He told Phil, "I wouldn't worry. Sometimes 76 is slow. There could have been an accident. I'll find out what's going on. Give me a call on my cell phone when she shows up."

~~~

Jeremy shook his head. His colleague and friend, Phil, was often scattered. He'd probably told Mary Jane the wrong day or time. He gave the Philemon home phone a call and hung up on the answering machine. Phil was such a technological incompetent—no cell phone, but at least he had an answering machine. Jeremy decided to take a spin around town. The small town of Lackey boasted only a little over 4,000 people. Mary Jane's red Toyota Prius should be easy to spot.

He drove by the movie theater and Andy's restaurant where he knew Mary Jane and the other nurses often went after shifts. No red Prius. As he drove past the intersection of Main Street and Route 76, he saw flashing lights to the north. Mary Jane had to take 76. Maybe something happened to hold up traffic.

At the intersection of 76 and Anderson Road, a policeman directed traffic. Shards of glass sparkled in the intersection. Off to one side, a hook and chain tow truck loaded a smashed-up car onto its back. A big pickup truck with a dented front end sat to the side, waiting to be towed away. Jeremy winced; the smashed-up car was red. He pulled over, parked, and headed toward the policeman in the intersection, Frank Thomas. It had to be either Frank or Miguel Torres, the two youngest members of the Lackey police force. They usually drew the evening shift.

After Frank waved a truck through the intersection, he motioned for Jeremy to join him. "It was a bad one, Councilman Terrell. The lady in the red car over there didn't stand a chance. The pickup was so much bigger. He t-boned her right on the driver's door. She was dead before anyone could reach her."

"What kind of car is it?" Jeremy asked, panic spreading in his voice.

"One of those hybrids, a Prius, you know the one the nurse from over at the hospital drives." Taking out his notebook, he continued, "Mary Jane Philemon, 201 Harcourt Street. The ambulance has already taken her body away."

"Oh God. That's my friend's wife. He's stuck at the Henderson airport waiting for her. Do you know whose pickup it was?"

"Yep, we know it. It belongs to Jake McMahan. When we got here, he'd taken off. Miguel has gone over to the McMahan house. You know, the big house a couple of blocks down Anderson. We had to go back to the station to get the other cruiser. I bet Miguel finds Jake, and I bet he'll be drunk as a skunk."

Before Jeremy could leave, Frank stopped him. "You say he's at the Henderson airport?"

"Yes," answered Jeremy.

"Look, Councilman Terry, the next thing I've got to do after I finish up here is the notification of the next of kin. Could you do it for me?"

Jeremy couldn't think of a reason to say no. "Okay." He walked to his car in a daze. He didn't know how to proceed. After sitting in his car thinking for a few minutes, Jeremy made a decision. He headed to the house of Margaret O'Brien, the president of Lackey College. Lackey, where both he and Phil were history professors, was a small place. The president knew each of the faculty members. Old timers like Jeremy and Phil were friends. Margaret would know what to do.

The president's house sat back from the street, a big, sprawling structure. It took Jeremy a minute to figure out which entrance to use. He rang the doorbell and waited. Nathan, Margaret's husband, answered the door. Jeremy didn't know Nathan well, so he introduced himself and gave a brief description of the situation. Nathan ushered him in yelling for Margaret to come quickly. Jeremy repeated the news to Margaret.

"Poor Phil," Margaret said, "He's waiting at the airport? And he doesn't have a cell phone?"

"No, no cell phone. Maybe it's for the best. I don't think we should break this over the phone."

"I guess not. Come on Nathan, we're going to have to get to the Henderson airport as fast as we can."

Jeremy had always liked Margaret's decisiveness. It was on full display as they hustled to the garage and fired up the big SUV. They didn't talk much as Nathan drove.

~~~

At the airport, Phil was frantic. *What had happened?* Mary Jane was an hour and three quarters late. The flight from Philly had disgorged its passengers. They were all gone now. He seemed to be the only one still there. He tried phoning his house again. No reply. And he didn't get a reply on either of Jeremy's phones. *Where could Mary Jane be? Where was Jeremy? What could have gone wrong? Would he be stuck at the airport all night?* He prided himself on being calm and rational. At the moment, he was having trouble being either.

When Margaret, Jeremy, and Nathan came in, Phil knew they weren't there with good news. "Where is she? What happened?" Phil almost shouted as he rushed up to them.

Margaret said, "Let's sit down. We have bad news for you."

Phil looked at Jeremy, who gestured to the row of seats by Phil's suitcase. After they sat, Margaret said, "Mary Jane has been in a car accident."

"Is she all right?" interrupted Phil.

"No Phil. No, she's not. I'm afraid Mary Jane did not survive the crash."

Phil broke down sobbing. Margaret reached out and put her arm around him. She motioned to Jeremy and Nathan to come close. They all held their friend as best they could. After a long while, the others backed away, and Phil looked up. "How?" he croaked.

Jeremy answered. "The truck was traveling fast. It was a direct hit. The policeman said she was dead before anyone could reach her."

"Where did it happen?" It didn't really matter. Still, for some reason, Phil wanted to know.

"At the intersection of 76 and Anderson. You know, the last stoplight north of town."

Phil nodded. "I guess you'd better take me home." He was surprised he could function at all. *Maybe this is what it's like to be in shock.* What would he do without Mary Jane? She was his best friend, his only love, and his almost constant companion. His life revolved around her. What was he going to do?

Nathan picked up Phil's briefcase and suitcase, and they all trooped out to the car. Phil got in the back with Jeremy. There didn't seem to be anything to say, so no one spoke. When they pulled up in front of Phil's house, Jeremy said, "I'll take your 211 class tomorrow. Don't worry about it."

Margaret added, "Yes, don't worry about anything at school. We'll cover for you. And you know we all want to help in any way we can. Please let us help."

Phil got out of the car and wheeled his suitcase toward the front door. It was dark. Mary Jane hadn't left the porch light on; normally they would have come through the garage. He fumbled trying to insert the key. When he finally got the key to work, he turned and waved to Margaret and the men. As he entered, he realized the house would always seem empty to him. Suddenly, he was very hungry. He hadn't had dinner, only a candy bar since lunch. He and Mary Jane had planned to stay in Henderson for dinner. He opened the refrigerator. There it was, staring him in the face—her yogurt: lemon, and his yogurt: strawberry.

~ 2 ~

AFTER A SLEEPLESS NIGHT, PHIL recognized he had to function. He had to find things to do. Knowing he coped better when he had a project, he made a list. *Maybe I can get through the day.* So, what do you do when someone dies? Call the next of kin, call the funeral home, write an obituary, arrange for a memorial service. There would be no burial. Mary Jane wanted her ashes scattered in the Lackey College forest. Phil wasn't sure he could accomplish everything on his list.

First, though, he had to find out more about the accident. Mary Jane's sister, Martha, would want to know. He expected Martha and Jerry and probably their two kids would come to the memorial service. He'd also have to call his Uncle Morris, his father's younger brother, who now lived in a nursing home. Then there were Mary Janes relatives in Panama. Her grandmother was still alive, but at 95 she couldn't hear over the telephone. He would call Enrique, Mary Jane's uncle.

Phil looked out the window at the downpour. *How appropriate.* He got an umbrella and headed for the garage. He was in luck; a parking space was close to the police station. Phil didn't know the chief, Bill Richardson, but had seen him around town. Richardson, right out of central casting, was a big, red-faced man who looked like he'd consumed plenty of donuts.

After Phil introduced himself, the chief expressed his sympathy for Phil's loss. "Accidents like this don't happen very often in Lackey. This one was a real tragedy. And I'm sorry about how Frank handled the notification. I reamed him out. We should have done it."

Phil was confused. "My friend Jeremy—you know Jeremy Terrell, he's on the city council—he came to the Henderson airport and told me. It was fine."

"Good, so what can I do for you?"

"I don't know any details about the accident. I'm going to have to contact my wife's sister. I don't know what else I have to do. There must be something else. Where's the body?"

"The body's at the funeral home."

"I should have guessed. Now, what can you tell me about the accident?"

"Oh, I'm sorry. I guess Councilman Terrell didn't give you the details. Come to think of it, there isn't much to tell. The accident was at the intersection of 76 and Anderson. Your wife was killed instantly when the McMahan pickup slammed into her driver's side door."

"Wait," Phil interrupted, "the McMahan pickup?"

"Yes, the pickup was driven by Jake McMahan, you know, the son of Samuel McMahan who used to own the mill."

"I think I know who Jake is. Doesn't he have a reputation as a heavy drinker?" Phil got louder. "Was he drunk? Was my wife killed by a lousy drunk driver?"

"Calm down, Professor Philemon. We have the situation under control. Yes, Jake had been drinking. In fact, he did not stick around after the crash. He walked home. His airbag worked, and there wasn't a scratch on him. Officer Torres found him at the McMahan house. The breathalyzer test showed an alcohol level well above the legal limit. He's in the cell out back as we speak. We're waiting for the district attorney to get here to formally charge him. I expect he'll be charged with leaving the scene of the accident and DUI. It's quite possible he'll be charged with vehicular manslaughter."

Agitated, Phil raised his voice. "He killed my wife! He damn well better be charged with more than vehicular manslaughter! It's out-and-out murder when a drunk gets into a giant pickup and rams into a smaller car."

"I know you're upset, Professor. Don't worry, we'll handle it. There is nothing anyone can do now. The wheels of justice are moving. We'll make Jake McMahan pay for what he did."

"Be sure you do," Phil said as he got up abruptly. He'd learned all he could at the police station. For some reason Phil couldn't put his finger on, the reassurances of the police chief weren't so reassuring.

Chief Richardson stopped him. "Don't leave just yet. We need to do a formal identification of the body. Can you come with me to the funeral home?"

"Huh, you know it was my wife," Phil said.

"Yes, but there are formalities. Look, it won't take long. Can you come with me to the funeral home? We can walk over right now."

Phil walked beside the police chief in silence. Main Street was quiet, which was good. Phil wasn't up to seeing anyone.

Phil didn't like funeral homes, and he tried to avoid going to funerals. He cringed as he entered the flower-scented front room. The police chief was well known, and an attendant led the two men into the back room. A sheet covered a body on a table. Phil didn't want to follow, but he knew he had to.

The chief went over to the table, checking to see if Phil followed. When Phil got beside him, he lifted the sheet. Phil gasped and turned away when he saw Mary Jane's face. Chief Richardson replaced the sheet and said, "That's your wife, Mary Jane Philemon?"

All the breath left his body. "Yes," he stammered.

"I'm sorry to do this, Professor, but we have to."

Phil just nodded as they left the room.

"I'll leave you here with Barbara, she can tell you about the details."

Phil was numb. "Okay."

Barbara, the funeral home lady, knew how to deal with people in grief. She spoke very slowly and clearly. Actually, the details were easy. He knew Mary Jane wanted to be cremated. Phil felt a little callous saying, "Whatever's cheapest." Luckily, he and Mary Jane had talked it over. She'd been emphatic; too many people spend too much money on burials.

After the paperwork, Phil walked back to his car carrying a folder from the funeral home. When he got home, everything seemed so normal. Still, it wasn't and never would be. Mary Jane was gone. He suddenly felt very tired. He wasn't used to taking naps. Today it seemed the only thing to do. He went right to sleep on the empty bed.

Phil woke after an hour and a half. He didn't feel refreshed, but his stomach rumbled in hunger. He fixed himself a grilled cheese sandwich and had one of his yogurts. Now he had to get back to his list. He went to Mary Jane's desk where she kept the out-of-town phone numbers. He didn't know what hours Martha kept. She was the bookkeeper for her husband Jerry's big ranch. There was only one number in Mary Jane's files, so he dialed it.

"Big G Ranch," Martha answered cheerily.

"Martha, it's Phil. I don't how to tell you this, but I have really bad news."

"Oh no."

He plowed ahead. "Last night Mary Jane was in an auto accident. A big pickup slammed right into her driver's side door. She didn't have a chance. She died before anyone could get to her. I had been at the airport in Henderson waiting for her to come pick me up. I didn't even hear about it until a couple of hours after it happened... Gosh, I'm rattling on. You don't care about where I was."

"That's okay Phil, I understand. It's an awful lot to take in. My little sister, dead! What can I do?"

"I don't know yet. Tell Jerry and the kids. I'll call Enrique. There'll be a memorial service. I don't know when or anything. I expect you'll want to come. Also, come to think of it, there are pieces of Lopez furniture you should have. Our wills say everything goes to the surviving spouse. I know Mary Jane would want you to have the chest, the two chairs, and the end table. They came from your parents' house."

"Phil, we can handle the details later. I'm so sorry for your loss. I know it's a lot to cope with now. Try to rest. God bless you."

Martha had been great. Still, it was one of the most difficult phone calls Phil had ever made. He wandered around the house aimlessly. Signs of Mary Jane were everywhere, but she wouldn't be there again.

~ 3 ~

PHIL LAY ON THE BED again. This time sleep didn't come. He started to think about Mary Jane. He had a vivid memory of the first time he saw her. Though he hadn't known it at the time, he had been sent to an Army hospital in Hawaii. He heard her before he saw her. She said, "Look, this one is starting to come around." He opened his eyes to see what must have been an angel peering down at him. She was beautiful, light brown skin, brown eyes, full red lips, and darkish red hair, auburn, he supposed, and the brightest smile.

"Welcome to the waking world, soldier."

"Where am I?" he croaked.

"You're in Hawaii, in the Army hospital, and we're glad to see you awake."

"I got shot."

"You sure did, in the left calf. The bullet broke your tibia. And then you had two surgeries, one to set the bone in Viet Nam and one here to remove a few bone fragments. You've been out for several days. I think the medic in Viet Nam gave you too much morphine. We kept you asleep for the surgeries."

Phil remembered getting shot while walking along the dike on a rice paddy. His company had been shot at several times before, typically by a guy with one magazine and little ability to aim his weapon. When they heard shots, they'd all dive down and return fire. Phil knew they didn't have the faintest idea what they were shooting at. They were trying to get the other guy to run for cover.

This time was different. He was hit, and it hurt like hell. He had fallen down screaming. A moment later, the medic rushed over and jabbed him with something, morphine, if the beautiful nurse was right. Phil didn't remember anything after the injection.

The nurse checked his vital signs, sticking a thermometer in his mouth, taking his blood pressure, and checking his pulse. After the thermometer came out, the nurse went to write down the results. After completing her notes, she came back to his bedside, grabbed his right hand, and asked, "Can you feel that?"

"Yes." He sure could.

She repeated the procedure with his left hand and his right ankle. She avoided his left ankle, covered by a big cast. "All things considered, you're in good shape, Private."

He wanted to keep her attention as long as possible, so he asked, "Am I going to recover? Will I ever walk again?"

"Yes, you're young, and you were in good condition when you got shot. While you have the cast, you'll have to be on crutches. After that the physical therapy people will have you walking on your own in no time."

He managed to ask her name. "Mary Jane Lopez," she said as she gave his shoulder a friendly pat and readied to leave.

"Come see me again," he said as she left. He remembers feeling like he sounded extremely needy.

Needy or not, she came back often. Clearly, part of it was her job as a nurse in the post-op ward, but part of it was more substantial. They could talk easily. They both came from small towns. She was from a very little place in Iowa. Her dad, from Panama, was the local doctor. Her mother had grown up in another small town in Iowa. Mary Jane wanted desperately to leave Iowa, and Army nursing seemed like a good way out.

Mary Jane thought Phil was odd—a college graduate who was an enlisted troop. He explained officers signed up for three years. Two years as a draftee was a shorter hitch. It would get him to graduate school faster, exactly what he wanted.

When he got transferred to a different ward, he navigated halls of the hospital on his crutches to visit her on breaks. They started to "date" then. First, they went to movies on base. When he became more proficient with his crutches, they went off base. They visited Honolulu. As small-town people, they found the city fascinating. They were amazed at many of the same things.

Phil didn't believe the romance would last, as much as he wanted it to. The Army was not going to want to keep him, an infantry soldier who walked with a pronounced limp after the cast came off. The doctors told him the limp would eventually go away. Still, he wasn't fit to go back to any infantry unit. Right before his discharge from the hospital, he got orders to report to Oakland to be processed out.

As Phil got ready to board the plane to the mainland, he and Mary Jane said a tearful goodbye. They both promised to write. Phil remembered wondering if a long-distance relationship could last.

He went home to Apadoca, Arizona. He didn't like Apadoca. His father had uprooted the family from Hershey, Pennsylvania when Phil was twelve. Phil liked Hershey, and his dad loved his job at the chocolate factory. His dad idolized Milton Hershey, the founder of the town. Phil was actually named Milton after Mr. Hershey. When Phil's dad did not receive an anticipated promotion, he started looking and found a job at the copper mine.

Apadoca was a hole, literally a hole. The open pit copper mine came right to the edge of town. The mine had actually swallowed a couple of houses. Because of the mine, it was always dusty. The dust didn't stay outside. It seeped into every corner of the house, making his mother furious. Often it was extraordinarily hot, and there wasn't much to do. Apadoca was close to the middle of nowhere. And even if you could get away to somewhere, somewhere was only Phoenix.

Although glad to see his parents and a couple of his high school classmates, Phil didn't want to stay long. Because his dad was a big shot in the mine, Phil got a desk job in the purchasing department. Though not thrilling, the pay was good. He wrote to Mary Jane every day and applied to almost every history PhD program in the US. Three months after his release from the Army, he got a letter admitting him to the history program at the University of Wisconsin. He was thrilled.

Despite the expense of long-distance, he called Mary Jane, happy to hear her voice. She was thrilled for him. He remembered her saying, "Wisconsin is almost Iowa."

He left for Wisconsin well before the start of classes. Upon arrival, he fell in love with Madison. The town was beautiful, and the university was so impressive. After living in Arizona for so long Phil loved the idea of a university beside a big lake. The large university had close to 30,000 students. Lackey College, where he'd been an undergrad, had about 800 students. It was only a little bigger now. Wisconsin dwarfed Lackey.

Phil's stomach fluttered on the first day of classes. He hadn't had many academic thoughts as a soldier and questioned his ability to take notes. He worked very hard. Despite the demanding classwork, he still corresponded faithfully with Mary Jane. He was overjoyed when she told him she'd come up from Iowa for the second week of her leave.

It was great having Mary Jane in Madison. She was even more beautiful than he remembered. She was a big hit with his graduate school colleagues. Phil was sure they wondered how he got such a good-looking girlfriend.

You could have knocked Phil over with a feather when, on the third day of her visit, Mary Jane asked, "Where do you think this is going?"

"Gosh, a long way, I hope. A long way," he answered, startled.

"Me too."

It got complicated then. Neither of them remembered a formal proposal. Still, from then on, they knew they were going to get married. They made it official a couple of days later. Phil used up a good chunk of his money from the job at the mine on a diamond ring. The wedding occurred six months later, right after Mary Jane got out of the Army.

Wait, the ring! Mary Jane always put her rings on after she finished in the operating room. She would have had her rings on when she drove to pick him up.

Phil leapt out of the bed and hurried to the car. He drove to the funeral home. As he opened the door, he almost knocked over Barbara, the lady he'd spoken to earlier. Hurriedly, he said, "I'm Mr. Philemon, I was here this morning. I have a question; what do you do with jewelry?"

"Oh, you mean in a case like your wife—when there's an accident?"

"Yes, I suppose most times people have a chance to remove any jewelry."

"I'm so sorry. Of course, we save any jewelry. I was supposed to give it to you this morning. You were in such a hurry. We decided to give it to you when you came to pick up the ashes."

"I'm here now. Is it easy to get the jewelry?"

"Sure, sure, excuse me," she said as she hustled into the interior of the funeral home. She came back a few minutes later with a small bag.

Phil looked in the bag. It contained Mary Jane's engagement ring, her wedding ring, and a necklace. He looked up and said, "Thank you so much. It's nice to have these things."

When he got back home with his little bag, a car sat in front of his house. Phil recognized it as Jeremy Terrell's Audi. Phil always felt a little inferior in his VW. His Passat was bigger than the A4. Still, it was a VW not an Audi. As Phil went to meet them, he could see the Terrells were holding pots.

"Beef Stroganoff and salad," Linda said. She handed a pot to Jeremy and gave Phil a hug. "We're so sorry. Mary Jane was such a wonderful person. I'll miss her terribly." She had tears in her eyes.

Phil invited them in, put the dinner in the refrigerator, and joined them in the living room. An awkward silence settled around them. Phil filled it. "Did you know the pickup belonged to Jake McMahan?"

"Yes, I did. I knew last night. Frank, you know, the young guy on the police force, told me. I didn't think it was an important detail last night."

"And he was drunk!" Phil surprised himself because he sounded loud and angry.

"Yes, Frank guessed he was drunk. I didn't know for sure."

"I went to the police station this morning, and the chief said they had Jake in one of the cells. He's probably going to be charged with vehicular manslaughter. I hope they do, at least that! Driving drunk in a great big pickup! He's just fine, but Mary Jane's dead."

Jeremy did not have any response and Linda didn't either.

Phil finally spoke up somewhat sheepishly. "I guess I'm not very good company right now."

Linda responded, "No, no. It's such a shock. We're all really down. I don't know how you're holding it together."

"I called Mary Jane's sister and broke the news to her. It was no fun."

The Terrells edged toward the door. Jeremy said, "Let us know what we can do. Don't worry, we'll take care of your classes. There's only a week of classes left; we can handle it."

Phil remembered his list. "Wait, wait. There's one thing I'll need help with. I have to write an obituary. The funeral home gave me samples. Can you come over tomorrow afternoon and help me write it?"

Jeremy and Linda nodded energetically. Jeremy added, "I'll see if Sally Joins can come along too. It might be good to have the editor of the paper as a helper."

"Good idea," replied Phil. A few moments later he waved goodbye to his friends. As he walked back toward the kitchen, he wondered why he had been so weird with Jeremy and Linda. It wasn't their fault Jake McMahan had run into Mary Jane. He got a bit freaky when he thought about Jake.

~ *4* ~

A WEEK LATER, PHIL WOKE to sounds downstairs. He had finally become used to the house being still. Now he could hear noises from the kitchen. Martha must be fixing breakfast. He got up, showered, shaved, swallowed his morning pills, and dressed. In the kitchen, he saw Martha had cooked him a breakfast of French toast.

Phil enjoyed having Martha there more than he'd anticipated. It was funny. Martha didn't look at all like Mary Jane. Martha was almost six feet tall. Mary Jane was half a foot shorter. They had the same coloring. On closer inspection, he could see a faint family resemblance.

This morning at ten a.m. Linda Terrell and Mary Jane's nurse friend Beth were coming to go through Mary Jane's things. In anticipation of leaving shortly after the women arrived, Phil gathered up Mary Jane's computer. A couple of months ago they'd tired of sharing the same computer, so they'd bought two new ones. Phil didn't see any reason to keep Mary Jane's laptop. He thought he could take it back to Ralph's store where they'd bought it.

At five after ten the doorbell rang, and Linda and Beth stood at the door. Phil introduced them to Martha.

"I'm going to leave while you do this. Feel free to take any of her clothes, and Linda and Beth can decide where to take left-over stuff.

Also, except for the two rings, you can decide what to do with the jewelry."

"I think I'll take a couple of her cute uniforms," Beth said. "If I can get rid of twenty pounds, they should fit. The uniforms can be my challenge clothes, you know the ones you keep trying until they finally fit."

Phil wondered if it wasn't more like thirty pounds Beth needed to lose. Such thoughts were better left unsaid. He grabbed the laptop and its cords and headed out the door.

He made the short drive to Ralph Williams's store. Phil had always liked Ralph and seen him as a smart guy who had worked very hard to make a go of his computer-repair/sales store. He hadn't always been such a hard worker. When Ralph was a student at Lackey, Phil had bailed him out by providing a summer school independent study Ralph needed for graduation. They'd been friends ever since. He and Mary Jane had Ralph over for dinner often. The social life for a thirty something in Lackey wasn't great.

When Phil arrived, Ralph and his assistant, a Lackey student named Jim Simmons, were behind the counter. They were an odd pair. Ralph was a short, slightly tubby blond with a round face. Jim was well over six feet tall and had dark hair and complexion. Jim's experiment with facial hair showed little success. Phil remembered Ralph kidding him by accusing him of having a "football mustache... you know, eleven on a side." Neither of them seemed to be doing anything when Phil opened the door.

"Phil, it's great to see you," Ralph said, coming around the counter and grabbing Phil's hand. "I'm so sorry about Mary Jane. It's awful!"

"Thank you," Phil responded. He held up the laptop computer and asked, "Think you can sell this?"

Ralph took the computer from Phil. "Why don't you come to the back room so we can talk? Jim can mind the store."

Phil followed Ralph to the back room. He had always found the room amazing. The bins attached to the walls were stuffed with what looked like random computer parts. A work bench held three computers sitting with their guts exposed. As far as Phil could tell, it was an exercise in chaos. They sat in two chairs in the back.

"So, what do you want me to do with this?" Ralph asked, holding up the computer.

"I want you to sell it. I have my new computer. I don't have any use for it."

"I can't. It wouldn't be right for me to make money because of your wife's death. It's your computer; you should sell it. You could get quite a bit for it on eBay."

"I don't know the first thing about how to sell stuff on eBay. I want you to sell it. We bought it here. You can vouch for its quality."

Ralph looked concerned. "Phil, I don't think you understand. It isn't right for you to give me the computer. I buy computers and fix them up before I sell them. People don't just give me computers."

After a moment's thought, Phil had an idea. "Okay, look, what if I use you like a consignment store? I'll give you the computer, you sell it. We'll split the proceeds. Then I'm not giving you the computer, and I don't have to figure out how to use eBay or mess with it in any way."

"Okay. It's not normal. It's a special case." After a moment, he added, "I'll have to wipe the hard drive. You're sure there's nothing you want to keep?"

"No, there's nothing."

Ralph set the computer on the desk and stared at Phil. "How are you doing?"

Phil was surprised by the serious look on Ralph's face. "All right, I think. It was such a shock. You never think anything like that'll happen to you."

"But how's it affecting you?"

"It's hard, an odd combination of big things and little things. Sleeping alone in the bed is hard. Often, I don't get a good night's sleep. Everything in the house reminds me of her. I think of things I want to tell her, and she's not there. We were close; we shared so much."

"Are you getting enough to eat?"

"Too much. The ladies at the church seem to have a rotation set up. Each day food appears. My refrigerator is stuffed with leftovers. I wish they'd stop. Martha threw out the excess food as soon as she got here. They'll probably stop after the memorial service. It's the day after tomorrow."

"Yeah, I know. I'll be there."

"I keep thinking about the senselessness of it all. Jake McMahan had no business being drunk behind the wheel. And driving a giant pickup truck. Those things are a menace even when the driver is sober." Phil could feel his emotions taking over. "You know, the police let him out on bail."

"He's been charged with a crime, hasn't he?"

"Yes, and I hope they throw the book at him. He should fry!"

Phil knew Ralph was taken aback by his emotional outburst.

"Have you been meeting with your lunch group?" Ralph asked.

"No. They've all asked me to come back, but I'm not quite up to it yet. I should try to go next Wednesday."

There was a brief silence. "Mary Jane's sister is here for the memorial service?"

"Yes, Martha, she came yesterday, and it's been good to have her." Phil tried to calm himself. "Her husband will be here tomorrow. He's driving one of their farm trucks. They're taking back a few pieces of furniture from Mary Jane's family."

"Anyone else coming in from out of town?"

"Yeah, this afternoon I am going to Henderson to pick up Andrew and Melissa, Martha and Jerry's two kids. It'll be good to see them. The only family I have is an uncle who lives in a nursing home. He can't make the trip. Mary Jane's other relatives are in Panama, so they're not coming."

Phil stood, and Ralph followed him out into the front of the store. "Thanks for taking the computer, and thanks for talking to me," Phil said as he walked out the door.

After Phil left, Ralph looked at Jim and said, "Poor Phil, he's in bad shape."

~~~

When Phil got to his house, Martha was the only one there. "We've finished up. Beth and Linda are taking clothes to the thrift store. There are only a couple of things I didn't know what to do with."

"What?"

"First, this," Martha said, holding up a small jeweled box from their family in Panama. "It should go back to Enrique. I already have one. I guess if we wrap it well, we could mail it."

"Good idea."

"The only other thing is this stack of books. It's got Mary Jane's high school yearbook and similar things. I wasn't sure you wanted me to get rid of them."

"I'll look at them. Thanks for saving the yearbook. I'll definitely want to keep it."

~ 5 ~

A WEEK AND A HALF after the memorial service, Phil got to the courthouse early for Jake McMahan's hearing. He'd never been in the courtroom before. It was new. Phil thought it reflected the newest design ideas. The cavernous room lacked windows. Probably a security feature. Skylights provided natural light, so it wasn't as gloomy as a big, windowless room might have been.

Only a few people were in the courtroom at any one time. Most of the business of the court was routine. He didn't know what to expect. While he'd watched quite a few crime dramas on television, it didn't appear to have been good preparation.

Phil did learn a few things. Lots of people in the county had drinking problems, and others couldn't seem to make scheduled meetings with their parole officers or on-time payments to the court. For the most part, the people in the courtroom were from two groups: young lawyers in cheap suits and working-class people from the rural parts of the county. Phil didn't see anyone he knew.

As he sat in the courtroom, Phil wondered what he wanted out of the day. He'd been pointing toward this hearing since the accident. He knew he wanted Jake McMahon punished. He knew it deep in his bones. Why? It wouldn't bring Mary Jane back. He wouldn't gain anything from it. Why was it so important to him? He was usually a calm, rational person, but he wasn't calm or rational about Jake. Maybe he needed closure. He sure hoped he'd get it.

He'd been mulling over punishment ever since his brief meeting with the assistant district attorney to discuss the possibility of Phil testifying during the sentencing portion of the trial. Phil had been firm then. He wanted Jake punished. He'd surprised himself. He'd been definite, even angry. He wasn't sure he'd made a good an impression on the guy.

There was a short recess before Jake's case. There was quite a bit of coming and going. After the recess started, Ralph Williams slid beside him on the right. A few seconds later Jeremy Terrell sat on his other side. It felt good to have his friends show up. Phil looked around at the audience. The courtroom was much fuller now. He was surprised to see Margaret O'Brien and most of his Wednesday lunch group. He nodded to them. He had a brief flashback to Mary Jane's memorial service. The church had been full—full of friends. As he turned back around, he took a breath, trying to calm his nerves. His palms were sweating. He was glad he wore a sports coat because he was sure his pits were lathered up, too.

After a brief silence, the bailiff gave the "all rise" command. The judge came in. At the same time Jake McMahan came forward to take a seat beside his lawyer. Jake was a big guy. His shirt lapped over his belt a little because he had a beer gut. Phil thought he looked like the frat boy type he'd seen in Wisconsin.

The assistant district attorney sat at the other table. The judge announced the case: "The State versus Jonathan P. McMahan." Then she called for both lawyers to approach the bench. The audience couldn't hear the muffled conversation, but at several points, it looked as if the judge was quizzing the district attorney guy who kept shaking his head. When the lawyers returned to their seats, the district attorney didn't look happy. On the other hand, Jake's lawyer looked very pleased. The judge then said, "Mr. McMahan you are charged with leaving the scene of an accident. Do you plead guilty or not guilty?"

Jake stood up. "Guilty."

The judge then sentenced Jake to pay a $5,000 fine and to serve three months of probation. "Exit by the door to the left and pay the clerk. The probation department will contact you to arrange the terms of your probation."

Phil sat back in his seat, unable to breathe. What had just happened? He leapt to his feet. "What about the other charges, DUI and vehicular manslaughter? He was drunk. He killed my wife!" Phil yelled.

"Order in the court," the judge declared as she banged her gavel.

Ralph and Jeremy tried to drag Phil down to his seat, without much success.

"I want to know what's going on here. This is a travesty! This can't be justice. What happened?" Phil turned to Jake McMahan, who'd stopped on his way out of the court, and said, "You can't get away with this. You killed my wife. I'll make you pay for it!"

"Bailiff, remove this man from the courtroom!" the judge said. "And sir, one more outburst from you, and I'll have you locked up."

Ralph and Jeremy grabbed Phil and hustled him out of the courtroom before the bailiff could get to him. Once outside, they let Phil go. Tremors coursed through his body. "What just happened? How can the case be over? There wasn't even a trial! I don't understand."

"We don't get it either. Clearly, there are things we don't know. There has to be a way to find out what the conference with the judge was all about," Jeremy said.

Ralph added, "We should be able to talk to the district attorney. You deserve to know what's going on. Still, you must calm down. You're in no shape to talk to anyone now."

Phil looked at his two friends, shook his head, and walked away. They hurried up beside him. Jeremy said, "Phil, we're on your side. We want to know what's going on as much as you do. Still, you've got to control yourself. Your performance in there almost got you in big trouble. You are lucky the judge didn't find you in contempt of court."

"Jeremy's right," Ralph added. "There's got to be an explanation. First you have to calm down."

Margaret O'Brien approached. When she got to them, she announced,

"I called the district attorney's office. We have an appointment at two o'clock to find out why they dropped the other charges."

This calmed Phil down a bit. Margaret was sharp, and she had a way of taking charge.

"I don't understand." Phil had no other words.

"Neither do any of us," Margaret said. "There has to be an explanation. We should learn what it is at the meeting. Jeremy, you and Ralph take Phil to lunch. The four of us should meet here at one forty-five to go to the meeting."

At lunch, they were silent until after they ordered. Phil looked at them. "I guess, I have to thank you guys. If you two hadn't dragged me out of the courtroom, there's no telling what I would have said or done. I don't know when I have been so out of control. I had so much bottled up inside. It all let go."

"We understand," Jeremy said. "There's no reason to apologize. We're all shocked at the speed at which the hearing proceeded. It was over before it even got started."

"And I didn't come across as a college professor with my performance in there."

"It wasn't your most professorial moment," Jeremy replied.

"I have to calm down and do a much better job at the meeting with the district attorney. I can't figure out why they dropped the other charges. They had all the evidence they needed."

"You know, Jake's dad, Samuel McMahan, used to run this town. Maybe he got to the police chief or the district attorney," Jeremy suggested.

"I hadn't thought about his dad," Phil said.

"Guys, this is no time for conjecture," Ralph said. "It's futile for us to try to guess what happened. We have a meeting coming up. We should be able to find out then."

~ 6 ~

THEY RETURNED TO THE COURTHOUSE at one forty-five. Margaret came five minutes later. On the way to the office, Margaret explained how she got the appointment. The district attorney, Will Jasper, had been a law school classmate of her husband Nathan.

Jasper looked sharp in his business suit. He was much more impressive looking than his assistant who Phil had worked with before. Margaret made the introductions. Mr. Jasper knew Jeremy because of Jeremy's service on the city council. He didn't know Ralph. When Margaret introduced Phil, Jasper said how sorry he was for Phil's loss. Phil restrained himself from saying he hadn't acted like it.

After the introductions, Margaret got right to the heart of the matter. She described the scene in the courtroom and the group's surprise at the dropping of the DUI and vehicular manslaughter charges.

Will Jasper cleared his throat. "We didn't want to drop those charges either. We were forced to."

"How so?" interjected Phil.

"There were no witnesses to the accident, so those two counts relied critically on the results of the breathalyzer test administered when the police got to the McMahan house. And we were unable to use those test results as evidence."

"Why not?"

"The policeman administered the test in the McMahan house. Technically, he can't gather evidence in a person's house without a warrant. As the lawyer for the accused was quick to point out, we can't use evidence gathered illegally. And the judge agreed. Without the evidence that Mr. McMahan was drunk, our case fell apart. I understand he got a stiff sentence for leaving the scene of the accident. That's the best we could do."

"Let me understand. You can't use evidence gathered in a house unless you have a warrant?" Phil asked.

"Yes."

"So, if the officer had arrested Jake for leaving the scene of the accident, and then taken him to his police car for the breathalyzer test, the test results would be admissible?" Phil pressed his case.

"Yes."

"Where is the justice in this? If Jake had stayed at the scene of the accident, the officer would have given him the breathalyzer test there. Again, the test results would have been admissible."

"Yes, that's usually what happens."

"So, Jake committed a crime, leaving the scene of an accident, which became the reason he could walk away from much more serious charges. It's perverted. Commit a crime so you can get away with two other crimes."

"Professor Philemon, you have to understand. He didn't get off because of anything he did. He got off because of a police error. As you say, if the officer had simply arrested him for leaving the scene and tested him in his cruiser, there would have been no problem. The rules of evidence are clear on this."

"He got off on a technicality. Again, where is the justice? Everyone in this room knows he was drunk. The breathalyzer test results were clear. He was drunk. And while drunk he plowed his great big pickup truck into my wife's little sedan and killed her!" Although Phil tried to control himself, he was on the edge of losing it.

Jeremy jumped in. "Phil's right! If he hadn't committed a minor crime, the system would have surely found him guilty of the more serious charges. It seems wacky. Surely you can't think justice happened in court today."

"I'm not going to claim the legal system is perfect. Still, if we let police misconduct pass, we won't be living in a country I'd like to live in."

"Police misconduct!" Ralph interjected. "It wasn't police misconduct. I know the policeman. He is a friend of mine, and he is an honorable man. A young officer, trying to do his job, made a mistake." Ralph ran his hands through his hair, agitated.

"The law is the law, and in this case, we followed the law. I am sorry about the outcome, but this office followed the law. It's our job."

Phil stood up, and almost shouting, said, "Can you tell me the case would have turned out the same if the accused wasn't the son of Samuel P. McMahan, the richest person in town? There is a different justice system for the rich, and you proved it today!"

Though the district attorney's face had grown red, he controlled himself. "I didn't agree to this meeting to be browbeaten. I did it as a favor to Margaret. I have another meeting scheduled. I told Margaret I could only spare fifteen minutes. I have to leave." With that, Will Jasper stalked out of his office.

The four of them looked at his back as Mr. Jasper hurried out the door. Margaret broke the silence. "I think we just learned the difference between the law and justice. If Jasper's right, everything was legal. They followed the law. I agree with everybody. Justice was not served."

"And there is no way to appeal this ruling, is there?" Phil asked.

Jeremy replied, "I don't think there is any basis for appeal. The district attorney won his case. The accused pled guilty. The defendant isn't going to appeal either. The case is over."

Phil was shaken. "I don't know what I expected to feel after the hearing today. I know I wanted Jake McMahan to pay for what he did. Driving a big pickup truck when drunk is criminal. If Jake had been punished, maybe I could have started to put this all behind me. Now I feel angry and helpless."

"We all feel the same way, Phil," Margaret said. "It's going to take quite a while to learn to live with this unexpected outcome."

After a short silence, Ralph said, "I guess we'd better get out of this guy's office. I don't think he'd like to find us here when he comes back."

They got up and trooped out the door. Outside, they lingered in front of the courthouse. No one knew quite what to do. While they didn't want to leave Phil alone, at the same time they didn't want to intrude.

Finally, Phil said, "I'm going to walk home. I didn't drive. I had so much nervous energy this morning; I walked here."

"You sure you don't want a ride?" said Jeremy.

"No," Phil replied. "I have a lot to process. Sometimes walking helps."

On his walk, Phil tried to figure out why from the very beginning he reacted so strongly when he thought of Jake, his drinking, and his big pickup. It was just so irresponsible. So evil. He wanted Jake to pay for his behavior. He knew making Jake pay wouldn't bring Mary Jane back, and punishment might not change Jake. His concern wasn't for anyone else who might be hurt by Jake later. He needed Jake punished to make himself feel better. Staring it in the face didn't make Phil feel too good. It was a reality. If anything, today's outcome made the feeling worse. He needed revenge, but that hadn't happened today.

By the time Phil reached his house, he was thoroughly depressed. He went inside and flopped on the bed. Eventually he slept.

~ 7 ~

PHIL SLEPT COMPLETELY THROUGH THE afternoon and woke up at six-thirty. He thought he should fix dinner. Nothing in the refrigerator looked appealing. He turned on the TV. Nothing there was interesting. He wandered around the house picking up the clothes he'd thrown down before his nap. There was nothing to do—no one to talk to.

Every time he tried to get interested in something, his mind reverted to rehashing events at the courthouse. He alternated between reliving the actual hearing and reliving the meeting with the district attorney. The district attorney wanted Phil to be mad at the police. He couldn't do it. The policeman in question was Ralph's friend and very new to the police force. As much as Phil wished the policeman had done the breathalyzer test anywhere else, he couldn't get mad at a person trying to do his job.

But the justice system—that made Phil angry. How could a technicality ruin the whole case? The police weren't doing a frivolous search trolling for any kind of evidence. It was a directed search to find a very critical piece of information. Every time he thought about Jake getting off on this technicality, he got madder.

Also, he was sure Jake's lawyer had a big hand in the whole thing. The lawyer wasn't interested in justice, only in his fee.

He directed his anger at Jake, too. When he started yelling in the courtroom, Jake smirked. Phil suspected Jake hadn't learned a thing from this whole episode. He'd confirmed daddy's money could get him off.

At nine, Phil couldn't stand it in the house anymore, so he decided to go for a drive. He drove through the campus. Next, he drove through the small downtown area. Almost all the businesses were closed. Andy's Restaurant had a small crowd, and Chin's had an even smaller one. It was a two-restaurant town. No wonder the students went to Henderson when they could. Finally, he turned down 76 and came to the intersection with Anderson Road.

He turned onto Anderson and saw the big McMahan house in the distance. He drove to the house and parked across the street. What could he do? He wasn't a violent man. He wasn't going to shoot Jake. And he couldn't beat him up. He'd be wiped out in a fight with Jake. And he'd made a rather dramatic threat in court. So, even if he could find a devious way to harm the man, he'd be an instant suspect.

Phil felt so helpless. There was nothing he could do. All his life he had been a doer. He believed hard work led to success. When he went to graduate school, he knew several of his colleagues were much smarter. He succeeded where some of them failed, because he worked harder and was a dogged researcher.

No amount of hard work was going to help now. He couldn't figure out how to create a project out of this mess. He stared over at the McMahan house. The lights were on. They were doing fine. The $5,000 Jake had to pay was a pittance to the McMahan's. Phil didn't think parole would affect Jake's lifestyle much. The contrast between how he felt and how he thought the McMahan's were feeling didn't do anything to lift his spirits.

He couldn't mount the energy to drive further. He sat there and relived the day's events. Again, everything turned out the same. Phil's anger boiled, and Jake McMahan smirked at him.

At eleven-thirty a police cruiser pulled up beside him and motioned for him to roll down his window. Phil complied.

"What are you doing here?" the young policeman asked.

"Sitting in my car, minding my own business. Is this a no parking area?"

"Look, Professor Philemon, I know who you are, and I know what happened in court today. We got a call from the McMahan house. Could you please go park somewhere else? Please."

"Okay, I guess I should be going home anyway."

Phil drove off, but the run-in with the policeman bothered him just the same. It was one more piece of evidence of the pull the McMahan family had. Still, maybe it was good they were bothered. Then again it had been no big deal for them to get the police to have him move.

The next days dragged by. Phil couldn't interest himself in anything. He ate sparingly and slept a great deal. He didn't have any ambition. He didn't answer the phone. He let it ring and ring. He didn't listen to the messages. He only went outside to collect the morning newspaper and the mail. Otherwise, he stayed in staring at the walls and trying, unsuccessfully, to stop rerunning the events at the courthouse. He didn't shave, shower, take his pills, or brush his teeth. There wasn't any reason to do anything. Nothing he could do would help.

~ 8 ~

A WEEK AND A HALF after the hearing, Jeremy woke Phil from one of his frequent naps by pounding on the front door. Phil let him in.

"Phil, I came by to see if you want to go to Wednesday lunch."

"Is it Wednesday already?"

"Yes, it is. I thought about getting you last Wednesday, but I decided against it. What's happening to you? You look awful. Your clothes are a mess, and you look like you've lost weight. Are you trying to grow a beard?"

"No. I guess I'm depressed. There doesn't seem to be any reason to do anything. I haven't shaved or showered. Do I smell?"

"Frankly, I don't want to get close enough to find out."

"Anyway, I don't think I'm up to the Wednesday lunch this week."

"You obviously need to change what you're doing. You can't just mope around the house like this. You need to get out. I know it's probably dirty pool to say this, but Mary Jane wouldn't be proud of the way you look now."

Phil turned away. It was dirty pool to bring up Mary Jane. Still, it was true. She would be horrified to see him like this. He turned back. "Okay, okay, I'll go. What time is it?"

"It's eleven. I came by early because I thought it might be hard to convince you to come. I'll be back at eleven-fifty. You should have enough time to clean up. I'll drive."

Phil let Jeremy out the front door. In the bathroom he looked at himself in the mirror. Jeremy was right. He looked awful. His clothes were a mess, and they were hanging off him. He had a scraggily salt and pepper beard, more salt than pepper. And his hair was a mess.

After a shower and a shave, he felt a little better. Still, his clothes didn't fit right. He was dragging again by the time Jeremy got back. He felt so bad, so useless. Meeting his lunch group might not be a great idea. They were usually full of fun. Phil didn't think he'd fit in.

~~~

The Wednesday lunch group was a long-standing tradition. They'd been meeting for at least fifteen years, maybe longer. Except for Sally Joins who edited the local newspaper, all the group were professors at Lackey College. Jeremy and Phil were from the history department. Bert Holman was a physicist. George Nathan taught political science. William Lin was from economics. And Bob Latham taught math. They met in the back room of Andy's restaurant, which suited them. It was the only part of the restaurant not in range of a big-screen TV showing Andy's favorite right-wing news channel.

Andy Roberts, who owned and ran the restaurant, knew they weren't fans of the news channel. He liked to kid them telling them they should eat in the regular restaurant to see what real people thought. Over the years Andy and the group had developed a weird sort of camaraderie. They kidded each other a lot. Eventually a few of the lunch group took up the habit of showing up a little early and asking Andy what the "real people" were thinking. On many occasions, this pre-lunch discussion provided the first topic of conversation for the lunch group.

When Phil and Jeremy came in, Bert and George were in a discussion with Andy interrupted by quick looks at the TV. They broke off their conversation and came over to Phil. "I heard about the court hearing. It was awful," Andy said.

The others had been there, and they all nodded in agreement. "Jeremy told me what you guys found out at the district attorney's office," Bert said. "Talk about getting off on a technicality."

"Yes... I still haven't really come to terms with it. It seems so wrong. It doesn't fit my sense of justice," Phil replied.

Jeremy motioned to the others. "Let's go to the back room. There's no use standing and talking when we could be sitting."

Bob, William, and Sally came in a few minutes later. Phil looked at his friends and felt a little better. Maybe he could get back to living among people again. He decided to start the conversation. "So, what were you two and Andy talking about when we came in?"

"Okay, we're all here. I can start," Bert said, "The news Andy runs out there had a story about sun spots causing a cooling of the sun. According to their source, the sun is going to go out in three or four hundred years. We're going to suffer through an ice age pretty soon."

"What?" several people blurted out.

Before Bert could answer, the waitress came in and took their orders. He continued. "According to their source, sunspots are flaring up. Sunspots are sort of tears in the surface of the sun. This source thinks the sunspot flares are going to cause a cascade leading to a decline in the sun's energy."

"Bert, who's the source? Is he a reputable physicist?" William asked.

"I've never heard of the guy, Dr. Lawrence White, and I've never heard of his lab, the International Physics and Natural Science Laboratory."

"Sounds impressive," Jeremy said.

"While I'm not as plugged in as I might be, I think I've heard of every major laboratory. I've never heard of this one. When I get back to the office, I'm going to check. I have a suspicion it's completely bogus."

"So, you think this is fake science, or pseudo-science?" William asked.

"Yeah, I think so. It's just so contrary to the thrust of climate science."

Bob jumped in. "And think of the source. I don't think the people who watch the right-wing channel put much faith in climate science. It's very convenient for them to have a contrary view out there. This way they can talk about the 'controversy' about climate. It reminds me of the tobacco companies and the 'controversy' about the health effects of cigarettes."

"I suspected as much," Bert said. "Still, I'm not going to dismiss it out of hand."

The food arrived, and the conversation waned for a while.

After they finished their meals, Phil addressed the group. "I don't know how unusual my situation is. Jake McMahan was guilty, but he got off on a technicality. It seems like an incredible injustice to me. What I don't know is... is it rare? Or are sharp lawyers finding fault with police procedures and getting guilty people off all the time?"

After a pause, Bob said, "A couple of years ago there was a case in a town near where I grew up. This guy, Martinez, Dennis Martinez, I think, killed his wife. He tried to make it look like a break in. The police found the tools he used to fake the break in. But, a little like your case, the police didn't have a warrant for the search, so Martinez got off. It was a big scandal."

"It's quite similar, and maybe even more careless on the part of the police," Phil said.

"I bet you could find lots of other examples," Bert added. "It can't be a large percentage of the cases. Still, there are so many cases. You're going to wind up with quite a few guilty people getting off on technicalities. The law is all about technicalities."

"I'm sorry Phil, there's a big difference between the law and justice," Sally said. "Even in this small town, lots of cases turn out very differently than I think they should. Often the difference between two outcomes comes down to the craftiness of the lawyers involved. Some of those guys are sharp, and others are real nincompoops."

The waitress cleared their plates, and they settled the bill. They always divided the check evenly no matter what anyone ordered or how much wine anyone drank. As they were getting up, the discussion turned to what they were going to do for the summer. Several of them had plans to travel overseas. Others were going to visit children and grandchildren. Phil had no plans. He and Mary Jane had been talking about visiting her family in Panama. Now she was gone. Listening to the others with all their exciting plans put Phil in a sour mood again.

~ *9* ~

JEREMY DROVE PHIL HOME FROM lunch. "Thanks for rousting me out.
It was great to see everyone. I guess I need to get over to the department
soon. The mail's probably piling up," Phil said as he got out of Jeremy's car.

Phil entered his house and looked around. Wow, he'd let the place go.
A big stack of unopened mail sat on the counter. Oddly, he had brought
the mail in every day but never opened it. Half-read newspapers were
scattered in several places. There were a few dishes on the dining room
table and even more stacked in the kitchen sink.

After he cleaned up a little, he attacked the mail. One of the personal
letters was from Phil and Mary Jane's financial advisor, Henry Jones, an
insurance agent who also acted as an advisor.

Dear Phil,
I am so terribly sorry to learn of Mary Jane's accident. Please drop by my
office at your earliest convenience, and, if possible, bring an official death
certificate. We will need that to make a claim on her life insurance policy.

Sincerely,
Henry

Phil scratched his head. Life insurance? He didn't remember buying any life insurance. Then he remembered. Mary Jane's parents had purchased life insurance policies for both Mary Jane and Martha perhaps twenty-five or thirty years ago. Mary Jane had been surprised by the size of the policy.

Another envelope had a return address from an insurance company Phil didn't recognize. It contained a check for the assessed value of Mary Jane's Prius. *Wow... I'm surprised they settled so quickly.*

~~~

The next morning Phil got up, showered, shaved, and took his pills. After breakfast, he read the newspaper cover to cover for the first time since Mary Jane's accident. He found a short article on the controversy about the cooling of the sun he'd heard about at Wednesday lunch. The MIT professor they interviewed said the TV story was the first he'd heard of it. None of his measurements of the sun suggested big changes. Phil didn't like the right-wing channel's political slant, and this was evidence it affected the stories they chose. Bert was right. The idea of a cooling sun was probably nonsense.

At nine-thirty, Phil decided to take a death certificate to Henry's office. The funeral home had provided him with several copies. He hadn't had to use any of them so far. Maybe that meant he hadn't done everything he needed to do.

Henry was not busy when Phil arrived. He greeted Phil, and they shook hands. "I'm so sorry about Mary Jane and the accident and all."

Phil never knew what to say, so he just sat down. Henry was about ten years younger than Phil. Phil felt odd having an "advisor" younger than him. Henry was also very short, about five-foot-three, Phil thought, and had a full head of bright red hair. His appearance made him seem even younger.

"I brought this death certificate," Phil said holding up the envelope. "Your letter talked about a life insurance policy."

"Yes, it's an old policy. It's been fully paid for several years. I think Mary Jane's parents took out the policy. It looks like they made a lump sum payment to fully cover the policy twelve years ago."

"I remember now. When their estate was settled, one of the stipulations was to finish paying for the life insurance policies they'd taken out on Mary Jane and her sister Martha."

"The policy's a big one, Phil. You're in line to receive two million dollars. It's a million-dollar policy with a double indemnity provision for accidental death."

"Wow." Phil couldn't respond beyond that.

"I'll take the death certificate."

Phil handed it over, still in shock. Two million dollars. He had no idea of the amount involved. What should he do?

"I know it's a lot to take in. You've become a wealthy man, Phil. Here, let me pull up your accounts on my computer."

Henry busied himself with his computer. For the most part, Phil put his financial plans on automatic pilot. He and Mary Jane felt they were behaving sensibly, and sizeable inheritances from both sides helped. Now everything had changed. Phil didn't know what wealthy people did with all their money.

Henry interrupted Phil's thoughts. "Here, take a look," he said as he turned the computer monitor so Phil could see it. With the insurance money, his total amounted to over four and a half million dollars.

Phil sat back. "Won't taxes eat into the two million from the life insurance?"

"No, life insurance proceeds aren't taxable income. The money's tax free."

"Wow, I'm speechless. It's a lot to take in. I guess I'll be getting the check from the insurance company?"

"Yes, I suspect it'll be a certified check. It'll come to you. I don't know how soon you'll get it. Insurance companies can be slow to pay claims."

"Actually, I've already received a check from an insurance company. It's for the damage to Mary Jane's car. It was totaled."

"That was quick. I bet the check for two million will take longer."

Phil got up. "Thanks Henry, this is incredible news. I don't know how to react."

"I know. Be sure to come in when you get the check. We should put it into your brokerage account, so it can work for you."

Phil nodded to Henry and walked out. He was glad he had walked over to Henry's office. With his new resolve to get out of his funk, he needed to get more exercise. Now, he was rich. What was he going to do? He wandered over to the Lackey campus. It was quiet, and Phil sat in front of the fountain at the center of the quad.

William Lin came out of the social science building. When he saw Phil, he waved and headed over. William was easy to pick out. He was big, well over six feet tall, and heavy, maybe two hundred and fifty pounds. He'd played football at a small college. He liked to say he was the only Chinese defensive tackle in the US. "It was great to have you back at lunch yesterday," William said as he sat beside Phil.

"Ah, Professor Lin, an economist. I think I need an economist."

"I'm not sure you're right. What's up?"

"I just came back from Henry Jones's office—the insurance guy. He acts as our financial advisor. Now, please keep this in confidence, but it turns out a long time ago Mary Jane's parents bought a life insurance policy on her. The idea was to protect the grandchildren if their mother died. As you know there were no grandchildren, so I'm the beneficiary. I'll be getting a check for two million dollars, and it's tax free."

"Holy cow, two million dollars! Phil, you're rich!"

"Yeah, I guess so. Mary Jane and I were doing okay. We were set up for a comfortable retirement. Now this changes everything."

"I know what I'd do. I'd be out of here as soon as I could go. No more blue books or papers to grade, no more students complaining about grades, and no more committee meetings. Nothing could hold me back."

"Gosh, I hadn't thought of retirement. So, you'd take early retirement. I thought you liked your job."

"I do, I like my job, but it's a job. I certainly wouldn't do it for free."

"Maybe it wasn't an economist I needed to talk to after all."

"Yeah, I see my job as mostly an economic arrangement I have with the college."

"Wouldn't you miss it?"

"Yes, I'd miss parts of it. On the other hand, every fall it's getting more and more difficult to get back the enthusiasm. And Cindy and I would like to travel. I have relatives back in Taiwan I'd like to see. And Jeff and his wife have two kids. We don't see them often enough. I would retire early."

"Well, I'm different. Sure, I'd like to travel more. To tell the truth, I'm not much of a hobby person. I don't know what I'd do with myself if I retired."

"Let me cycle back to what I said earlier. No more blue books, no more papers, no more useless committee meetings, and no more students complaining about grades. There's a lot of this job I wouldn't miss at all."

"I can't disagree. Please keep this under your hat. I only recently found out about it myself. I don't want it spread all around town."

After William left, Phil walked to the humanities building and emptied his mail box. He found his mail easy to dispose of. He hardly ever got any important mail anymore. If people had important things to say, they sent it by email. He realized he hadn't checked his email in a while. He could check from home, so he put it off. He looked around his office. William would give all this up and take early retirement. Phil hadn't given much thought to his retirement, maybe sixty-five or seventy, not now. He was only fifty-nine.

As he walked home, he wondered what to do. Though the two million dollars opened lots of possibilities, he wasn't sure what they were. He didn't have Mary Jane, so what difference did it make? *I have the money because she died. That's awful.* Maybe he should give it away. He hadn't earned it.

~ *10* ~

IN THE EVENING, HE TRIED to remember the name of the guy Bob had mentioned, the guy who'd gotten off because the police didn't have a warrant. Martinez, that's it. Bob grew up in a suburb of Cleveland, so Phil googled the *Cleveland Plain Dealer*. On the *Plain Dealer* site, Phil typed Martinez in the search bar. After a great number of irrelevant hits, he found a long story on the case of interest.

The story started out with a profile of Dennis Martinez, the accused. Little was known of him until he started working for a family-run furniture store. By all accounts he was a good salesman. After three years, the family promoted him to sales manager at a store in the suburbs. Two years later, Martinez married Lily Johnson, the daughter of the furniture store owner. After the wedding, Mr. Martinez was promoted again, this time to vice president of the company.

When Lily's father died two years after the marriage. Lily took over as company president. Acquaintances said Dennis and Lily didn't socialize very much. No one could name people who were close friends with Martinez or Lily. They were members of a country club. Dennis was an avid golfer.

A year after her father died, a car accident left Lily paralyzed and confined to a wheelchair. Four months later, she was found murdered in her house, the apparent victim of a burglary gone wrong. Soon after her body was found the police arrested Dennis Martinez and charged him with murder.

The story continued with the trial. Dennis Martinez was found not guilty of murder because there was no evidence to contradict his story. He said he'd come home to find his house broken into and his wheelchair-bound wife dead. She'd been strangled. Based on the evidence presented, there was no direct connection between Martinez and the crime. A juror was quoted as saying he wondered why they'd bothered to bring charges. There was nothing to back them up. The jury only deliberated for a half hour.

Apparently, the reporter questioned the police. She found lots of evidence linking the husband to the murder. The police found the tools used in the faked break-in. Paint samples on the knife used to pry open the door matched paint on the door jamb. And the husband's fingerprints were the only ones on the tools. The police hadn't found the tools on their initial investigation. Two policemen came back later and discovered the tools. This evidence wasn't allowed to be shown to the jury because Mr. Martinez's lawyer had been able to suppress it. The critical search had been conducted without a warrant.

Martinez sold the four furniture stores his wife had owned. As her sole heir, he had every right to sell them. Lily had been a wealthy woman in her own right. As her heir, Martinez liquidated her stocks and moved to Florida within a month of the end of the trial.

When Phil finished reading the story, he was upset. There were clear parallels with his case. Evidence gathered in a search without a warrant was not admissible in court. Dennis Martinez and Jake McMahan had both gotten off because of a police error. Phil couldn't blame the police. In the Martinez case, they'd found the critical evidence. He bet no burglars were ever found. Dennis Martinez killed his wife in cold blood and got away with it. He was more reprehensible than Jake McMahan.

Phil started to wonder what good it did to find this case. Finding other cases didn't make him feel better. In fact, it made him feel worse. Dennis Martinez got away with murder and walked away a rich man. It was maddening. The police, and anyone who read the Plain Dealer story, knew he was guilty. Justice was not done. The law had been followed, but justice had not been done.

There has to be a way of getting a guy like Dennis Martinez. Al Capone was only convicted of tax evasion. Then people watched the known criminal, waiting for him to make a misstep. There was no police task force waiting for this Martinez guy to make a mistake. He was probably living in a big house in Florida and playing lots of golf. He was rich and had no reason to mess things up.

Phil knew how he felt about Jake McMahan, and there were probably relatives and friends of Lily Johnson who felt the same way about Dennis Martinez. Something should be done about guys like Jake and Dennis. They'd slipped right through the justice system. Despite their obvious guilt, they'd both walked. What could be done? And what role could he play? Phil didn't know.

For the rest of the week intermittently Phil tried to fight his depression. Most days he wasn't very successful. He avoided going to his office at the college, which wasn't like him. He cleaned the house a little. Still, often, he just let the phone ring. Phil knew he had to snap out of his funk, but he couldn't. He simply didn't know what to do with himself.

~ *11* ~

THE NEXT WEDNESDAY, PHIL GOT to the lunch group a little early. Jeremy and Bert were talking to Andy, so he joined them. "This guy doesn't have any credentials," Bert said. "No one has ever heard of him. None of the legitimate guys who study the sun's activity have readings close to his. I think it's complete crap!"

"Yeah," Andy said. "I hear you. Still you should recognize the people who watch my TVs won't agree with you. All they'll hear is the *New York Times* claims the cooling sun story is false. The reporter will never out and out say the story is false, just the *New York Times* says it is."

"There are ways to tell who's an expert no matter who reports their findings," Bert said. "Experts in physics qualify for grant funding. They qualify for grant funding by publishing the results of good research. And to publish you have to convince reviewers you have new, interesting findings."

"So, you're telling me an expert is someone other experts think is an expert," Andy shot back. "You're not going to convince these people. They don't trust universities. They think all you egg-head professors are scamming them. All college ever gave them, or their kids, is a load of debt."

The others arrived, cutting off the conversation.

"Bob isn't going to make it today. He and his wife are off to England. I think they left last Friday," Jeremy reported as they sat down.

"I guess we can get by without a mathematician," Sally said.

They all nodded. Bert couldn't contain himself. "You wouldn't believe what Andy just said. The guy responsible for the cooling sun nonsense is a nobody. As far as I could find, he's not a physicist. At least he's not a member of the American Physical Society. And his lab is a phantom, too. I gave up after I made a couple of calls. None of my friends had ever heard of him or his lab either."

"What did Andy say?" William asked.

"Yeah. Andy claims it wouldn't matter. People like him will see a claim that this guy's work is bogus as another claim by a person with a different view. And the only way they'd hear about it is when a TV commentator mentions a story in the *New York Times*. And they wouldn't believe anything in the *Times*."

The waitress interrupted them. When she departed, George continued the discussion. "I believe it. There is a lot of good research showing most people don't know what to do when presented with divergent opinions. They tend to believe the expert who agrees with what they thought in the first place."

"Isn't that bad? And this isn't about opinions; it's about reality. Haven't we lost a lot when there are two competing realities out there? There are already enough things reasonable people can disagree on. I'd hope we could agree on things we can measure," Bert pleaded.

Jeremy spoke up. "It's not that simple, my friend. How do you measure the heat of the sun? It can't be easy. You can't send a research assistant up there with a thermometer."

"No, it's not research assistants with thermometers," replied a slightly exasperated Bert. "But it's not too difficult to take accurate measurements."

"I bet it's not straightforward. There are calculations involved, right?"

"Yes, but they're simple calculations."

"Simple or not, I think Jeremy's point is a good one," Sally said. "If there are calculations involved, and maybe even if there weren't, people won't believe scientists. I think we've lost a lot when people don't believe in science. There's a lot of evidence faith in science has fallen off."

Bert responded, "I know, and it burns me up."

"We can see you're upset," George said. "It's interesting. For quite a while I've been wondering how to reconcile two facts. First, like we're saying, people have lost faith in science. Second, the percentage of the population with a college degree is going up, and the percentage of the population with exposure to higher education has gone up even more. How do you square those two facts?"

"I hate to suggest the obvious conclusion," Jeremy said. "Maybe we're not doing a very good job."

William interrupted. "I don't agree with your conclusion Jeremy."

"Why not?"

"I think we're doing a fine job for the most part. It's the people we don't teach who have lost faith in science, not the ones we've taught. It's part of a bigger social split."

"Go on, explain yourself. I want to hear this," Jeremy said.

William continued, "You know about the widening income gap between the haves and the have nots?"

He got nods around the table.

"The haves are mostly college educated and can afford to send their kids to college. For the most part the have-nots are less well educated, and they feel like the haves look down on them. They hear things like they live in flyover states. And they're characterized in lots of other unflattering ways."

"What does it have to do with not believing science?" asked Bert.

"I think these people, the ones from the lower end of the education/income spectrum, think other people talk down to them. And scientists are part of it."

"So, you think the science doubters are part of a larger split in the country," Sally said.

"Yes, I do. And it's a big problem. The widening income distribution is a huge deal, and I think it drives a great number of splits we are seeing in our country."

"So, the economist is telling us it's all based on economics," quipped Jeremy.

"No, it's not all economics. Nevertheless, economic factors are important."

"We've drifted into the social sciences. It's time for me to get back to work," Bert said, getting up. The others followed.

~ 12 ~

RALPH WAS ALONE IN THE back room of the store when Phil walked in after lunch. He came out in response to the bell over the door. "Phil, it's good to see you. I tried to call you yesterday. You weren't home. I left a message. Is that what brought you in?"

"Actually, no. I forget to check the answering machine all the time. It was Mary Jane's job. What were you trying to call me about?"

"I sold the computer—Mary Jane's laptop. Maybe I could have gotten a little more for it, but this guy seemed to need it. I didn't think you were interested in me holding out for a big price. Anyway, I got $1,000 for it. Close to what you paid for it for new."

"The money doesn't matter. It doesn't matter at all. In fact, I want to talk to you about money. Do you have a minute?"

"Sure."

"It's kind of a private talk. Could we go into the back room?"

Ralph nodded, and they headed into the back room. Ralph cleared a chair for Phil.

"It's weird," Phil said hesitating. "Okay, I'll start this way. I got a letter from Henry Jones, the insurance agent. He acts as our financial advisor. When I got to his office, he told me there was a life insurance policy on Mary Jane. It's a million-dollar policy—remember Mary Jane's father was a doctor. There's a double indemnity provision in the case of accidental death. I'm about to receive a check for two million dollars tax free."

"I can see why the price for Mary Jane's computer didn't matter! It's chicken feed. Wow, two million dollars and tax free."

"You are only the second person I've told about this. I don't want it spread around. I've got to figure out what to do."

"I'm not the one to talk to. My parents didn't have two nickels to rub together, and this store isn't exactly a money machine. I've never had any money. I wouldn't know what to do with it if I did."

"I talked to William Lin from the economics department. He said he'd retire if he were in my position. I've never even thought of retirement. He's right. I can afford to retire. He was brutal about it. He's only working for the money."

"What would you do if you retired?"

"I don't know. Mary Jane and I had lots of travel planned for our retirement. She wanted to go to Panama to see relatives. And there are other places I might want to visit. Still, travel wouldn't be the same without her."

"What about history and teaching? You were very active at the college. Wouldn't you miss it?"

"You know, maybe not. It's odd. While my first reaction to William's notion was negative, the more I think about it, the better it seems. To be honest, after my last book, you know the one about the transition away from farming employment, I haven't developed momentum on another research project. It isn't like me to be without a project. Maybe it's a sign?"

"Gosh, I always envied you guys at the college. I thought you had the perfect job. You get to work on a beautiful campus. You get good salaries and benefits. And you have the summers off. It's hard to think of giving it all up."

"Yeah, I know it's a great job. But, in the end, it's just a job. I don't know."

"You've got a lot to think about. I wouldn't rush into anything. I think the standard advice is not to change anything for a year after a big shock. It's good advice. I wouldn't make any big changes."

"I know the advice, but I don't know if I can follow it. Let's change the subject for a minute."

"Okay."

"What happened in Jake McMahan's hearing wasn't so unusual. Police make mistakes all the time. Here, I have the url for an interesting case," Phil said as he handed a three by five card to Ralph.

"You want me to look at this right now?"

"If you don't mind. The article isn't too long."

"Okay," Ralph said as he fired up a computer on the desk. In a few moments, Phil could see Ralph had the *Plain Dealer* story up.

Ralph finished the story. "Wow, this guy sounds like a real scumbag. He clearly killed his wife, and he got away with it. The tools weren't found during a search with a warrant. A guilty person got off."

"Not only did he get off, he walked away a rich man. He sold the business and all her investments. He is living as a rich man in Florida, and the people there probably don't even know what a sleaze ball he is."

"I agree. So, it's interesting. Why bring it up?"

"Good question. I don't know. Maybe somebody should do something about cases like this Martinez guy and Jake McMahan. Guilty people shouldn't get off on technicalities. It's just plain wrong for guilty people to avoid punishment."

"Calm down, Phil, I can see you are wrapped up in this. It's not going to do you any good to get all upset."

"Yes, I know. The McMahan case still strikes a raw nerve. Actually, the other case is more egregious. It was out-and-out murder and still he walked. I know I can't do anything about it. Still... someone should, don't you think?"

"Is there anything anyone can really do?"

"Maybe there isn't, but there should be. I've been thinking about it a lot. I know it's wrong. It's not my place..."

"I don't know what can be done. Everything was legal. These cases are closed."

The outside bell rang, interrupting their conversation. Ralph got up and went out. Phil followed him. Mary Jane's friend, Beth Watson, stood there. She smiled when she saw Ralph and Phil. "Hi you two. I'm not interrupting anything, am I?"

"No," Phil said. "I was about to go. Thanks for talking with me, Ralph."

Phil walked out the door. He looked back and saw Ralph and Beth in a close conversation. Phil wondered if the visit was all business. He hoped not. It would be nice if Ralph had a girlfriend.

As he got in his car, he thought Ralph was probably right. There was nothing to be done about people like Jake McMahan and Dennis Martinez. There were flaws in the justice system, and they got lucky. Still, it wasn't satisfying.

~ 13 ~

ON THURSDAY, PHIL DECIDED HE needed to get away for a while. He packed a few things in a small suitcase and drove to Cleveland. He enjoyed the drive, though there was nothing particularly scenic about it. It was good to get away. Staying around Lackey with all its memories wasn't good for him.

He splurged and stayed in a nice hotel downtown. He'd never stayed in such a fancy hotel before. What the heck, he had money. The next morning, he visited the Rock & Roll Hall of Fame. Phil wasn't musical. In fact, he had no sense of rhythm at all. Nevertheless, he enjoyed himself. In the evening, he took in an Indian's game. As with most sports, baseball was better in person, and it was always thrilling to go to a big-league park. Still, the game was too long.

The next day he went to the offices of the *Plain Dealer* to look in their public archives. He knew he could have done an online search, but he enjoyed the archives. The smell of newsprint pervaded the place. He found lots of stories on the Dennis Martinez trial. The article he'd found earlier was a good summary, so he didn't learn much. Martinez killed his wife and walked because the police goofed. Also, his research didn't uncover any mention of the crime ever having been solved.

Phil thought there were more Dennis Martinezes out there, so he went to the Cleveland public library and got on a computer. To start, he googled "got off on a technicality" and then tried "evidence without a warrant." He tried other search terms and eventually found eight interesting cases. All the accused people were definitely guilty of murder, and because the district attorney or the police had not crossed every t and dotted every i, the accused got off completely free.

Phil knew what had happened with Jake McMahan was not unique. His research here showed him maybe it wasn't even unusual. *Wait, I'm not being fair. There are thousands of court cases every year. I'm finding exceptional cases—they aren't tough to find.*

Phil walked around downtown Cleveland for the rest of the afternoon remembering the times he and Mary Jane had wandered around Honolulu. After a while he decided these kinds of memories weren't good for him. In the evening he went back to his hotel in a funk. Nothing on the big-screen TV interested him. He decided to go to bed early. Going out for dinner by himself didn't have any appeal. He wasn't hungry, anyway.

He couldn't sleep. He started to think about what he could do about the miscarriages of justice he'd found. It was frustrating. He felt he was right on the edge of coming up with an idea, then it faded.

~ 14 ~

AFTER A LONG, LONELY WEEKEND, Phil went to the history department on Monday. He looked around his office again. He even scrolled through the "Ideas" file on his computer. None of the suggested topics sounded interesting. In fact, he couldn't figure out what a few of them were.

He decided he should talk to Jeremy who served as department chair. Phil had been chair ten years ago, so he knew what Jeremy was going through. Phil knocked on the door frame before going in the open office door.

Jeremy looked up. "Howdy stranger. I thought I would see you last week."

"Sorry. On the spur of the moment I decided to take a short trip."

"Where did you go?"

"I went to Cleveland. It's not a bad drive. I saw the Rock & Roll Hall of Fame and took in an Indian's game. I felt like I needed time away from the house."

"You could come in here, you know."

"Yeah, I guess that's what I want to talk about."

"What's up?"

Phil told Jeremy about the life insurance policy. "Wow. Your retirement worries are out of the picture."

"Only a couple of people know about this, so please don't spread it around. Right now, I don't know what to do."

"What do you mean?"

"When would you retire? I ran into William right after I heard about the money. He said he'd be out of here in a flash if he was in my shoes. He'd take early retirement. It's tempting."

"Phil, I'm surprised to hear you talk about leaving. What about the next book? Your three books were all big. You're a real scholar, one of the best on campus. People look up to you. I've met people at conferences who say, 'Lackey College. Doesn't Phil Philemon teach there?' You can't be thinking of turning your back on being a historian. And what about the students?"

"Yes, I know. Let me quote William. 'No more blue books, no more papers to grade, no more useless committee meetings, and no more students complaining about grades.' While there are great things about this job, some of it sucks. And if I wanted to write another book, I could do it as a retiree. I bet they'd still let me use the library."

"Now, I have to speak as your department chair. You can't walk out on me. What do we do with the courses you're scheduled to teach next semester? Students have already signed up for them."

"I've thought about a replacement. Didn't Martin come in last year moaning about having retired too early? Wouldn't it be easy to have him come back in a temporary job while you searched for a permanent replacement?"

"Have you already talked to him?"

"No, no, I'm just thinking out loud. I'm not sure I'm going to retire early. I only thought it was fair to let you know I'm thinking about it."

"I can handle it. Martin is a good idea. I'll give him a call if you do decide to go. Still, you shouldn't retire. Take a leave. You're too young to retire, and the department needs you. The college needs you. Please don't do anything too hasty."

As he walked out of Jeremy's office, Phil thought the last plea was a bunch of bull. The department needs you. The college needs you. It was beneath Jeremy. No one was indispensable. Phil was sure they could hire a replacement who would be great. Graduate schools were full of bright people doing very interesting, exciting things. Nobody needs me.

Phil went home and piddled around for a while. At loose ends, he decided to review his notes from the Cleveland library. The cases were interesting. The details were different, and in every case, a guilty person walked away free.

Phil knew the arguments for police following procedures. Details mattered. If the police could finesse the details when they wanted, we would be taking steps in a very dangerous direction. Lawyers would no doubt tell him the cases he'd found were the price the country had to pay to live in an orderly, free society. He wouldn't want to live in a country where the police could break in without cause and search anyone's house when they wanted. While Phil knew the arguments, these cases still bothered him. Couldn't the rules be fudged in clear cases of guilt?

Phil realized he'd spent the better part of the afternoon reviewing the cases and taking more notes. He'd had a similar kind of concentration when he'd worked on his dissertation and wrote books. Clearly, he concentrated on these cases.

Phil wandered around hoping something would gel. He thought hard about who he was and how he worked. Occasionally, he thought he knew what made Phil Philemon tick. Now he wasn't sure. Then again, he knew he worked best when he turned things into a project. It was why he liked writing books. They were big projects. They took hours of concentration. How could he make his fascination with these miscarriages of justice into a project? If not a book, what?

Phil also knew he wanted to get back at Jake McMahan. His next project had to focus on revenge. He went to bed pondering how to accomplish his two goals: get a project to absorb him and get back at Jake McMahan.

He awoke the next morning with more clarity. He knew what he had to do. He finally had an idea he thought would work. He wasn't sure he could pull it off, but he knew he had to try. The more he thought, the more entries for the to-do list formed in his mind. He got up and started the list. It turned out to be quite long. It was good to have a project. Maybe in the end he would find he couldn't follow through, but for now, he felt energized to be starting.

~ *15* ~

PHIL WENT TO THE LACKEY library on Tuesday morning. The inspiration for this trip was a quotation from *The Poisoner's Handbook: Murder and the Birth of Forensic Medicine* by Deborah Blum, a book he had assigned in his 20th century American History class. Blum had said something like this: poison is the coward's way to kill. It was true. A situation simply had to be engineered in which the person in question ingested the poison. If he was ever going to get his revenge on Jake McMahan, this might be the way.

Phil sat down and opened *Poisons of the World*, the book he'd found in his search of the library's holdings. It had been published in the seventies by a professor from Cambridge and contained detailed discussions of all known poisons organized by chemical families. In the index he found an entry for nonlethal poisons. Phil was sure he couldn't kill anyone, even Jake. Maybe he could make him sick? There were about sixty entries for nonlethal poisons. He wrote down the page numbers.

After a couple of hours and checks by most of the page numbers on his list, Phil found an interesting entry for poisonous dart frogs. Poisonous dart frogs were among the most lethal poisonous animals. There were several types. A few of the frog poisons weren't lethal, at least in small doses. Phil found the frogs fascinating. They came from the jungles of

Central and South America. Native tribes used their poisons to coat the tips of darts they used in blow guns. This gave the frogs their name.

Phil wrote detailed notes on the various varieties of poisonous dart frogs. After finding the frogs, he made quick work of the other references to nonlethal poisons. While other nonlethal poisons caused people to become violently ill, none of them had lasting effects. This made the poisonous dart frog more interesting. Its poison could cause lasting effects. The poison was a neurotoxin. It could cause permanent paralysis. He'd have to do more research on the internet. Still, what he'd found was promising. He put the book back on the shelf where he'd found it.

~~~

Phil didn't notice Sherry Ahearn who had started work in the Lackey College library the previous week. Sherry had been delighted to find an opening she was qualified for so close to her mother. Her mom struggled with living at home but refused to go to a nursing home near Penn State where Sherry had previously worked. The Lackey opening had been a godsend. Being an alumna of Lackey was a bonus. She didn't expect to see many people she knew. It had been twenty-two years since she'd left Lackey. There were probably a few professors still here. She wondered if they'd remember her.

The library was dead at the start of the summer. There were only two patrons as far as Sherry could see from her perch at the reference desk. She looked over as one of them closed his book and got up. She recognized him. It was Phil Philemon. He'd been one of her favorite professors. She'd taken two of his courses. Truth be told, she'd sort of had a crush on him when she was a co-ed. Maybe she should go over and say hi. Then again, perhaps she shouldn't leave her post. She didn't know how finicky the Lackey staff was about such things.

In any event, Professor Philemon shelved his book and marched out of the library without casting a sideways glance. Shelving the book bothered Sherry. While people thought they were helping the librarians, too often they put the books in the wrong place. She looked around. Absolutely no one was there, so she went over to where Professor

Philemon had been and looked at the shelves. Everything seemed to be in the right place. One of the books wasn't shoved in all the way. She thought it was the book Professor Philemon was looking at—*Poisons of the World*. Odd. No telling what professors are interested in.

~ 16 ~

PHIL GOT TO THE LUNCH group early, but neither Andy nor any of the group were in the main room. Bert and William were already in back when Phil got there. Phil had a big announcement for the group. On Tuesday afternoon, he'd told Jeremy he wasn't coming back. He didn't want a leave; he had decided to retire. At Jeremy's urging, he'd gone over to talk to Margaret. He was surprised when Margaret's secretary, Susan, let him in right away. Margaret greeted him warmly. Phil told her about the insurance and his decision to retire. At first, he didn't know how to feel when Margaret wasn't at all bothered. As the discussion continued, he found himself a little miffed. She didn't seem to want to talk him out of it. Margaret said she envied Phil. She was going to retire soon herself, maybe in a couple of years.

After everyone had settled at the table in Andy's back room, Phil spoke up. "I have an announcement. I'm taking early retirement. I have told my chair, Jeremy, and even Margaret knows. Except for them, you're the first to know."

"Wow, Phil why?" Bert blurted.

Phil filled them in about the two-million-dollar life insurance payment and his talk with William. "When you let yourself think you could live pretty well without working, it becomes hard to figure out why you are.

I might well get back to my writing someday. For a while I think I'm going to travel."

"As you know, Phil," William said. "I think you're making a great decision. It's clearly the decision I'd make if I were in your shoes."

"Not me," Bob said. "They're going to have to carry my cold, dead body out of the science building. I'm never going to retire."

"Oh, I'm going to retire eventually," Bert said. "Not any time soon. You recently finished a book, didn't you, Phil? Did it play into your decision?"

"Yes, a little. I haven't gotten any traction on my next academic project."

At this point George spoke up. "I want to change the subject. Guess who showed up on campus?"

He received a lot of blank looks.

"Phil, you and Jeremy might remember her. Bert and William, I think she was before your time. Sherry Ahearn, from maybe twenty-five years ago. You remember; she was an older student. She was an incredible fox back then."

"George, I'm scandalized you would talk about one of the students that way," Sally said mockingly.

"You don't know who I'm talking about. Back in the day, Sherry Ahearn had a good chunk of the faculty lusting after her. She was twenty-seven or twenty-eight when she started. I think she had a failed marriage right out of high school. Anyway, she wasn't much younger than Phil or Jeremy or me back then. And she was a truly beautiful girl."

Phil said, "Sure, I remember Sherry Ahearn. She took a couple of my classes. What's she doing back at the college?"

"She's in the library. I saw her behind the reference desk. I thought I recognized her, and I was right. I checked with Mildred at circulation."

"I would have never figured her for a librarian. I tried to talk her into graduate school. Despite my advice she left here for a big job in business in New York. She was a smart cookie. I figured she would be a captain of industry by now," Phil said.

"A smart cookie, huh. I thought she was more like a hot tomato,"

George said.

"I've had enough of you guys," Sally said as she stood. "See you next week, and maybe you can have elevated your thoughts by then."

As they left Andy's, Phil's colleagues all shook his hand. He might be retiring from the college, but he assured them he'd still come to Wednesday lunch.

After, he walked to campus. He wanted to make a trip to the library before going to Ralph's store.

When he got to the library, he headed for the section on travel books. He took two books off the shelves, one on Panama and one on Costa Rica, and searched for an empty chair.

As he sat down, he saw Sherry Ahearn, at least he thought it was her. He got up and went to greet her.

"Hi, Sherry," Phil said. "I recently heard you were back on campus. It's me, your old history prof, Phil Philemon."

"Yes, yes, I recognize you," Sherry said with a big smile. "I was so sorry to hear about your wife. I think I may have met her at one of the history cookouts when I was a student."

Phil still didn't know how to respond to people. "Thank you," he stammered. He quickly changed the subject. "I'm surprised to see you here. If I remember correctly, you had a great job in business when you left. There was no talking you into doing graduate work."

"While the job paid well, it didn't end well. My trip through the business world is a long story. I finally figured it wasn't for me. Several years ago, I went back to school and got an MA in library science. I'm much happier as a librarian."

"I'd like to hear the long story."

"Here is the short version. I ended up having several very bad personal experiences in the business world. I made good money, however, I was miserable. As a librarian I don't make as much money, but I'm much happier."

"How did you end up back here?"

"I should probably say because of all the wonderful memories of my undergrad days. The truth is my mother just turned ninety, and she needs me."

"I remember, she lived on a farm not too far away."

"Wow, you have a good memory. Yes, and she still lives in the farmhouse. I tried to get her to move to a senior living facility near Penn State where I worked. She wouldn't budge. Now she has a roommate."

"You moved in with her?"

"I think it will only be temporary. I'll have to see."

"So, you were fortunate we needed a librarian."

"Yes," Sherry replied. "It was incredibly good luck. I'm not quite sure what I would have done about Mom if I hadn't found this job."

"It's good to see you. I'd like to hear the long story. Now I've got work to do before an appointment this afternoon. Welcome back."

"Thanks, Professor Philemon. Stop by, and I'll give you the long story."

"Call me Phil, please—no more Professor Philemon."

"Okay."

Phil returned to the travel books. *Sherry Ahearn is more attractive now than she had been as an undergraduate.* She still had dark hair, big, bright blue eyes, deep dimples when she smiled, an unlined face, and a very nice figure. When she was an undergrad, she was a little too flashy or wore too much make-up. Phil couldn't put his finger on it. Now she was more subdued, maybe not trying as hard.

Phil went back to the books on Panama and Costa Rica. He sat down and took notes on the sections he thought would be useful for his upcoming trip. He had decided to hand carry the jeweled box to Mary Jane's relatives. And he wanted to find out more about Costa Rica and go there on the same trip. The travel books had lots of useful information. After an hour of note-taking in the quiet library, he found he wanted to wave goodbye to Sherry Ahearn. It was odd behavior, but she returned the wave with a smile.

~ 17 ~

AT FIVE TWENTY-FIVE PHIL found Ralph about to close his store.
"Do you have time to talk?" Phil asked. "I have an idea I want to try out
on you."

"Let me lock up, and we can go into the back room," Ralph said. When
they were seated, Ralph asked, "What's up?"

"It's complicated, so let me start at the beginning. You know all about
Jake McMahan and my wife. For the longest time, I've been trying to
figure out how I can get back at Jake.

There isn't a way. I made a fool of myself in court. If anything
happened to Jake, I'd be an instant suspect. Even so, it kept gnawing at
me, driving me crazy."

"It's got to be hard. There's nothing you can do. You're right. You'd be
the instant suspect."

"Do you remember the story I showed you about the guy who killed
his wife in Ohio?"

"Yes, so what?"

"It got me thinking. It turns out he wasn't so unusual. He killed his
wife, and because of a legal technicality, he got away with it. I found
quite a few similar cases."

"That's interesting. What does it have to do with you?"

"I think something should be done about these miscarriages of justice. And I'm working on a plan. I think I can dispense justice in these cases."

"Hold on, Phil. This isn't like you at all. You're a history professor. What do you know about dispensing justice?"

"I forgot to tell you—I took early retirement. I don't need a salary anymore, so I'm no longer a history professor."

"Wow, that was sudden. Aren't you supposed to keep things the same for a while?"

"I know, but everything's different now. Let me cut to the chase. I'm developing a plan. A plan to poison murderers who got off on technicalities. I need a helper. I want to do this, but there are parts of it I don't know how to do. I think you might be able to help."

"Wait a minute. You want me to help you poison people?"

"Yes, it's mostly technical things. I'm going to need cameras so I can investigate the people. You're good with technical things like cameras. And I'll need a fake ID—aren't there parts on the internet where people can get fake IDs? You could find them."

"I don't know, Phil. This sounds way illegal. I can't poison people."

"Yes, I know it's illegal. I'll take all the risks. You won't be poisoning anyone. I'll do that. What I need is technical assistance. You know I'm not good with computers and things like that."

"I don't get it... how is this going to help you feel better about Jake McMahan?"

Phil laid out his entire plan to Ralph, and they had a long discussion. Phil knew he was laying a lot on Ralph. It came completely out of the blue. Ralph was skeptical, and Phil couldn't blame him. Still, he could tell Ralph was intrigued about the technical aspects of what Phil had outlined. They finally agreed the first step was getting the poison. They left any final decisions until after they saw whether Phil could procure the poison.

That evening, Phil reviewed his research on the poison dart frog again. He reconfirmed his decision to try to obtain the poison from a variety called the Golduclearn Poison Frog (Phyllobates vittatus). He chose this frog because it was in the middle of the list—number six—of the most poisonous dart frogs. Its poison caused pain and paralysis, not death to organisms as large as humans. Like many of the poisonous dart frogs, it was brightly colored. It had bright orange stripes on its black back and green mottled legs. It was a native of Costa Rica, which was also useful for Phil. Costa Rica was next to Panama where Mary Jane's father came from.

Tribesmen in the jungles of South and Central America used a gruesome procedure to extract the poison from the frogs. They would capture a frog, confine it, and poke a stick down its throat and out its leg. The frog would become agitated and start to sweat the poison. The tribesmen would then dip their darts into the poison.

The poison dart frogs were peculiar. Their toxicity derived from their diet of ants, mites and termites. Taken out of the wild and fed a different diet, they did not develop poison. Because they were so brightly colored and safe if fed the appropriate food, people kept them as pets. They made a colorful addition to terrariums. Phil wasn't interested in these domesticated frogs, he wanted the poisonous ones from the wild.

~ *18* ~

TWO WEEKS LATER, PHIL WAS happy to get off the plane in Miami. While he had been extraordinarily nervous at security in the airport in San Jose, it had gone smoothly. And he'd been waived through customs in Miami. He was tired. Earlier, he'd planned to make it most of the way to Pennsylvania. Now he decided to only drive for about six hours.

As he drove, Phil reviewed his trip. It was good to see Enrique and the Lopez clan in Panama City. He and Mary Jane had visited them a couple of times before, so he didn't have too much trouble keeping all the names straight. Bringing the jeweled box created quite a stir. Enrique decided it should go to his oldest granddaughter, Rosa.

After a couple of days in Panama City, Phil felt himself souring. He tried to stay upbeat, but there were too many memories of Mary Jane. Also, his Spanish was rusty, and he had trouble understanding Enrique's mother and a few older relatives. Finally, on the fourth day, Enrique took him to the airport for his flight to Costa Rica.

He and Mary Jane had visited Costa Rica once in the past, so he'd seen most of the sights. This visit wasn't a tourist trip. He had a particular destination in mind. He rented a car at the San Jose airport and made his way to Quepos on the Pacific Coast. Quepos was interesting. There were lots of brightly colored buildings on the main drag. Phil was a bit disappointed. It appeared Quepos was a fishing village on the way to becoming a tourist trap.

After a so-so night in mid-priced hotel, Phil got into his car and drove to the edge of town. There he stopped beside the road and put on his wig and fake mustache. It wasn't too difficult getting things right using the rear-view mirror. After he was satisfied with his disguise, he headed to Nuevo Landres, located a few miles south of Quepos.

Nuevo Landres wasn't actually a town. It was more like a crossroads with a name. In any event, Phil found what he was looking for—the grandly named Costa Rican Reptile and Amphibian Center. The building didn't match the name. It was a small, slightly decrepit wooden place. Phil had watched Ralph find the place on the internet. He didn't know how he'd done it.

Phil parked in front of the building and walked inside. After his eyes adjusted to the dim light, he could see lots of movement. Many snakes slithered around in glass cages. Phil wasn't fond of snakes. They gave him the willies. Also, the place stunk. It reminded Phil of one of his favorite quotations from a Douglas Adams book. Adams described a place as smelling like "the armpit of a vacuum cleaner." This place smelled just like that.

A couple of minutes after Phil arrived a man came out of a back room. Phil walked up to the counter and exchanged greetings. Then Phil took a card out of his pocket and read it in Spanish. He didn't trust himself to wing it for this purchase. The man's eyes got big when Phil mentioned the poison dart frog. The man didn't reply immediately. Phil got nervous. After a pause, he asked, "You have it, don't you?"

The man seemed to wake up. "Yes, yes," he said. "It's expensive." Then he took out a piece of paper and wrote down a price, both in Colon's and in dollars.

After looking at the price, Phil responded, "I can pay. Dollars."

"Good, good," replied the man. "US dollars, good."

Then the man went into the back room from which he'd emerged earlier. Phil waited in the front room with all the snakes. Phil got up his courage and looked more closely in the glass cages. Several were filled with snakes, and frogs were in other cages. Several of the little frogs were very brightly colored but Phil didn't see any matching the pictures of the frog he wanted. After about five minutes, the man came out with a little jar of poison and showed it to Phil. Phil had no idea what he was looking at, so he paid the man and got out in a hurry.

As he drove north in Florida, he realized he didn't remember much of anything after he purchased the poison. He'd gone back to Quepos and spent two days there wandering the beaches. Then he went back to San Jose, spent an afternoon, and taken the plane to Miami the next day. He'd put the jar of poison in his shaving kit in his checked luggage, so he wouldn't have to explain the contents.

Phil continued for several hours before stopping at a nondescript motel. All the motels seemed to be the same to Phil. There was nothing to do, so he went to bed after a quick dinner. He found it difficult to sleep. As he lay there, he wondered what he was doing. Before his trip, the plan had been theoretical. He had the poison now, which made it real, not a theory. Could he really do it? Could he be actually harm people? He went over the arguments in his head. He'd been convinced of his arguments when he'd presented the project to Ralph. Now he was having second thoughts. He didn't like having second thoughts. He tossed and turned and finally slept.

In the morning the motel had a good breakfast, which was nice. In the middle of South Carolina, he started to think about the next steps in his plan. Clearly, he needed Ralph more than he'd first thought. When he'd broached the idea, Ralph had been very skeptical. As he'd explained, mostly he needed Ralph for technical assistance. He did not need Ralph to actually do anything. As they talked about the details, Ralph became more and more intrigued. The topic that seemed to swing Ralph his way was the discussion of surveillance equipment. If he was going to be successful, he needed to know what these people were doing. Ralph told Phil it would be easy to obtain very small cameras to focus on a house. These cameras were motion-activated. When you picked up the camera after a week or so, you didn't have to fast forward through hours to see the important minutes.

Phil had left it at that for the time being. There was no use pressing

Ralph further unless he successfully obtained the frog poison. In the back of his mind, he wondered if the guy in Costa Rica had sold him mud in a jar. He had no way of knowing what he had, and he couldn't think of a way of finding out. The guy had been full of warnings about the extreme dangers of the stuff. Phil was sure he had said something about plastic gloves when he'd handed over the package. Still, it could have all been a subterfuge.

The rest of the trip passed without event. He finally rolled into Lackey at about midnight, glad to be home. He was dead tired. Long drives had been easier when he was younger. Before he went to bed, Phil squirreled away his poison in the safe he'd bought. He hid the safe behind a box he used to store out-of-season clothes.

~ *19* ~

HE WOKE UP LATE THE next morning and had to hustle to make it to his Wednesday lunch. He knew the lunch group would be missing a couple of members. Jeremy was on his trip to the Balkans, and William was off visiting his grandkids. Still, they would have enough attendance for a good conversation.

Phil ran into Bert and Andy when he arrived for Wednesday lunch.

"Welcome back, Phil," Bert said.

"Oh, were you gone?" Andy added with a smile.

"Yes, I went to Panama to see Mary Jane's uncle and his family. Then I took a short trip to Costa Rica."

Bert changed the subject. "Andy told me about another story on his TVs. A guy's offering places on an interplanetary ship he is promising to build. He's trying to sell people on the idea of moving to another planet before the sun goes out."

"Even when the legitimate scientists all came out saying it's nonsense, a certain fraction of people don't believe them. I wonder how many takers he's finding for this spaceship scheme?" Phil asked.

"Not very many yet. The idea is new," Andy said.

"There are probably enough dumb people with money who'll buy tickets," Bert said.

"Bert, my friend, it's not about dumb. These people will see it as covering their bases. It may not be very likely. Still, what if it happens? It's going to appeal to them the same way insurance does," Andy responded.

The others joined them, so they adjourned to the back room. When they were assembled, they asked Phil about his trip.

"So, it had two parts. First, I went to Panama City to see Mary Jane's family. Her uncle Enrique is a nice guy. Mary Jane's grandmother and four cousins live there, and the cousins have several kids. Anyway, afterwards I spent a few days in Costa Rica."

At this point the waitress arrived. After they'd placed their orders, Bert reported what he had learned from his talk with Andy. After they heard the basic story, several people started to talk at once.

"Let Sally go first," Bert said.

"Bert, as I understand it, scientists aren't sure where, or even if, there's a planet out there capable of supporting life. Where's this guy's spaceship headed?"

"You're basically right. We have hazy ideas about planets orbiting other stars. They might be in position to have the right atmosphere to support life. Then again, they might not. If this guy claims to know where he's headed, he's lying through his teeth," Bert answered.

"My turn," Bob said. "So, if I buy a ticket on this guy's rocket or whatever, isn't it actually a ticket for my grandchild or my great grandchild or my great-great grandchild? How does he figure out how to deal with that? The buyer isn't going to be alive to go himself."

"The only way I can see it working is if he is asking people to buy shares in a company. The company will build the spaceship, and a certain number of shareholders will be eligible to go," Bert said.

"I guess you're right. I think if William were here, he'd tell us a corporation never dies. It's a major advantage of corporations. The shares get passed down," George said.

"I think this guy's a huckster. He's going to disappear with the money of any fool he gets to invest," Bert said.

"Andy thinks he'll get investors. They may not believe the cooling sun business, but what if it's right? He says they'll see it like insurance. If you're rich enough, you can afford to buy insurance against all kinds of things," Phil said.

"And come to think of it," said George. "What if it's global warming, not the sun going out? Given predictions I've seen, it might be a good idea to get out of here either way."

"No one knows where to go," Bert said

Bob asked, "Who said, 'There's a sucker born every minute'?"

"P. T. Barnum," Sally answered. "And Bob, I think it's apt in this situation. Bert is right; this guy, whoever he is, is a huckster, like Barnum."

"It's discouraging," Bert said. "We toil away in our science labs, and crazy stories like this cooling sun business still are believed by lots of people. I'm going back to work. I can't let this discourage me too much."

"The march of science won't wait?" Bob asked.

"Nope," Bert got up. His leaving broke up the group.

~~~

Phil went to Ralph's to report on his success at obtaining the frog poison. He was pleased with Ralph's reaction. He said he'd read the Dennis Martinez story again, and he was warming up to Phil's plan. He would only commit to this one project. If it succeeded, he might sign on for more. He wanted to see how things went.

Phil then filled Ralph in on the additional things he thought he'd need. Ralph said, he'd start working on the list right away. Fake IDs would be fairly easy, and it wouldn't be hard to get a credit card in one of the names. He'd already looked online for cameras, and he knew which one he'd order. Phil walked out of Ralph's store happy with the progress he was making.

~ *20* ~

PHIL WANDERED TO THE LIBRARY after visiting Ralph. When he got there, he went to the reference desk to see Sherry Ahearn. She smiled when she saw him. "Welcome back stranger. I understand you just got back from a trip."

"There are no secrets around here."

"If you didn't know how small a place this is before now, you weren't paying much attention. I do want to hear about your trip. However, I've got a staff meeting in a couple of minutes, so now's not a good time."

"Okay, and maybe the library isn't the best place for a story about my trip." Phil paused. Then he said, "You owe me the long story about leaving the business world for the library. Could you meet me at Andy's for a cup of coffee after work? I can tell you about my trip and hear your long story."

Sherry seemed surprised, then said, "Sure, that'd be nice. I can't stay long. I get off at five but have to be back at Mom's no later than six-thirty or six forty-five."

"Andy's at five then. See you there. Have a good staff meeting."

"If possible," Sherry said as Phil turned and left the library.

At four forty-five Phil walked to Andy's. The main room was like a lot of other restaurants. To Phil's mind it was overly decorated. Old advertising posters were all over the walls even behind the big screen TVs. He was seated in a corner booth when Sherry walked in at five after five.

"Good meeting?" Phil inquired.

"No, just routine stuff. As usual, it lasted longer than necessary. Librarians spend lots of time being quiet and telling people to be quiet. When they get a chance to talk, they can't stop. Enough about my meeting. I want to hear about your trip."

"Okay, I was going to do ladies first, but I'll go since you asked."

"I insist."

"I flew into Panama City. Mary Jane's uncle lives there. Mary Jane's father's from Panama. Actually, her grandmother is still alive. She lives with Enrique. And there are cousins and their spouses and children."

"So, you had a lot of people to visit."

"Yes. Enrique is a successful accountant there. He has a very nice house. As I mentioned, he has a large family; Catholic you know. It's odd. While Mary Jane's dad had a serious falling out with the church, Enrique's still a big time Catholic."

"How did you talk to them? Do you speak Spanish?"

"Yes, my Spanish is passable. From twelve on I grew up in Arizona, and Spanish was a survival skill for a teenager there."

"I thought you were from Hershey; you talked about it so much in class."

"I was born in Hershey. We moved to Apadoca, Arizona when I was twelve. Anyway, it was funny. My Spanish is better than most of the older crowd's English, so I spoke Spanish with them. On the other hand, the younger bunch's English was better than my Spanish."

"Was it difficult to switch languages all the time?"

"No, just tiring. I got confused. Still, usually I could carry on reasonable conversations."

"What happened after Panama?"

"I took a short trip to Costa Rica. I figured while I was close, I should take in another country. Costa Rica is nice, more civilized than the rest of Central America. I didn't have to use my Spanish very often. There are enough tourists, so English is spoken in most places like hotels and restaurants. Enough about me and my travels. I want to hear the long story about how you became a librarian."

"I remember you guys in the history department telling me I should go to graduate school, and maybe I should have."

"Yes, you should have," Phil said.

"I didn't. I was feeling old then. I had a disastrous first marriage. It was so stupid, marrying right out of high school. I was thirty when I finished college. My classmates were mostly twenty-two. I felt like I'd wasted so many years, and I had a very good job offer in New York City. I don't quite know why they hired a history major. I guess I stood out in the interviews."

"In lots of ways, I'm sure. You had a great undergraduate record, and you were very mature compared to the others they probably interviewed."

"Mature... that's a nice way to put it, Phil. Anyway, I was feeling old. My job had been basically in sales, and I was good at it. I made lots of money. I was partly on salary and partly on commission. I got promoted after a year, and I liked New York. It's a very exciting place to live. I'm a small-town farm girl. I had a great time those first years in the city."

"What did you sell? When a person tells me they were in sales, I always want to know what they sold."

"It doesn't sound very exciting. I sold packaging."

"Packaging. You mean boxes?"

"All right, I'll give you the full story. My company made display packaging, those see-through plastic packages lots of things come in."

"You mean like those plastic bubbles pills come in? They're hard to get into?"

"Yes, and it's more than pills. It's a big business. I had a great job. I worked with the product development group. Together with an advertising agency, the product development group came up with a packaging plan for a client. I sold them on using our packaging. It was interesting and creative. I got to see how things were designed, and I learned a lot about sales. I liked working with the people. I loved the job."

"Then why become a librarian?"

"It had more to do with my personal life than with my job. So here goes. I guess my first marriage had deeply scarred me. I didn't date at all in New York City. Then along came William Burris. He was hired a rung above me in the company. He took what seemed like a real interest in me and my performance, which flattered me. One thing led to another, and we started to date. I know you shouldn't mix business and pleasure. We were discreet. I fell for him, and I was sure he loved me."

"What happened?"

"He proposed, and I accepted. We knew one of us would have to quit the company, and he offered to start looking for another job. I was thrilled. It all seemed perfect. Then late one day I came into his office unexpectedly and found him wrapped around his young secretary. He had her blouse and bra off, and there was no mistaking where they were headed."

"It must have been awful."

"It was mortifying. As I look back on it, I shouldn't have been surprised. Bill was a bit of a flirt, and his secretary was pretty and young. Maybe there were other clues I should have seen. Let's face it, I was head over heels in love. He could do no wrong. But then he did... In a way, it's the story of my life—a replay of my first marriage. While I didn't recognize it when I fell for Bill, he was a lot like Joel, my first husband. They were both charmers, but they couldn't give up the chase. I thought I could be enough for them. I was wrong both times. Luckily, I found out about Bill before we got married."

"I'm so sorry."

"That's all water under the bridge," Sherry said with a wan smile. "On with my saga. After I split up with Bill, I waited a while for him to move. He was supposed to be looking for another job. He stayed, and he was my boss. I couldn't do it, so I quit. My decision was a big surprise to everyone. No one knew the real reason. After I quit, I applied for every job in sales I could locate. I had good experience, and I thought I'd get good letters of recommendation. The job search process was brutal the second time. Excuse me, Phil. Men are such bastards. On two occasions,

I was propositioned during job interviews."

"That's awful! Did it drive you to library school?"

"Not directly, I decided to wipe the slate clean by getting an MBA. I tried, but it didn't work for me. The second semester, my accounting professor made a pass at me. I was furious. This time I didn't go silently. I went to the dean. It didn't work. The guy did nothing. I felt completely let down. I finished the semester then dropped out."

"The next year I did get another job in New York. I had to take a pay cut, and the work wasn't nearly as interesting. And I ran into bosses who were more interested in my body than my ideas. By then I'd had it with men. Still, they couldn't be avoided. I recognize now the key guys in product development at my first job, and in the advertising agency too, were probably gay. I didn't give it much thought at the time. They were good coworkers—easy to work with. Everywhere I turned in my new company there were leers and suggestive comments. Male chauvinist pigs, every one of them."

"And that drove you to library school?"

"Yes, I kept the job for a miserable two years. I saved as much as I could to afford the two-year library degree. I figured I loved books. I liked college campuses. And I was going to get as far away from the business world as possible." Sherry paused and then said, "Gee, I've prattled on. I've unloaded a lot on you. I guess I needed to talk. And I don't want to sound like I hate men."

"I understand. It's good to talk. Unfortunately, I'm not sure you're completely out of the woods yet. Most college professors are men. And I'm sure many of them are probably male chauvinist pigs, too."

"I developed a strategy to deal with them. When I arrived for Library School at Penn State, I entered my dowdy period. I let my hair grow out, hid my figure in sloppy clothes, and didn't put on makeup. I know this might sound conceited, but starting when I was a teenager, people, mostly men I guess, noticed me when I walked into a room. Not during my dowdy period. I didn't have any more problems with instructors.

"When I got a permanent job at Penn State, I dropped the dowdy look. I did it slowly. It was funny. I got lots of compliments. They thought I was finally getting myself together. I didn't have any trouble with men in the library, either. Men who work in libraries tend to be nice guys.

"I've been thinking about this a lot. I think the business world warps men. Most of the bosses are men, and for the most part the women are in subservient positions, secretaries and so forth. This gives men the notion women can be bossed around. The worst of them take it too far. Also, and I hate to admit this, a few women use their sexuality to get ahead. It's a whole system problem. It's not like that in libraries. Libraries have basically flat org charts, so there aren't many supervisors, and in many cases more than half of the supervisors are women. It's just different."

"I'm so sorry. I guess I saw the same problems in my wife's experience. She'd been an Army nurse, and she had a few bad experiences during her tour in Viet Nam. The Army has strict nonfraternization rules, but they get ignored all the time."

"I didn't know she was in the Army."

"Yes, we met there. She was my nurse in Hawaii. I got wounded in Viet Nam, and she was the first person I saw when I woke up in Hawaii."

"You got shot in Viet Nam and woke up in Hawaii?"

"Yes, apparently the medic in Viet Nam gave me too much morphine. The last thing I remember after my leg got shot was the medic rushing over and putting a needle in my arm. The doctors in Viet Nam set my leg and decided to keep me under during the medivac flight to Hawaii. I had another operation there to get rid of bone fragments. When I finally woke up, Mary Jane was smiling down on me."

"Wow, was it love at first sight?"

"Yes, I guess so. It's hokey. At least for me it was love at first sight. She was so beautiful and so nice to me. I was kind of disoriented at the time. She explained things to me. She was wonderful."

"Did you get married when you were in the Army?"

"No, the Army threw me out too soon. They didn't want a gimpy infantry man, so I got an early release. We were married after Mary Jane got out of the Army, in the summer after my first year in grad school."

Phil looked up. The restaurant was filling up with its dinner crowd.

"Look at what time it is; don't you have to go?"

"Oh, yeah," Sherry said, looking at her watch. "It's been so nice to talk to you, Phil. I'm not sure I've told another soul about all this. It helps to talk. Thanks so much for coming to the library and inviting me." She reached over and gave his shoulder a squeeze as she got up and walked out of the restaurant.

Phil watched her walk away. She was in her mid-fifties now. Still, like she said, almost every man turned his head to follow her out. She's so gorgeous; it's no wonder she has had trouble with men. Then he stopped himself. He knew he shouldn't think that way. It wasn't her fault guys hit on her. He'd never thought being beautiful was a burden. On the contrary, it opened doors for people. On the other hand, maybe Sherry's experience, and Mary Jane's too, suggested a downside.

~~~

As Sherry got into her car, she wondered what Phil thought about her story. She hadn't shared it with many people. I come across as a coward. She hadn't fought; she'd run. Phil seemed to be sympathetic not judgmental. Maybe it was okay to share her story with him.

~ *21* ~

TWO WEEKS LATER PHIL WAS on the road, heading south along I-95 toward Hilton Head, South Carolina. It had been difficult to track down Dennis Martinez. According to the Plain Dealer piece, Martinez had moved to Florida. Initial internet searches had not turned up anyone in the right age range with the same name in Florida. Searches of records of housing transactions finally located him. The transaction was the sale of his Florida house. Even though Phil was extremely discouraged, he plugged away. He finally found a record of a lot purchased in a small town outside Hilton Head, South Carolina. The purchaser, a Dennis Martinez, listed a current address in Florida.

When Phil thought about it, it made sense. Martinez was an avid golfer. As far as he knew Hilton Head was mostly golf courses. Also, if Martinez was trying to put his Ohio past behind him, moving was a good idea. It certainly hadn't been easy to find him. Phil was ninety-nine percent sure he had the right guy. If he could make the surveillance cameras work, he'd erase the one percent doubt.

Phil was nervous about getting the cameras positioned correctly. He had to hide them as much as possible. Also, he had to get them focused on the house. It was best to have one on the front of the house and one on the back. And of course, it was important to be able to plant and retrieve the cameras without being seen.

Under Ralph's direction, Phil had tried out the cameras. Using one of the trees in his yard, he'd focused the camera on the Owens' house across the street. After two days, he was amazed at the results. Ralph had showed him how to download the camera images. Though the camera was tiny, it had an incredibly clear picture. It showed Ben Owens coming out each morning to get his paper and Betty getting the mail each afternoon. Also, both were in several other views including forty-five minutes of Ben mowing the lawn. Otherwise the videos showed traffic and several neighbors walking their dogs. Ralph showed him how to zoom in and out, fast forward, and view the video in slow motion.

Back in South Carolina he drove by the address, 105 Meridian Drive in Billington. Billington was right off the road to Hilton Head. The house was quite new. There was a stand of trees across the street, not another house. Phil decided the trees would be a nice place for the camera facing the front of the house. The back would be easy, too. The house next to 105 was under construction. It was framed, and the roof was on. He could use one of the trees on the side of the lot to mount a backyard camera.

After a quick spin around Billington, Phil drove to the Savannah airport to pick up a rental car. He used a fake driver's license and credit card Ralph had procured for him. Also, he wore the fake mustache and hairpiece he'd used in Costa Rica. His picture on the fake driver's license matched perfectly. Everything worked, even when he told the rental agent he wanted to pay cash. Despite that, the agent still wanted to see a credit card. It was the same routine at the motel. They took his credit card but didn't object when he paid with cash.

There'd be a little traffic early Sunday morning. A few people from Billington probably commuted into Savannah on Sunday. He planned to arrive at first light. He'd practiced mounting the camera several times, even in the dark. He wouldn't have to work in the dark. Still, knowing he could gave him extra confidence.

He didn't sleep well in the motel. There was nothing wrong with the bed, and it was quiet enough. He tossed and turned, nervous. He finally got out of bed at four-thirty and got dressed, putting on the vest with the cameras in its pockets. He checked and double checked to be sure he had everything he needed. He paced around the motel room a few times and finally left. The little Korean car started right up. *Wow, this is incredibly loud. I guess any noise sounds louder in the middle of the night.*

When the morning light was right, Phil drove slowly up to 105 Meridian with his headlights off. He'd put on the latex gloves. He and Ralph thought it unlikely the cameras would be spotted, but they wanted to eliminate any possibility the equipment could be traced back to them. Ralph had filed off the serial numbers. Phil even remembered to turn off the dome light, so it didn't come on when he opened the car door.

He got out and placed the camera on the tree he'd chosen the day before. He then got back in the car and drove slowly past the construction site. When he got to the far side, he pulled over. He got out, closing the door as quietly as he could.

He walked to the back of the new house, glad to see the construction site had been cleaned up very well. There were no boards to trip over. It was barely daylight now, so he had to be careful. He found a good tree and planted the second camera. He reached as high as he could to place the camera so it had a view over the fence surrounding the swimming pool in Martinez's back yard. He retraced his steps. When he took off the latex gloves in the car, his hands were soaked. He checked, and he was sweating almost everywhere a person could sweat.

~~~

He got back to Lackey midday on Monday. The night before he'd stopped at one of those cookie cutter motels. He'd not slept well. After the thrill of actually making progress on his project, he started to have second thoughts as he drove. He wondered about the feasibility of the project. What if the cameras didn't show anything? And he still had nagging doubts about the whole enterprise. It seemed so roundabout.

Nothing seemed to have changed on his long weekend away. He walked into town. It felt good to walk after being in the car for so many hours. Ralph was alone in the store when Phil arrived. They went into the back room knowing the bell would ring if anyone came.

"I think everything went perfectly. He didn't have any across-the-street neighbors, only a stand of trees, so the front view was easy. And a house was under construction on the next-door lot. It was easy to plant the camera focused on the backyard."

"You're sure you turned on the cameras."

"Yes," Phil said. "I remembered to turn the cameras on, the last step in the routine you taught me. We practiced it enough. And I am pretty sure they're aimed correctly."

"Those cameras have a fairly wide-angle lens, so precise aim isn't important."

"A fence wrapped around a swimming pool in the backyard, so I tried to get the backyard camera up high."

"It sounds like you did a great job. I guess we have to wait a week to see how it turned out."

"I think we should fly down to Savannah next Saturday. I'm not sure I'm up to the same drive again."

"Okay," Ralph said after a pause.

"It's on my nickel, Ralph. I'll pay. And I'll make the reservations. We can use names on the IDs we got. What did we choose for you?"

After Ralph filled him in on the details of his fake identification, Phil said, "I'm going to have to charge the tickets on the credit card. I had to put it down at the motel and at the car rental place. In both cases they both took cash for the actual payment. I don't think there's any way to pay cash for the airline tickets."

"Yeah, I don't think you can avoid using the card. We rented the mailbox in Sounder. You'll need to go over there to pick up the bill. Then you'll have to get a money order to use to pay the credit card company. You need cash to get a money order, but it'll work. The credit card company might think it's weird. A guy has a credit card and no checking account. I don't think it'll bother them much."

"It should work. So, what did you do this weekend?"

"Surprisingly enough, I had a date."

"Do tell, and who was the lucky young lady?" Phil asked with a smile.

"Beth Watson, you know—the nurse. She was a good friend of your wife's."

"What did you do?"

"We went out to eat in Henderson and then went to a movie. I had a good time. I hope she did. She seemed to."

"I'm sure she did. It's nice you two have found each other. It must be tough in Lackey. There aren't many eligible people in your age range."

"You're right. I wouldn't say we've found each other yet. It was only one date."

"I bet there will be others. I hope our short trip to Savannah doesn't ruin your love life."

Ralph laughed. "There is no love life to ruin yet. Still, I would have probably asked her out this weekend if we weren't going."

"What about Friday night?"

"Phil, it's okay. I'll deal with it. You seem more anxious about it than I am."

Phil laughed. "I hear you. I'll back off. She's the first female you've shown any interest in, and I don't want to be the reason things get messed up."

"Don't worry. If things don't go right, it won't be on you."

~~~

When Phil left the store, Ralph heaved a big sigh. I guess Phil's going through with it, and I'm along for the ride. Ralph had been skeptical about Phil's project at first. He'd gone along because Phil had been so earnest. He needed help, and Ralph could provide it. Getting the fake IDs and buying the cameras had been easy and kind of fun. Now he was going down to South Carolina to help. Phil had assured him he wouldn't have to do the actual poisoning. It was fine with Ralph. He'd never thought the whole thing would get this far. On the other hand, this guy Dennis Martinez seemed like a real no-good. He guessed he'd be going down to South Carolina. Maybe he could keep Phil out of trouble.

~ 22 ~

ON WEDNESDAY, PHIL GOT TO Andy's a bit early. As usual, Andy and Bert were in a heated discussion. Just as Phil walked up, Bert said, "I think it's the difference between living in the city and living in the country."

Andy answered, "Yes, I think partly. People who live in the country don't want the government looking over their shoulders. They don't think what they're doing is anyone else's business. People who live in cities are all crammed together. They know what they do affects others, and they can sure see how what others do affects them. I think where you live changes your mindset."

"Look at you guys agreeing," Phil said.

Andy and Bert looked at him and smiled. Bert responded, "Sure, we agree on a few things, but mostly we agree the other guy is wrong."

Andy laughed. "You're right, Bert; you're usually wrong."

"And so are you," Bert added. "Come on, Phil, let's get to the back room."

When the group collected, only one member was absent. Jeremy was still on vacation. After they placed their orders, Bert started the conversation. "Surprisingly, Andy and I found something to agree on."

"What's that, the time of day?" William asked.

"No, we agreed the split in the country has a big urban-rural component. For the most part, people who live in the country don't like government interference in their lives. They want small government. People in cities are different. They see how government can help. They are more likely to think we're all in this together. They tend to be fine with a bigger government role."

"You've got your finger on part of it. There's more to it. Farmers sure want government help with price supports. And be they urban or rural, lots of small government types are concerned with what goes on in bedrooms and doctor's offices," Sally said.

"Yes, it's more than an urban-rural divide," George added. "People don't mix very often. Even people who live in the same town go to different grocery stores, eat in different restaurants, and live in different neighborhoods. People who live in the country don't mix very often with people who live in the city."

"We used to have TV programs in common. Now there are so many channels we don't even watch the same stuff," Phil said.

"Let me get my two cents in here," Bob said. "I think the political divide has lots of dimensions. People watch different news programs, so they get a different slant on the world. People live in cities, and they live in the country. They have a different set of life experiences. People have different levels of education. They have different ways of analyzing things."

"I hope the educated people are better at analyzing," William interrupted.

"Yes, but you interrupted me," Bob continued. "There are other ways people are pulled into different camps. There is a big income divide. People are rich, and they're getting richer. Other people are poor, and they're getting poorer."

"You hit it," William interrupted again. "The data are stark. The income of a family at the twentieth percentile hasn't grown in a long time. Corrected for inflation, it's actually gone down a bit. Meanwhile a family at the ninetieth percentile has seen its income grow considerably. And those as the ninety-ninth percentile have seen their income skyrocket."

"There's no American dream for those low-income folks," Jeremy said.

"Nope, none," William answered.

"I've thought a lot about this," Sally said. "And you professors have a good take on things. However, you're missing the key issue."

"The key issue?" Bob asked.

"Yep, the key issue—the rate of change of modern life. Things are changing fast, and some people are comfortable with it and others not so much. Take the urban-rural divide. City people have adapted to all the changes. For the most part, city folks are okay with immigration, cell phones, the internet, using Apple-pay at Starbucks, and eating in ethnic restaurants. Their life isn't close to the life their parents lived."

"What about country folk?" Phil asked.

"People in the country are different. They're not all bumpkins, mind you. Still, the pace of change has been slower. While they have immigrant labor and cell phones, they're living much the same life their parents lived."

"So, Sally, where is Lackey, Pennsylvania?" George asked.

"It's a mix. We're a small town, and there are lots of farms around. So, we're part country. The college, you guys and the students, brings a little city. You're not afraid of change, and for the most part the students aren't either. Little college towns like Lackey are one of the places where there's more mixing than normal. Dinner time at Andy's is often an interesting mix of college folks and town folks."

"You left out one thing, Sally," William said. "You left out the deindustrialization of the U.S. Our economy used to crank out lots of high paying factory jobs. Most of them have disappeared."

"Fair enough," Sally said. "You can put those people on the list of those left behind. I still think it comes down to how you have or have not adapted to changes. If you don't deal with change well, you're in one group. If you easily adapt to changes, you're in the other group."

"Yes," George said. "A conservative doesn't want change. He or she wants to conserve things. Sally understands the words."

"Wow, with so many things separating us, we may never find common ground," Bert concluded.

"On that sad note, I guess we'd better get back to work," George said as he got up.

~ 23 ~

PHIL AND RALPH GOT OFF the plane in Charleston. They were both a little tired; changing planes in Philly was never fun. They got a rental car and headed south to Savannah. Everything went very smoothly. Phil checked into a motel while Ralph stayed in the car. After Ralph got into the room, he put in the black hair rinse and applied fake tattoos on his forearms.

Phil was pleased. "If I had to give a description, I would say you were the black-haired dude with the tattoos."

"I look pretty tough, huh."

"For sure," Phil said with a laugh.

Very early the next morning, another Sunday, they drove to Billington. No one was up and about that early. They were sure no one saw them pick up the cameras.

Back in the motel room, they fired up Ralph's laptop. After one dog walker, the camera from the tree across the street picked up Dennis Martinez getting his Sunday paper. Relief ran through Phil. It was the same Dennis Martinez from the pictures in the Plain Dealer.

The rest of the first day went quickly. The motion activated camera picked up Dennis leaving in his Mercedes and then returning. It also picked up various other cars passing by his house and the same dog walker. Monday wasn't much more interesting. Again, Dennis started out each day getting the paper in his robe and slippers, and his hair looked like he'd just gotten out of bed. Things got interesting on Tuesday. Other than to get his paper, Dennis did not go out Tuesday morning. At about eleven-thirty a car pulled up. A tall, dark-haired young woman in a short skirt got out and walked up to the front door.

"Wow, look at her," Ralph exclaimed. "She's a real babe. Let me back it up and use the slow motion."

"Calm down, Ralph."

Ralph reversed the video and got the young woman getting out of the car and walking up to the door in slow motion.

"I was right, she's a real babe," Ralph said. "Look at that short skirt, and she's got a dynamite body. Dennis is opening the door. Wow, did you see what he did? He greeted her with a slap on the butt."

"Yes, I saw it. Looks like Dennis has a girlfriend."

"It's too bad we don't have a camera in there right now."

"Enough already, we've got lots more of this video to look at."

Ralph put the video back to regular speed, and they kept looking. Cars came and went. Ralph reverted to slow motion when the girlfriend left the house in mid-afternoon.

"She is a real looker. And look, her hair is wet. Maybe she took a swim or a shower after sex."

"If it's a swim, we'll see it on the backyard video," Phil said. "Right now, we need to finish the front yard part."

"Ah shucks, this is the only interesting part."

The video of the next several days went by with little change in the routine. They saw Dennis come out to get his morning paper, drive away, and come back each day. He got his mail when he came home. He didn't seem to have any guests. On the Friday footage, the car that had brought the girlfriend on Monday pulled up in front of the garage. Ralph quickly activated the slow motion. Two women got out of the car this time. They went around to the trunk and got out cleaning supplies.

"It's her again, the taller one," Ralph said. "She's dressed differently. The bandana on her hair makes her look different. It's her. It's the girlfriend."

"Back it up again, I wasn't focusing on her. The shorter one is certainly not the girlfriend."

After Ralph reversed the video and played it again, Phil said, "I think you're right. I didn't see it at first. This outfit is so different."

"So, Dennis's girlfriend is one of his cleaning ladies. How about that?"

The rest of the front-yard video was routine. When they turned to the footage from the backyard, Phil breathed a sigh of relief. The camera covered the back of the house very well. Not much happened until they saw a deer go by at daybreak on Monday. Then on Tuesday afternoon, Dennis and his girlfriend came out of the house in their swimsuits.

"Slow motion time for sure," Ralph said. "Look at her. There is no hiding it, she's got a great body. Look at her in her bikini. He looks a little sloppy. She sure doesn't."

"I can't take their whole swim in slow motion. I grant you she's a very pretty girl. We already know about her."

"You're a real party pooper, you know that Phil," Ralph said as he speeded up the video.

The video showed Dennis and the girlfriend playing around in the pool for about half an hour and then going back into the house. The rest of the backyard video was uneventful.

"Okay, what did we learn?" Phil asked.

"We learned he has a great looking girlfriend who doubles as his cleaning lady."

"Yes, what else? Let's try to stick to the useful information."

"So, to plant the poison, you have to enter his house. Let's look at each time a person enters and leaves the house. We might be able to see if he has a security system," Ralph suggested.

"Good idea."

As they looked at the video from the front-yard camera, they had a hard time seeing the mechanics of opening the door when Dennis got the paper in the morning. When he opened the door for his girlfriend, they thought maybe they saw a security keypad. When they turned to the backyard video, Ralph got all excited and paused the video when Dennis and his girlfriend were coming out of the house to take their swim.

"I understand you like looking at her in her bikini. Why freeze it here?"

"Look, under her left arm. The alarm system should have another keypad there. You can see exposed wires. For some reason the keypad hasn't been installed. The house is new, right? I think they had a problem with the alarm system, and they had to remove the keypad. It could mean the door isn't alarmed."

Phil looked closely at the video. "I think you're right. I can see the wires. Are you sure they're coming from where the alarm keypad should be?"

"It's my best guess. I can't think of anything else it could be. Let's look at them when they enter to see if anyone makes a move toward a keypad on the other side."

After looking at the two getting back in again, Ralph concluded, "I don't think the back door is armed."

"I agree. That's an incredible piece of luck. What if the alarm people come back tomorrow? I mean, they aren't going to leave the house without an alarm for long. We should act soon. Our next task is to figure out where to plant the poison. I have an idea. Go back to the start of the front yard video."

"What do you want to look at?"

"Right at the start. Slow it down when Dennis comes out to get his paper."

They both looked at Dennis coming out. "I don't get it," Ralph said. "What's interesting about him getting his paper?"

"Look at his slippers. I have similar slippers. They're old. They slip on your feet, because the heels are worn down. He's doing it like I do. He's pushing hard with his feet to get his toes all the way. He does that to keep them on. I think we could plant the poison in his slippers."

"You think it would work?"

"It's got a good shot. Look at him, he's half asleep. I bet he just rolled out of bed. The slippers are one of the first things he encounters each morning."

~ *24* ~

THE NEXT MORNING, PHIL AND Ralph waited in a secluded spot for Dennis and his Mercedes to pass them. After the car zoomed by, they moved. Phil got out beyond the next-door neighbor's house and quickly went to the back of the Martinez house. Ralph drove on and parked in front of the construction site.

After Phil heard Ralph hailing the construction workers in a loud voice, he moved to the back door. Back home he'd practiced for several hours with the lock picks Ralph had purchased for him. While he was by no means an expert, it didn't take him long to get through the door. As he slipped on the booties he'd brought, he saw they were right. Where the alarm keypad should be a couple of wires hung loose. He quickly made it down the hall to the master bedroom.

It wasn't hard to find the slippers in the bedroom closet. Phil took a minute and a deep breath as he memorized where the slippers were located. Then he knelt down and took the package out of his vest. He had to be careful here, and though he had practiced, his stomach had lodged in his throat. First, he took the right slipper and exposed the inside toward the toes. He inserted a tack in the slipper being sure it stuck up through the fuzzy lining. Next, he took out the jar of poison. He was glad the latex gloves were easy to work with. Using a Q-Tip, he coated the tack with the poison. He'd only used a small amount of poison. If it worked as well as advertised, it should do the job.

He placed the slipper in its original location and packed up his materials, putting the Q-tip in a plastic bag. He was quite sure he wasn't going to leave any trace he'd ever been there. He got up from the closet floor and headed down the hallway. He almost jumped out of his skin when the doorbell rang. Martinez never had any visitors. Who could this be? He crept up the hallway. There were no more sounds. Then he heard a large truck pulling out of the driveway. He peeked out a window and saw a UPS truck.

Phil went to the front of the house and carefully looked through the long window flanking the door. A small package sat on the front porch. He could make out writing on the box. It said the Minnesota Slipper Company. Oh crap, Martinez ordered new slippers. His whole plan would be ruined. He opened the front door, scooped up the box, closed the door, and made his way to the back.

When he got out of the house, he could hear Ralph and the construction workers talking. They couldn't figure out a way for a signal, so Ralph was supposed to keep the construction workers busy for fifteen minutes. Phil had finished in ten minutes, so he had five minutes to wait. Then, it struck him; he'd opened the front door. The alarm on the front door was armed. The police were probably on their way. Phil had no time to wait for Ralph. He had to get away. And now he held the slipper box.

Frantically, Phil scanned the backyard. His best bet would be to go through the yard. Dennis had a screen of trees on the far side of his swimming pool. If he could make it to the trees, he might be able to make it to the next street over. Of course, he might run into dogs or fences. Ralph would eventually find him. Phil hustled past the swimming pool and into the line of trees at the far edge of the Martinez lot. He paused and looked around. The next house, the one backing up to Martinez's lot had a tall fence about ten feet in front of him. He decided to head away from the construction site. He had to move quickly and not make noise.

The next house also had a big fence. Now he was behind Martinez's neighbor's house, so he felt a little safer. Thank God for these trees. At the far edge of the neighbor's lot, he saw a way to get to the next street, the one paralleling Meridian. The house fronting on that street sat on a big lot. The house itself was on the far side from Phil, so he could make it through a line of trees on this side without being seen. When he got close to the street, he felt much better. He took off his vest and wrapped it around the slipper box to disguise it a little. He sat in a little clump of trees about thirty feet from the street and tried to plot his next move. He had to stay hidden in case the police responded to the alarm. Maybe they would search the neighborhood. He thought people in his situation spent too much time running and not enough time hiding. *If I hide too well, how will Ralph locate me?* They'd developed no contingency plans for this kind of event.

~~~

Ralph finished his conversation with the workers who were roughing in the plumbing on the new house. He had learned quite a bit about the house, the neighborhood, and the plumbing business. He had posed as a construction worker interested in maybe moving south from his native Indiana. As he got to his car, a vehicle pulled into the Martinez driveway and skidded to a stop. Ralph could read the sign on the side of the car, the AAA Alarm Company. Two guys in uniforms got out and ran to the front door. *Phil better not be in there.*

He decided to drive away from the Martinez house. He didn't want to have to answer any questions from alarm system cops. After driving around in the subdivision for about ten minutes, Ralph drove back by the construction site. The alarm system car was no longer at the Martinez house. He paused after the Martinez house. Phil did not come running to jump into the car. Ralph was not surprised. He'd been wracking his brain to try to figure how Phil had tripped the alarm. *Now what should I do?*

As he figured it, there were two options: either the alarm system guys had Phil, or he had hightailed it out of there when he realized he'd tripped the alarm. He couldn't do anything in the first case. If his second guess was right, where would Phil go?

Ralph thought about it for a while. Phil wouldn't have walked out along Meridian. He could easily have run into whoever answered the alarm. He probably went out through the backyard and tried to hide or to make it to another street. Ralph realized he'd been pausing in front of the house much too long, so he started moving. He had been around quite a bit of the neighborhood, but he had not been on the street behind Meridian.

Ralph drove out Meridian, turned right on the cross street, and then right on Johnson Drive, the street in front of the houses backing on the lots on Meridian. As he drove slowly down the street, Phil came out of the woods fifteen feet in front of him.

Phil got into the car with a big smile. "I hoped you'd show up soon. Let's get out of here."

Ralph sped up. "What happened? An alarm system car pulled up when I finished with the plumbers. Two guys in uniforms rushed into the house. It really spooked me. I didn't know what to do. I didn't want to stick around, so I drove off the other way. I just went by, and the alarm system car's not there anymore."

"I don't know anything about any alarm system car. Everything was going smoothly, until a UPS truck came. You must have seen it."

"Yes, I did. I didn't think much about it."

"Look at what they left." Phil positioned the box so Ralph could read the label.

"New slippers. The whole thing would have fallen apart if he got new slippers."

"Yes, so stupidly I opened the front door and grabbed this box. When I got out of the house, I realized I'd probably set off the alarm. I couldn't wait for you back there for five minutes. I finally made it across to this street. Then I waited. I figured you'd probably troll the neighborhood looking for me."

"That's what I decided. I also thought the alarm system cops had you. I couldn't do anything if that had happened. I tried to be positive. Actually, I haven't been looking for you for long."

"From my vantage point, it seems like it's been forever. If we ever do this again, we'd better have more contingency plans. This worked out okay. In the future we should have plans for what to do if things mess up."

"Yeah... no. We're going to get you a cell phone. A simple text message would have made this a whole lot easier."

~ 25 ~

WHEN THEY GOT BACK TO the motel, Phil put away his vest. On the ride there, they agreed they'd been incredibly lucky at Martinez's house. Phil definitely needed a cell phone, and they were going to do more planning. While it's difficult to think of every contingency, they should have done better.

Since they'd been able to deal with Dennis Martinez so quickly, they had plenty of time to make a trip to Spartanburg and the BMW tour. Ralph was anxious to leave the motel. After they packed, they carefully picked up the plastic bag with the Q-tip. They needed to find a place to dispose of it.

They ditched the plastic bag in a dumpster outside a truck stop. Then they took the interstate north. After a couple of hours, they got off and took small roads. When they saw a barbeque joint on the edge of a small town, they stopped. Surprisingly, at two o'clock in the afternoon, several vehicles were parked in front. Most of the vehicles were pickups.

"It looks like the locals like this place," Ralph said.

"And I don't think we will stand out much. Look at those tattoos on your arms. If you had a southern accent, you'd be one of the boys."

The restaurant was about half full. Several people were at the bar, and many of the booths were occupied. The clientele was mostly men in work clothes. In a back booth there was also a family with small children. Since no one made any attempt to greet them, Phil and Ralph seated themselves in a booth. After about five minutes, a bored looking waitress came over, plunked down two glasses of ice water, and handed them menus. "Can I get you all anything to drink before you order?"

After they ordered, iced tea for Phil, who specified unsweetened, and a beer for Ralph, Ralph looked at Phil and said under his breath, "You all."

"What did you expect? At least it wasn't y'all. Think about where we are."

The family with the children left. Lunch time had to be about over. After a few minutes, everyone turned their heads as the door opened, and two men and a teenage boy walked in. They sat in the booth behind Phil and Ralph. One of the men called out, "Sally, what's a man gotta do to get service in this joint?"

The waitress yelled back, "Bull, hold your horses. You're not the only one in the restaurant. I'll get to you all when I'm good and ready."

After a few minutes, Sally came over with water and menus for the newcomers and took their drink orders. Then she leaned over to Ralph and Phil and asked, "Ready to order?"

They both ordered the barbeque sandwich. As Sally turned away from them, the guys in the other booth got their order in. Apparently, they were locals who didn't need much time with the menu. After Sally went away, almost everyone in the restaurant could hear the conversation of the newly arrived threesome.

Bull said, "Look, if Jimmy here wants to go to college, he might not stand a chance. Most of the spots are already taken by niggers and chinks. You know colleges reserve a bunch of spots for the niggers. White folks with better grades and test scores can't get in. And chinks, you go to any college campus, you'll see, they're overrun by chinks."

Ralph's eyes got big when he heard "niggers" and "chinks." Phil gave him a warning look.

The father replied, "It can't be that bad. I know a bunch of Jimmy's older friends who're going to college."

Bull would have none of it. "Yeah, there are white kids from rich families who go, but if you need help, you won't get it. Colleges give most of the scholarships to niggers. They get the most places, and they get all the scholarships, too. And the chinks are out-of-state students; they can pay the big tuitions."

One of the locals at the bar yelled out, "Why you running your mouth about college, Bull? The closest you ever got to college was a Clemson football game."

"Shut up, Jack. I know lots about college. I keep up with the websites. What they call affirmative action is part of the attack on whites by people in DC, New York, and California. They've given all sorts of favors to niggers because they know they'll vote for them. It's why they want to let all those Mexicans and whatever in to the country. They want to dilute the white vote."

"I don't know," Jack said. "I don't know if you could get many white folks to do the jobs the Mexicans and South Americans are doing now."

"BS!" Bull shouted. "The only reason those Mexicans get hired's because they'll work for next to nothing. They are driving down pay, so it's hard for a white man to earn a living."

"You all hush up now," Sally yelled. "This ain't no debat'n society. Folks come here to eat in peace and quiet." She looked over to Phil and Ralph's table.

Their food came, and it was followed quite rapidly by the food for the three sitting in the next booth. This quieted things down considerably. The barbeque was good, and Phil and Ralph finished everything. They paid, cash of course, and left a nice tip for Sally.

When they got into the car, Ralph said, "Wow, did you believe that guy Bull? Come to think of it, maybe he was very aptly named. What a bunch of bull. Get me out of the South!"

"Yeah, part of it is the South. Still, I bet a lot of what he said might come out of the mouths of our neighbors. Have you heard the description of Pennsylvania as Philadelphia and Pittsburgh on the ends and Alabama in the middle? There's an awful lot of racist white folks in our state, too."

Ralph paused. "I've never heard it before... I guess I can see where they're coming from."

"Think about the people you went to high school with—the ones who didn't go to college. Do you think they might share Bull's views?"

"Come to think of it, I know a few who do."

They got to Spartanburg in time to make a quick tour of the museum at the BMW Zentrum. It was interesting, and it thrilled Ralph, who was a bit of a car nut. As a result, they closed the place down. The real reason they were in Spartanburg was for the factory tour they'd booked for the following morning.

They found an out of the way motel and checked in. They decided to get rid of Ralph's disguise. It took him quite a while in the shower to turn his black hair back to its natural light brown. After Ralph looked like himself, the two of them were ready to take a couple of pictures the next day. They were supposedly taking a trip to Charleston and Spartanburg. While they hadn't actually been to Charleston, they could fake it. Pictures of Ralph from the BMW tour would be a nice touch.

They found the next morning's BMW tour incredibly interesting. The initial stamping of parts, assembly, and painting was completely handled by robots. The fascinating thing was the way each car was handled separately. The robots read a bar code telling them what kind of car they were building, and they assembled the right parts. After a part was attached, actually glued in some cases and welded in others, another robot swooped in with a laser to ensure everything aligned properly. The painting robot arms changed paint colors with each car. Again, they must have read bar codes. The whole thing was very impressive.

After they moved on from the painting, Phil asked, "Have you counted the number of workers we've seen?"

"No, maybe there were two guys with clipboards wandering around where the robots were assembling the cars. It's mostly robots."

When they got to the part of the plant where engines were assembled, they saw more manual labor. The final assembly line did have quite a few workers. In the end, the impression was machines did most of the work and all the heavy lifting.

As they exited the plant, Ralph asked, "What time is it? Do we have time to go through the museum again? We were rushed yesterday afternoon."

Phil looked at his watch. "Sorry, Ralph, we have to make it back to Charleston, turn in the car, and make our flight. We've got to go."

~ 26 ~

WHILE PHIL AND RALPH WERE doing their tour of the BMW plant, Maria Gutierrez got out of her car in front of Mr. Martinez's house. She was surprised he didn't greet her at the front door. At times he wanted her to come straight to the bedroom. This must be one of those days. She let herself in with Lupe's key. Maria walked toward the bedroom. Dennis, she had to remember to call him Dennis, was in the bed.

"Hi babe," he said.

"You want me in the bed already?"

"Take your time, you know how I like it."

Maria smiled. She did know how he liked it. She started to swivel her hips gently. She slipped her dress off one shoulder, then put it back and smiled at him. He smiled back. She unbuttoned a few buttons still swaying her hips. When she got her dress fully unbuttoned, she shook a little faster and then turned around and dropped the dress to the floor. She peeked over her shoulder and gave him another smile. She unhooked her bra, dropped it, and, cupping her breasts, did a spin. After a little more shaking, she slipped out of her panties, and turned around giving him a big smile and shaking her nude body.

She was surprised he wasn't smiling, and she didn't see the tent she usually created with her striptease. "What's the matter, baby?" she asked coming over to the bed and stroking the place that usually was the tent.

"I don't know. I thought... I thought... I don't know. Maybe your dance would help. It's weird. I can't feel my right leg. I thought, if anything would do it, you would. I can't feel it—nothing."

Maria looked concerned. "What's happened?"

"I think it started earlier this morning, and it's gotten worse. I thought you might help. It's not any use rubbing there anymore. Nothing's going to happen."

"Let's see," Maria said as she pulled back the covers. The bottom half of Dennis's right leg was red and swollen. "Your leg looks awful." Maria backed away in horror. She gathered herself and came back to the bed. "Does it hurt?" She gently poked his leg.

"It did earlier, not now. Now I can't feel anything."

"You need to see a doctor."

"I don't have a doctor here."

"I can drive you to the hospital."

"I'm not sure I can make it to a car."

"I think you need an ambulance. They'll get you to the hospital."

"Okay, I guess you're right. Dial 911 and tell them we need an ambulance."

Maria gathered up her clothes and quickly put them back on. She did not want to greet any ambulance workers naked. Then she called for the ambulance.

After the call she went back and helped Dennis get his pants on. The ambulance came very quickly. The people were nice enough, and they got him loaded.

~~~

Trick Ahearn got a call to go to the local hospital at one o'clock on Wednesday. They had a patient who might have been poisoned. As the chief of police for the county, he wasn't normally the one who would take this kind of call, but his detective was on sick leave.

When he arrived at the hospital, a nurse ushered him into Dennis Martinez's room. Martinez had bandages on his right leg and was sitting up in bed. The doctor in the room introduced him to the patient. The doctor explained Mr. Martinez had lost all feeling in his right leg. The only abnormality the doctors and nurses found was a small puncture wound in his foot.

"Do you know how you got the puncture in your foot?" Trick asked.

"I stepped on a nail or a tack. I took the thing out of my slippers when I felt it. I went out for the paper on Tuesday. It's funny, I only use those slippers to get the morning paper. I was still in my robe. I can't figure out how they picked up a tack. Then again there's a construction site next door. Maybe it came from there."

"Doctor Smithers, is this the kind of reaction one could get from a nail or a tack puncture?"

"No, it's not. It's the reason I called you. Mr. Martinez's tetanus inoculation is up to date. Even if he got a bad dose of the vaccine, this is not the way tetanus presents. This reaction is very strange. I think there's a poison involved."

Turning back to Mr. Martinez, Trick said, "I guess the tack or nail is long gone."

"I heaved it into the woods across the road. Maybe you could find it. It was little; it might be tough to find."

"You still have the slippers though?"

"Yes, they're back in my house."

"We're going to have to have our lab techs look at them. They can figure out if we're dealing with poison or what."

"It would be helpful," said the doctor. "We're having a devil of a time trying to figure out how to treat Mr. Martinez. None of our tests have been able to determine anything."

Trick took out his notebook and asked Martinez the standard set of questions about who he was, where he worked, and where he lived. Then he asked if Martinez thought he knew anyone who had any reason to want to harm him.

"I've been wracking my brain. I'm new here. I moved in a couple of months ago. I don't know many people. Most of my local friends are guys I've met on the golf course. I can't think my taking a little of their money on the golf course would be reason to poison me."

"What about where you lived before?"

"Maybe, there could be someone from Ohio. I used to live there. I lived in Florida for two years before I moved here. Again, I only had golfing friends in Florida. I'll have to think about it more. Maybe you piss a person off and don't even know it."

Trick left the hospital and drove over to Billington. The whole thing seemed weird to him. Who would put a poison tack in someone's shoe? When he got to the address on Meridian, he was impressed. Martinez had a nice new house. It wasn't big, because the guy lived alone. Trick let himself in with the key Martinez had given him, entered the alarm code, and looked around. The house was almost brand new. It was a little messy, but it had nice finishes. He could see a big swimming pool in the back. In the garage, he saw Martinez's Mercedes. He was a little envious. He and Sue and the two kids lived in less space than this. He didn't have a Mercedes, and they went to the public pool.

After a little more snooping around, he went back to the bedroom and found the slippers in the closet. The slippers were well used. The fuzzy lining had been worn down quite a bit. He picked up the right slipper with tweezers and looked at it closely. He could see a smudge of something rust colored. Next, he turned the slipper over and saw the hole where the tack had been. After this brief inspection, he dropped the slipper into the clear plastic bag. He made a few other notes. The only oddity was the missing alarm keypad for the back door. It might be easy to break in if the alarm wasn't functioning. He looked at the back door and the key hole. The key hole showed a little wear. Nothing unusual.

He looked at his watch. He had to get the slipper to the station. There wasn't anything more to do until they analyzed the residue on the slipper. He thought maybe they would have to get the state crime lab involved. There were a limited number of tests his guys could do. Since they knew the blood in the slipper was Martinez's, they didn't have to worry about doing any DNA.

~ 27 ~

RALPH AND PHIL GOT HOME late Tuesday night. Phil's plan was maddening. They couldn't stick around to see if they'd succeeded. They didn't want to be anywhere near the scene of the crime. All they could do was keep watch on the websites of local papers.

Andy, Bert, and William were in a heated discussion when Phil got to Wednesday lunch. "What's up?" Phil said as he shook hands all around.

"Andy's TVs ran another story on the cooling sun controversy. I can't see how this kind of nonsense isn't squelched when the science is so clear," Bert said.

"Bert, let it go. It's not doing you any good to worry about this. Let's get lunch," Phil said.

After they gathered, ordered, and started in on their wine, Bert couldn't contain himself. "When I got here, there was another story about the cooling sun. I can't believe the story is still getting airtime."

"Bert, you have to ignore it," Sally said. "Eventually, the story will fade."

Phil spoke up. "I want to change the subject. Ralph and I got back from our little trip to South Carolina. It was good to get away. I think it is one of the few vacation trips Ralph's ever taken. Running his store is awfully demanding."

William responded, "Yeah, lots of people have the yen to be their own bosses, so they open a store or a restaurant. They soon find they aren't their own bosses. The business is the boss. Unless you hire a good staff, you're on call all the time."

"So, what did you do? Why go to South Carolina?" Jeremy asked.

"We went two places: Charleston and Spartanburg."

"Spartanburg, the big BMW plant?" Bob asked.

"Yes, and the factory tour was absolutely amazing. Most of the work is done by robots," Phil said.

"No wonder lots of factory jobs have gone by the wayside," Sally responded.

"I'm sure robots and automation are a big part of the story, but I want to talk about another part of our trip. Remember when we were trying to understand what split the country apart, and Sally said it was about how people reacted to change."

"I think her analysis is spot on," Bob said.

"Well, I think there's another dimension to it. While Ralph and I were in South Carolina, on our way to Spartanburg we stopped for lunch in this barbeque place on the edge of a small town. You wouldn't believe the character we ran into there. This guy's name was Bull, or maybe it was a nickname. Anyway, I thought Ralph was going to jump out of his chair when Bull started talking. Anyway, Bull's convinced there's a conspiracy led by people from DC, New York, and California to put white people down. He railed against affirmative action and letting immigrants have jobs. None of us mentioned racism, at least not directly."

"You're right, Phil. A lot of the split is north/south. Attitudes toward race explain a lot," George said.

"There's more to it," Jeremy added. "I think we've all heard the one about our own state. Pittsburgh and Philadelphia on the ends and Alabama in the middle. I think racism is as big a problem in the north as it is in the south. Think about Lackey College. What do we have... forty-five black students? And we can only attract them by offering special scholarships."

"Bull complained about special scholarships for black students. He told this friend his kid would never get into college. All the spots were taken by blacks. Actually, he said 'niggers.' And even if the kid could get into college, he'd never get a scholarship. All the scholarships were reserved for niggers."

"Surely, he's exaggerating," Sally said.

"Yes, of course," Jeremy said. "Still, what Phil's bringing up is a big problem. We give substantial race-based scholarships, so Lackey has racial diversity. The whole issue is difficult. Why can't a white kid get one of those scholarships? It gets even worse when you realize a few of those black kids come from wealthy families. There are white students who need the money a lot more than they do."

"I really like Sally's idea," Bob said. "Let me try to see if racism doesn't fit in. So, from the start of our country, particularly in the South. In the North, too, blacks were thought to be inferior. They did jobs suggesting they were inferior. Along comes the Civil War, and afterwards blacks were supposed to be equals. A big change. Like Sally said, some people adapted to the change. Others had a more difficult time. In the South, where black slaves often outnumbered whites, it was a bigger and more sudden change than in the North where slavery wasn't as common."

"Let me throw another thing into the mix," said George. "The South lost the Civil War, right? So, I think losers are much more likely to resist change than winners."

"Yeah," William said. "Think about the difference between factory workers and guys who liked to tinker with computers. The factory workers don't like change. They don't like the robots at the BMW plant. It hurts them. Who knew IT would be this big a thing? When the boom in IT came along, those computer tinkerers liked the change."

"Fair enough, but you interrupted me," George said. "What I'm saying is, the shift toward racial equality was the result of a loss for Southerners. On the other hand, to the extent it affected them, it was the result of a victory for those in the North."

"Now I'm more confused than ever," Bert said. "I think I said this before. Listening to you social scientists makes my head hurt. What do you think, Sally?"

"I was impressed with myself when Bob was so enamored with my analysis. I have to say George has thrown a spanner in the works. I'm going to have to think about winners and losers. It's probably important, but it doesn't quite have a one-to-one fit with normal ideas about liberals and conservatives. There are rich conservatives. Guys who look like big time winners. And there are rich liberals. Again, guys who look a lot like winners. And there are liberal and conservative losers, too. It's a puzzle."

With Sally's summary, they ended their lunch conversation and went back to work.

~ 28 ~

PHIL WENT HOME AND CHECKED the South Carolina papers. He drew a blank. If he had been successful, Dennis Martinez should have experienced paralysis three days ago. It was only going to make the papers when it got reported to the police. Each of the papers he checked had a police blotter section. None of them listed admissions to the local hospitals. Of course, not all the papers published every day, so there was no use getting upset yet.

He decided to turn to the list he compiled in Cleveland. He narrowed down the list by location. He didn't have any other measure to use, so he looked for the closest likely candidate. Michael Miller lived in upstate New York in one of the counties bordering Pennsylvania. It should be an easy hour drive from Lackey.

Phil got on the internet and entered the url for the news story about Miller. He only had a faint recollection about the case. He'd not taken thorough notes. The Corning, New York newspaper, *The Leader,* ran the story. Phil chuckled wondering if a reader of the paper "followed the leader." The story summarized Miller's background, the death of his brother, and the ensuing difficulties.

Michael and his brother Matthew were partners in a car dealership they'd inherited from their father. Apparently, if you bought a Ford in

Corning, it was a "Miller-car." Though the boys were a year and a half apart in age, they were only one grade apart in school. The story had a cute picture of them aged about eight and ten from a newspaper ad. It also had pictures from more recent ads.

The boys had grown up in Corning and attended local schools. Neither distinguished himself in sports or anything the paper chose to mention. They went to college at different SUNY schools, but the colleges were the only inkling of a difference. After college both boys went to work for their father. Their father had a stroke and died five years after Michael, the younger of the two, joined the business. As the only two surviving family members, the boys inherited the dealership.

According to sources at the dealership, the boys basically got along. There was a hint of difficulties involved with dividing up tasks. Apparently, their father had not prepared them for leadership. "The old man had expected to run this place for another ten to fifteen years," one of the secretaries was quoted as saying. Still, the dealership seemed to be doing all right.

At the start of deer season the boys went hunting. This had been a family tradition, and they'd gone out the first day practically all their lives. Examples of taxidermy decorated the Miller dealership. Two years ago, Michael returned alive from the hunting trip—alone. Matthew was shot in what was first described as a hunting accident.

Michael appeared to be devastated by the accident. He stated that he and his brother had been hunting in their normal spot. They were both wearing blaze orange vests. As the hunt progressed, they drifted apart because Michael thought he heard a deer off to his left. When he was about thirty yards from his brother, a deer walked out of a thicket. As he raised his rifle, he heard a shot from the direction of his brother. The sound spooked the deer, and Michael missed his shot. Michael said he'd waited for a while. After no other deer showed, he decided to link up with his brother. After a bit of a search, he found Matthew. He was dead, face down in the woods with blood all over his hunting vest. He'd been shot in the back.

According to the paper, hunting accidents are not uncommon. Lots of hunters are out there on the first day of hunting season, and each one of them is armed. Michael called the local ranger to report the shooting. He gave the ranger his location and stayed with the body.

The first difficulty with Michael's story came from the ranger, Rick Adams. When Adams turned onto the forest road to get to Michael and the body, he saw only one set of tracks. It had rained a little the night before, so tire tracks were easy to spot on the dirt road. He found the Miller's car a mile and a half down the road. Adams knew this patch of woods. It belonged to one of the local farmers. Not just anyone was permitted to hunt in the woods.

Adams found Michael Miller in tears sitting on a log about ten feet from his brother's body. He listened to Michael's story. He then inspected Matthew's body. He was clearly shot in the back, probably by a rifle. There was no exit wound, so the bullet was still in the body. Adams called emergency personnel, and he had Michael walk to his location when he heard the shot. The spot was clearly in front of where the body lay, so Adams concluded it wasn't likely to be an accident involving the two hunters. Next, he asked Michael if he'd run into any other hunters. Michael said he hadn't seen anyone. He claimed to have heard a truck or a car out on the road shortly after the two shots: the shot that killed his brother and his shot at the deer.

The newspaper story then recounted the police investigation. A few things about Michael's story didn't add up. First, Adams reported to the police Michael told him he'd heard another car on the road, but Adams was sure the only tracks on the road were from the Millers' car. Second, the farmer who owned the patch of woods the Miller boys used said it was reserved for them. He only rented it out to one set of hunters at a time. Also, he was at home all day. While he'd seen the Miller car, he hadn't seen another car until the ranger came by. The final part of the case was the ballistics analysis. The bullet they took out of Matthew's body was a perfect match to a bullet the police shot from Michael's rifle. Michael was charged with first degree murder.

Of course, Miller hired a lawyer, and stuck to his story. Covering all his bases, the lawyer requested a chance for his own ballistics expert to test the evidence. The case against Michael started to fall apart when the police couldn't come up with the bullet. It was missing from the evidence room. Apparently, the police practically tore the place apart. They couldn't find the bullet.

The district attorney decided to drop the charges. As he told the reporter, the only solid evidence he had was the bullet. Michael's attorney could get the ballistics report thrown out of court because the bullet was missing. The testimony about the tire tracks wasn't going to be convincing. The ranger hadn't taken any pictures. And besides, another hunter could have used a different road. Even though it was over a mile away, there was another possibility. And the farmer couldn't be absolutely sure only two cars came by. Without the ballistics evidence, he didn't have a case.

Phil knew the answer. Still, he wondered if the report of the police's ballistics expert couldn't be put into evidence. It seemed so unlikely another person was involved. Michael Miller was guilty. The police knew it, the district attorney knew it, and Phil thought even Miller's lawyer knew it. The police screwed up. Or Miller bribed a policeman to get rid of the evidence. Like Jake McMahon and Dennis Martinez, the results followed the law, but justice wasn't served.

Michael Miller was a great candidate for his project. Next, he searched the internet. It amazed him how easy it was to find information. Michael Miller lived in a town a few miles outside of Corning. He'd recently moved, and Phil was able to pull up the house plans as well as several pictures of the house from the real estate listing. He also found phone numbers for Michael: his work phone at the car dealership, his home phone, and his cell phone.

Ralph would have to okay Michael Miller as the next target, so next he set up a meeting. They agreed to meet the next evening. Phil spent more time looking for information about Miller. Though he found other stories about the killing and the aborted trial, there was nothing as thorough as the story in *The Leader*.

He found it was almost nine-thirty, and he hadn't had anything to eat since lunch. Also, he hadn't quite disposed of all the mail he'd received while he was in South Carolina. He shook his head. He might be too wrapped up in this project. He couldn't let the rest of his life go to pot, so he got up and got busy.

~~~

On Thursday evening, Phil and Ralph met at Phil's house. Phil had his computer set up with the story from the Corning paper. He paced while Ralph read the story. When Ralph finished, he said, "It fits. He's as guilty as can be. And now he's the full owner of a car dealership. Plus, I bet he got life insurance settlements from his father and from his brother. I bet he's rich."

"I hadn't thought about the money angle. You're probably right. No doubt he profited very handsomely from the whole affair."

"No doubt."

"Am I right? Essentially, he got off on a technicality. The police ballistics report couldn't be entered into evidence, because the bullet went missing. There is no suggestion the police had done the testing incorrectly. His lawyer was simply grasping at straws. He got lucky when the bullet went missing. I think Michael bribed a policeman to get rid of the bullet."

"There's nothing in the story about him bribing anyone."

"Yeah, I know. Still, if you're the kind of guy who murders your brother in cold blood, I wouldn't think bribing a policeman would be a big deal. And he'd lived in Corning all his life. I bet he knew the police well enough to know who to bribe."

"Phil, there's enough here for me to say he belongs on our project. There's no use worrying about how or why the bullet went missing."

"Good, so you agree. We are heading up to New York to look into Michael Miller."

"Agreed."

"Look at what I found out about him. It was easy. I have an address, the layout of the house, and phone numbers. The internet is amazing."

"Wow, you even have phone numbers. I need to buy more equipment. I can't get away this weekend. Could you take a scouting trip?"

Phil thought it over. "You want me to set up the cameras this weekend?"

"No, not yet. I think it would be better if I got us more surveillance equipment. I think with more equipment we can listen in on his phone calls. I want you to scope out his house and the car dealership. We don't know how we're going to get him. It could be at home or at work. This might take longer than Dennis Martinez. By the way, I haven't seen anything in the papers I'm monitoring."

"Me neither. It's maddening."

~ *29* ~

ON SATURDAY PHIL DECIDED TO go to the Lackey football game instead of Corning. It was the first game of the season, and he wanted to assess the team's chances. A few of his students played quite a bit last year. Small college football was funny. Most of the players on the roster were freshmen or sophomores. With this set-up, freshmen played a lot. There could be big differences from year to year.

As Phil surveyed the stands, he saw Sherry Ahearn sitting at about the forty-yard line near the top of the stands. He caught her eye and was pleased when she waved for him to come join her.

"I'm surprised to see a librarian at a football game," he said as he sat down.

"I don't know why. You shouldn't have stereotypes about librarians."

"Fair enough. So, you like football?"

"Yes, I do. In truth, I like basketball better. For me, football started when I was a student at Lackey. It was high school football then. My little brother was a big high school football star. The whole family used to go to his games. I bet you've heard of him, Trick Ahearn. Actually, it's Richard. Everyone has always called him Trick."

"Sure, Trick Ahearn. Of course, I never put two and two together. So, he was your brother." Phil took a small sip of the soda he'd bought at the stand.

"Still is."

"What happened to him? I think I remember him as a running back. He was incredibly fast. Lots of colleges were after him. Wasn't it... well, almost a scandal when he didn't go to Pitt or Penn State?"

"Big-time football recruiting is such a mess. I remember my mother saying she'd be glad when the phone stopped ringing. And ten or twelve coaches came to the house to try to charm my parents. Trick loved all the attention. He let it drag out. When he finally signed with the University of South Carolina, everyone was really surprised."

"What happened to him? Did he go on to football glory at South Carolina or what?"

"It was tragic. Much to his disgust, they red-shirted him his freshman year. Then in his first game the next year, he was blindsided and blew out his knee. It was a bad injury. He went through rehab, but he lost a lot. He was never fast again. He finally quit football."

"What's he do now?"

"He stayed down South. He's the chief of county police for the county around Hilton Head. He's got a nice wife and two kids. He's doing okay. I think he wonders what his life would have been like if he hadn't had the injury. Pro football players make a lot more than county police chiefs."

Phil choked on his soda and tried to catch his breath. "You're right." This is too close for comfort. Chief of county police. Sherry's brother might be investigating the poisoning of Dennis Martinez. Maybe it was nothing. Still, it momentarily threw him.

When the game started, it became clear Lackey's good players played defense. They could hold the other team to 3-and-outs on most occasions. The Lackey offense was another story. Maybe the other team had a great defense. It was hard to tell. Still, it was hard to argue the Lackey offense was any good. The game featured a lot of punting. At half time Lackey led three nothing. Lackey's three points came as the result of a fumble recovery deep in the other team's territory. The best they could do was a field goal.

At half time Phil and Sherry wandered down to join the group of fans milling around near the stadium entrance. Phil led Sherry over to his friend Jim McSweeny, the Lackey basketball coach. After he introduced Sherry as a new librarian who liked basketball, Phil asked, "Any diamonds in the rough this year, Jim?"

The coach replied, "As a matter of fact, yes. You know how it is. All the best players go to division one schools. We're left with the others. Our hope is they're late bloomers, or we can coach them up. One of our freshmen, Nate Smith, was a good recruit for us—a six-two guard who could shoot. He was a step slow, so big-time programs weren't interested. Now, you're not going to believe this. He grew six inches over the summer. Now he's six eight and has all the skills he had as a six-two guard."

"Isn't he still slow?" asked Phil.

"He was slow for a guard; now he's fast for a forward."

"And he's still coordinated?" Sherry asked. "I've seen lots of tall teenagers who don't seem to know where all their body parts were."

"Good question. It was our big concern. Now, we haven't had any official practices yet. I've watched the guys playing a few times, and he seems as well-coordinated as before."

"Wow, a six-eight guy who can shoot," Phil said. "We should tear up the league."

"Now, Phil, don't jump the gun here. Nate is only one player. It takes about eight good players. We're in a tough league. I've learned over the years not to expect too much from freshmen. I'm willing to say we'll be better than last year, but no more."

As they were heading back to their seats, Sherry said, "The basketball coach was excited about the new player. Then he backed off."

Phil replied, "His coach's training came into play. Coaches don't like raising expectations. It's hard to live up to high expectations. Coaches always want you to expect little, so when they succeed, everyone is pleased."

"I get it. His coach's training slipped a little when he talked about the new player. I think he expects him to be very good."

The second half started, and their attention focused on the game. Trends from the first half continued. Neither team could move the ball. The game deteriorated again into a series of punts. Fortunately for Lackey, they had a slightly better punter.

Near the end of the third quarter, Phil said to Sherry, "I'm starting to think a successful offensive play for us is one where we hold on to the ball."

"Phil, you're awful. You've got to have more faith. There's always a chance we can break a big run or hit a long pass."

"I don't see any Trick Ahearns in Lackey uniforms. I don't think any long runs are likely."

Not two minutes later a running back from Lackey broke off a sixty-yard touchdown run. Phil and Sherry both stood and cheered. After the score, Sherry pounded Phil on the arm and shouted, "Oh ye of little faith. What do you say now?"

"Like I said before, another good play. He didn't fumble."

Sherry laughed. "You're awful."

The rest of the game reverted to form. While the Lackey defense started to wither a bit, they held on. The final score was ten to nothing. Phil and Sherry walked back to the center of campus and said goodbye to one another. Sherry begged off when Phil suggested going out for coffee or a drink. She'd promised her mother she'd be home right after the game.

~~~

At night, Phil piddled around the house and started to get into a funk. What was he doing with Sherry? It was nice to be with her at the game. At the same time, it felt like he was being unfaithful to Mary Jane. He found his feelings very confusing. The more he thought about things, the more he started to doubt himself. What he had done in South Carolina wasn't like him. Yet it seemed so right at the time. Now he was having second thoughts.

It might not matter... I don't know if I actually did anything in South Carolina. What if the poison wasn't poison at all? That guy in Costa Rica could have scammed him. And even if it was poison, did he have the right dose? Maybe Martinez just had a little numbness in his foot that went away quickly. Or maybe somehow the tack slipped between his toes. There were so many variables. Maybe he hadn't seen anything in the South Carolina papers because nothing happened.

He replayed the courtroom experience with Jake McMahon and got steaming mad all over again. Jake had seemed so smug. Was his project ever going to affect Jake? He didn't know. The silence from the South Carolina papers made him feel like a failure.

As he stewed, Phil reviewed his behavior. Originally, he'd planned to go to Corning. He'd told Ralph he'd scout out Miller's house and the car dealership. Saturday was the right day, not Sunday. He'd gone to the game instead. Phil believed people did what they wanted to even when they said they wanted to do something else. At a deep level did he not want to go to Corning?

Phil went to bed confused. He hated having doubts.

~ *30* ~

WHEN PHIL WOKE AFTER A less than satisfactory night's sleep, he decided he needed to talk things over. Ralph was the only one he could talk to. He'd said he was busy this weekend. Maybe he was with Beth Watson. After moping around all morning and fixing himself a very unappealing lunch, Phil decided to call Ralph. He got an answer on the third ring.

"Where are you?" Ralph asked.

"Oh, I'm home. I don't want to interrupt anything today. I know you're busy, but I need to talk. I didn't go to Corning this weekend. Can we get together Monday?"

"Sure... you okay, Phil?"

"I'm having doubts. It's maddening. We don't know what happened in South Carolina. I don't know, I think I'm confused. Listen, I'll pick you up after your store closes on Monday. Maybe we can go over to Henderson and get a bite to eat."

"Sounds nice. Are you sure you're okay?"

"I'll be fine. See you tomorrow afternoon. Five-thirty?"

"Works for me. See you then."

On Monday, Phil checked the South Carolina papers and again drew a blank. It was frustrating. He took a long walk through campus and to the campus woods. He remembered wondering if he'd ever be able to walk through these woods again. He found he could. He avoided the part with Mary Jane's ashes. His long walk gave him clarity. He'd fallen into a trap he'd run into before. All his eggs were in one basket. His project with Ralph was it. He had focused on it too much. If it failed, he had nothing. In the past, Mary Jane provided a balance. When he was too involved with one of his research projects, he always had her. She could shift his focus and keep him on an even keel. Now he had no balancing point, and the frustration of hearing nothing ate at him.

When five-thirty finally arrived, Phil picked up Ralph at his store. On the drive to Henderson, Phil explained his feelings to Ralph.

Ralph responded, "I don't think I have the same problem. I work hard at the store. After hours, I let it go. I don't stew over it. I play video games, and I have a group of friends. Lately it's been Beth more than others, and it's nice. Don't you have any hobbies?"

"No, I guess I don't. Mary Jane was my balance, and now she's gone."

After a pause, Phil asked, "Don't you have any qualms about what we did in South Carolina? I feel like I talked you into it. I'm feeling a little guilty. I also wonder if vengeance accomplishes anything. And our approach seems so roundabout."

"Don't worry about me. Listen, Dennis Martinez is a real scumbag. He killed his wife in cold blood and got away with it. I've got no problem with what you did in South Carolina. I've been thinking about it, and I want to play a more active role in all this. I know you said you only wanted me for technical assistance. I'm willing to do more. I was skeptical of the whole thing when you first brought it up. I wondered about being a vigilante. Now I'm fully on board. I think this guy in New York, Miller, deserves the same treatment we gave the guy in South Carolina."

"I never thought about being a vigilante. I guess it's the right word. I'm glad you're okay with it. Still, we'd better improve on what we did in South Carolina. As far as we know we didn't do anything, at least nothing has made the papers."

"It's frustrating. I know, but if we failed the first time, we can go back down there again. I think Martinez deserves two tries if that's what's needed."

Phil felt a little better by the time they got to the restaurant in Henderson. Villa Mexicana had been one of his and Mary Jane's favorites. His Arizona background gave him a taste for Mexican food.

Phil and Ralph got a booth in a corner and ordered. As they were devouring the chips and salsa, the door opened, and Jake McMahan and a couple of his friends walked in. Phil shrunk back in the booth and told Ralph to look.

Ralph whispered, "Stay calm. This had to happen eventually."

Jake and his friends looked a little tipsy to Phil. Their speech seemed slurred. Had they been drinking? In any event, they all ordered big Margaritas. Phil fought to keep his feelings under control. He couldn't stop looking at Jake and his friends.

Phil and Ralph's food arrived, which provided a diversion. Phil couldn't concentrate on eating. He mostly pushed his food around. He was so wound up seeing Jake; he couldn't focus. He became more alarmed when Jake's group ordered another round of Margaritas.

Ralph, leaned over and said in a low voice, "Calm down Phil. Don't let him spoil your dinner. You're going to run into him. Lackey's a small town."

"I guess so. All these feelings are hard to hold back. And frankly I'd feel better if he was drinking iced tea."

"Yeah, I bet two of those big Margaritas pack a punch."

Phil ate a little of his dinner, but he was too upset to do it justice. He decided to take the rest home. He paid the bill, and he and Ralph slipped out of the restaurant. When they got to their car, Jake's big pickup was parked right next to them.

"You don't suppose he's going to try to drive home after those Margaritas, do you?" Phil asked.

"I don't know. It's none of our business, Phil. Let's get in our car and go home. You're going to drive to Corning tomorrow. You'll need a good night's sleep," Ralph said as he got in the car.

Phil hesitated. He couldn't get into the car. He paced around the parking lot. Ralph got out and joined him. "What are you doing, Phil?"

"I don't know. I'm so wound up. I don't think I can drive home yet."

Just then Jake and his two friends came out of the restaurant. They were laughing and having a good time. All Phil could see was they weren't walking very steadily.

Before Ralph could grab him, Phil walked over to Jake, and said, "You're not going to drive home in this shape, are you?"

One of Jake's friends looked startled, and said, "Buzz off, mister. What we're doing's none of your business."

Then Jake recognized Phil. "I know you; you're the guy who threatened me in the court room. You've been haunting our house. Leave me alone. I can drive anywhere I want," he said as he brushed by Phil and piled into the pickup with his friends.

Phil had to jump out of the way as Jake backed up fast. As a result, the Styrofoam box he'd been holding dropped and spilled enchilada on the parking lot. As Phil stared at them, Jake and his friends sped down the road. "Wow," he yelled. "He made me out to be the bad guy. I threatened him in court, and I'm haunting his house. What about he killed my wife?"

"Look, he's a jerk. We all know it, but I thought our project was partly about avoiding him. And what does he mean about haunting his house?"

"Oh, that's a little embarrassing. The night after the courtroom fiasco, I drove around, and I parked across the street from his house. I simply sat there. Eventually the police came by and asked me to move on. The McMahans had called them. They recognized my car. It wasn't my finest moment."

"I guess not. Lackey's too small a town. You only did it once?"

"Yes, only once. Now he says I'm haunting his house."

On other occasions, Phil had realized Ralph was more mature than many people who had several years on him. Ralph came through again. "Look," he said, "Let's take a few more laps around this parking lot to get ourselves together. Your leftovers spilled. We need to clean it up and dump it in the trash. Then we can drive home in peace. It's not going to do us any good to confront him."

After a brief pause, Phil nodded. "You're right." He scraped the spilled leftovers back into the box and fell in beside Ralph.

~ *31* ~

ON TUESDAY PHIL DROVE TO Corning. He'd recommitted to the project on the drive home the evening before. During the drive, he'd half-way expected to see Jake's big pickup off the side of the road. No such luck.

His investigations on the internet made it easy to find Miller's house. It was in a nice subdivision with new houses. Phil thought lots of the houses were what would be called McMansions. Miller's house was on a cul-de-sac, not ideal for getting in and out. Mounting cameras wouldn't be easy, either. Phil now realized they'd been lucky in South Carolina. Martinez's house had a stand of trees across the street and the construction site on one side. It was easy to mount the cameras. Here, if you ruled out going into one of the neighbor's yards to use a tree, the only possibility was a street-light pole.

He cruised by the car dealership. He was impressed. It was a large modern looking place. What had once been Miller Ford was now Miller Ford-Kia. They had a lot crammed full of cars.

Phil parked in a downtown parking garage and walked by the dealership. It was a nice fall afternoon. He put on a hat and sunglasses. He took a slow walk past the dealership feigning interest in the cars. There were lots of people working in the dealership, and he picked up speed when he saw a salesman heading his way. Maybe Miller would be vulnerable if he worked at his office late. In the final analysis. Phil figured the house would provide more chances.

When he got back to Lackey, he went to Ralph's store to report. He didn't think he'd learned much. In Miller's case, the internet made it easy to get the details of where he lived and worked. Ralph agreed. He hadn't learned much, but he thought the trip was worthwhile. It verified what they'd thought. He also said he'd had luck. Equipment to listen in to phone calls was on the way.

~~~

On Wednesday morning, Phil continued his ritual of looking at the websites of the South Carolina papers. He almost fell off his chair when he came across a story with the headline, "Local Man Apparently Poisoned." Righting himself, he read the story. It was about Dennis Martinez all right. The facts were clear. Martinez's right leg was completely paralyzed, and the police were convinced it was the result of a deliberate act. Someone had placed a tack in Mr. Martinez's slipper. The police guessed the tack had been coated with poison. The police person interviewed was Trick Ahearn, just as he had feared. Anyway, Trick said the results of the analysis from the state lab weren't in. They couldn't say what the poison was. The article ended with a plea for anyone who knew anything about this affair to call the police.

Phil called Ralph and gave him the url for the story. "The chief of police for the county is Trick Ahearn. He's from around here. He's the younger brother of Sherry Ahearn, the new librarian at the college."

"Yes, and haven't you two been seen together? I mean you and Sherry."

"We're friends, nothing more. She was a student of mine a long time ago, and we've been catching up with each other. Nothing to talk about."

"You know how people in Lackey talk."

Phil felt stupid. "I guess I never gave it a thought. It's weird her brother is investigating the Martinez thing. It's a connection to Lackey I don't like having."

"I got the story up on my computer. There's not much there. It doesn't look like the police have much to go on. It's the way we want it. And it worked. You were so worried before. Feel better now?"

"Yes, it worked. I was so worried about the poison dosage and its effects. I mean we didn't have much to go on. Right leg completely paralyzed. About perfect I'd say. Let's hear it for luck."

"Yeah, I guess we were lucky. Now it's Michael Miller's turn. I'll let you know when the new equipment comes in."

~~~

After Ralph's store closed on Saturday, Ralph and Phil took off for Corning. They brought the cameras they'd used in South Carolina and the new phone intercept equipment. The new equipment amazed Phil. It had come in late Thursday, and they'd tried it out on Friday. Phil felt a little guilty snooping on his neighbors. Early in the morning they'd aimed the new equipment at the house across the street. In the evening, they replayed every phone call the Owens made. Then Ralph showed him another capability. Ralph's cell phone could intercept phone calls. After a bit of a wait, Ralph's cell phone showed the Owens' line was making a call. Ralph answered it on the first ring and acted like he was a Spanish speaker. Betty Owens apologized, saying she must have dialed a wrong number. When she redialed, Ralph let the call go through.

In Corning, they worked fast at Michael's cul-de-sac. At twilight, they pulled up to the light pole, and Ralph placed the camera on the pole. Phil was worried it could be seen by anyone who looked. It wouldn't be hidden at all. Ralph argued it was small. No one would notice it. Who looked at light poles? The only potential problem was someone seeing them place the camera or retrieving it.

They decided they weren't going to get any video of the back yard. They would only mount the phone intercept equipment on the fence running behind Miller's house. There was a little path behind the fence. It was Phil's job to get the equipment in the right spot. The only flaw in the plan would be if a dog got spooked as he walked along the path.

When it was completely dark, Ralph let Phil out close to the end of the path. Phil walked bent over so he could hide behind the fences bordering the yards. When he was a couple of houses away, he could see outside lights at the Miller house. When he got to Miller's portion of the fence, he could hear talking coming from the deck. It was a woman and a man. Phil peeked through the slats in the fence. He could make out two people on the deck. He couldn't tell who they were. He sat down and waited. He couldn't make out what the two were saying, but he could smell roasting meat. At least his nose worked. Dinner wasn't served yet. He might be in for a long night.

Phil wasn't concerned. He and Ralph had considered this possibility. After the difficulties in South Carolina, they'd had good plans. There were two possible pick up spots. Ralph would text Phil if he had to switch to the second one. As Phil waited, wishing he could understand what the people were saying, he felt his new phone vibrate. Ralph was already monitoring the second pickup spot.

After a time, he heard noises he interpreted as silverware clanking on plates. He took another peek. The two people were now seated at a table. A half an hour later, a door opened and closed. Finally, the lights over the deck went out. He got to his feet. Wow, was he stiff. He leaned over the fence and mounted the phone intercept equipment. It only took a few seconds. After he was sure the equipment was in place, he made his way back. He headed for the second pickup spot, a couple of blocks away from Miller's cul-de-sac.

He was relieved when Ralph drove up ten minutes later. "What happened?" Ralph said when Phil got into the car.

"He was out on his deck with a woman. It was all lit up. They were grilling. Boy, I sure got stiff sitting down with my back to the fence. After they turned out the lights, I mounted the phone intercept gizmo just like you showed me. We should be in business."

"I hope they don't have a cookout when we come to pick up the equipment."

"Then let's not make it on a Saturday."

The trip back was uneventful. It was a bother to have to get rid of the rental car. They thought it would be foolhardy to use one of their own cars.

~ 32 ~

PHIL WAS BORED AT HOME. There was nothing to do. The house was probably as clean as he could make it. He'd even cleaned out several closets. He found it wasn't difficult to get rid of things Mary Jane had accumulated. He made a couple trips to donate clothes Martha and the girls hadn't located. He wasn't sure why he had gone on the cleaning craze. He wasn't thinking about selling the house. Mostly he was bored. Of course, he reminded himself, he hadn't tackled the attic yet. But he'd had his fill of cleaning.

~~~

On Wednesday he got to Andy's a little early. None of his group was there yet, so he went over to talk to Andy. "What's happening in the real world, Andy?"

"A bunch of liberals are getting all upset when honest folks want to carry guns. I don't get it. What's wrong with carrying a gun?"

"It's not the wild west out there. Guns are dangerous. Lots of people are killed or injured with their own guns."

"They're idiots."

"I think you've made my point," countered Phil.

"What about the constitution? Doesn't it give people the right to have guns?"

"I think the constitutions talks about having a well-regulated militia.

I don't think people having guns at home is the same thing."

"The Supreme Court doesn't agree with you."

By this point in the conversation several other members of the lunch group had come in and were listening. "I don't think you two are going to agree on this one," Jeremy said. "Let's go to lunch."

When lunch group had all assembled, Bob spoke up. "Phil, I don't think you're going to convince Andy to favor any kind of gun control. The NRA has brainwashed people like Andy to believe any move toward gun control will lead to the government taking away hunting rifles."

"I hate those slippery slope arguments," Bert said. "Isn't the whole point of having laws about drawing lines? We can ban people from doing some things and not ban them from doing other things."

"Banning things like assault rifles isn't easy. How do you define an assault rifle?" Sally said.

"Aren't machine guns illegal? Doesn't there have to be a definition there?" Jeremy asked.

"I think the pro-gun anti-gun split is part of the urban-rural split we talked about before," Bert said. "If you're from rural America, you probably grew up there, and you probably had guns around. If you grew up in an urban setting, you probably didn't."

"You've got part of it," George said. "But part of it is east west. Westerners like their guns."

"Don't you mean the wild west," Bob asked.

"Wait," Phil said. "For my money, the best program about the wild west was Gunsmoke, and it was anti-gun. Marshall Dillon was always trying to get guys to check their guns before they came into Dodge City."

"I think people in the west have gotten over trying to be Marshall Dillon," Sally said. "And urban-rural or east-west, feelings about guns are one of the things driving the split in the country."

~~~

After lunch Phil went to Ralph's store. As was often the case, Ralph was in the back room. He came out when he heard the bell. "Hi Phil, what's up?"

"I'm back from my Wednesday lunch, and I didn't want to go home. Listen, I've been thinking you could use help around here. I could take care of the front of the store while you're working in the back."

"Phil, I know you. It's a nice offer and all, but you don't know much about computers."

"I wouldn't have to know much. I could certainly give the computer to the people when they come to pick it up. And I bet with a little training, I could write up descriptions of what's wrong with computers people bring in."

"There's more to it."

"I'm trainable, and I've got to think it's difficult for you to get repairs done when you have to bop out here every time a customer comes in. If I could handle a quarter of the customers, I'd be a big help. Maybe after a while, I could handle half of them. I don't want to pressure you. Think about it."

"I'm worried about why you want to do this. Is it because there is a lull in our other project?"

"Maybe. I don't know for sure. I've been at loose ends at home. I have cleaned and cleared out about as much as I can stand. I want to get out. I have to be around people more."

"What about the college, couldn't you do something there?"

"I've thought about going back. Maybe I'll go back next year. I'm sure they'd let me teach a course if I wanted to, you know, as an adjunct. Right now, it doesn't seem appealing. It's weird, I loved my job. Now I don't know. I think I told you before. I am a plunger. I like to have a project and really work on it, plunge into it. Our project has grabbed me, but it comes with these lulls. I need to get through the lulls."

"Okay, I'll take you on. I can't pay you."

"No, no, I never expected any pay. As you know, I don't need it. Show me what I need to know, so you can get back to repairing computers."

"Also, there's Jim to think about. He doesn't work too often. If we had three people in here, we'd be tripping over each other all the time."

"Fair enough. I don't want to push Jim out. After a trial period, if I work out, we can figure out a schedule. It shouldn't be hard to work around Jim's schedule. After all, he's a full-time student."

After Phil helped Ralph close the store, he felt good about himself. He certainly hadn't been bored. He'd only been able to handle two customers without Ralph's help. He could see how he'd get better. They couldn't get free to go back to Corning until Tuesday, so he figured working with Ralph would be a good way to pass the time. Often it was quiet at the store. He'd have a chance to think things over. Phil was sure it was going to be an improvement over staying home.

~ 33 ~

THE NEXT TUESDAY PHIL PICKED up Ralph right after closing time. Phil was careful to get a different color car for each trip to Corning. After a quick dinner in Corning, they approached the cul-de-sac at dusk. Ralph retrieved the camera even faster than he'd put it up. When he got back into the car, he smiled and said, "It's here undisturbed. I told you people never look at light poles. They're part of the background."

"Great. Let's find a quiet place to see if it worked."

They parked at the far side of the parking lot at a playground. It was deserted in the evening. Ralph fired up his laptop, and they began the video. They wouldn't have a chance to see it all. They just wanted to be sure everything had worked.

The picture was very clear. The first thing they saw was the newspaper delivery. It was followed by someone walking her dog around the cul-de-sac. Then Michael Miller came out of the house in a jogging outfit and picked up his paper. The first day was Sunday so there wasn't much coming or going. Except for the newspaper pick up no one came in or out of the Miller house.

On Monday morning after the newspaper pick up and the dog walker, a car came out of Miller's garage. The next thing they got was another car coming out of the garage.

Phil exclaimed, "There's another car coming out of Miller's garage. I don't think he's married. Maybe he has a roommate. This could make things more complicated."

"It's a wife or a live-in girlfriend. The second driver had on a red top. Not many guys would wear a red shirt."

"I bet we can figure it out. We have more than a week's video. Eventually, they have to come out to the mailbox or mow the lawn or go for a walk or something."

"I'm pretty sure the first one was Miller. And my bet is the second one was a woman. You heard two voices when you were waiting behind the fence. One was a man and the other was a woman, right?"

"Yeah, you're right. Sure, there were two of them having dinner. I should've expected both of them to be living there."

They looked outside. It was dark. They'd been so absorbed in the video they hadn't noticed.

"It's time to retrieve the phone intercept equipment. You ready?" Ralph asked.

"Sure, let me put on this black shirt. I hope they aren't cooking out again."

The retrieval of the phone stuff went smoothly. They headed back to Lackey right after Ralph picked up Phil. For the most part they drove in silence.

~~~

The next morning Phil reviewed the video on his computer. He learned quite a bit from the video. As they suspected, Miller had a woman living with him. She left for work, wherever it was, about fifteen minutes after Miller. Also, she usually got home an hour and a half before he did. Soon after she disappeared into the garage, she came out the front door to pick up the mail. She was young, petite, and had long brown hair. Phil thought she was nice looking. She wasn't the knockout Dennis Martinez's maid/girlfriend had been. Still she was a nice-looking girl.

On Monday evening, her car left at about six-thirty. Forty-five minutes later a pizza delivery guy came by. The wife or girlfriend got home at about ten-thirty. Otherwise there wasn't much activity on Monday.

Except for fetching the paper in the morning, Michael Miller didn't appear on the video at all.

The rest of the weekdays followed the same pattern: Miller got the paper, the two cars left, the woman returned and got the mail, and Miller came home. Most nights neither of them went out again. The one exception was Thursday night when Miller's car left the garage at 6:15 in the evening and didn't return until midnight.

The weekend was different. Miller mowed his front lawn on Saturday morning. After he finished the front, he switched to the back. Since the video was motion activated, this made for very choppy viewing. Miller would appear from behind his house, mow to the edge of the grass, turn, and then disappear behind his house. After three of these short videos, Phil fast forwarded to the end of the lawn mowing. Saturday afternoon, Miller and his lady friend took a walk. They were both in jogging outfits. At least as they were leaving and when they got back, they didn't appear to jog. Later the woman's car left and came back a couple of hours later. A grocery shopping trip was Phil's guess.

The Sunday video was uneventful, but Phil was intrigued by the second Monday video. It repeated the same pattern. The woman left a little after 6:00 in the evening, then came the pizza delivery, and the woman came back late. Phil thought, "Monday night football, the guy gets a pizza and watches Monday night football. The woman doesn't care for football, so she has some other plans."

After he finished his first run through the video, he plugged in headphones to listen to the phone intercepts. The readout on his computer gave the phone numbers involved and the times of the calls. Miller made a strange short call Sunday night. It completely baffled Phil. Monday afternoon at about five a call originated from a phone in Miller's house. From this call Phil learned the woman's name was Jill. Jill was calling Sheryl, who was apparently a friend. They chatted for a while. Phil learned Jill was a third-grade teacher, and Sheryl worked in a doctor's office. The purpose of the call was to confirm plans for the evening. Jill and Sheryl were going to dinner and a movie. It was a girl's night out. Their men were going to watch the stupid football game.

The next phone call was from Michael Miller. It came from a different phone. Phil guessed Jill used her cell phone, and Miller used the house phone. He could verify which phones were used later. In any event, the phone call was to a local pizza place to order a pizza. This jived with the Monday night pizza delivery.

Phil listened in on several other phone calls. The car dealership apparently stayed open late several evenings. Miller went home before closing. As a result, he got some work-related calls. Jill appeared to have a wide group of friends, and she liked to talk on the phone. Also, she called her mother most days. Jill's mother didn't like Jill's living arrangement, and she didn't like Michael Miller. Some of the phone calls were in hushed tones. Miller must have been in the house then.

The only nonbusiness calls Miller made were to his bookie. At least that's what Phil finally figured out. The calls were short, and there was a code of some kind. Phil heard combinations of team names and city names. Miller mentioned Washington, the Eagles, and Dallas in one call. Phil backed up to the strange Sunday call. It was to the bookie's number and only mentioned Tampa. Phil switched to the internet and looked up the Monday night football schedule. Sure enough, Tampa Bay had played playing the New York Jets that Monday.

The rest of the phone calls weren't very interesting. Phil learned more about Jill than he ever wanted to know. Phil did perk up with Miller's Sunday call to his bookie on the second Sunday. He put his money down on San Diego. They were playing Denver the next night. It seemed like an odd bet to Phil until he remembered there was a point spread involved.

When Ralph got to his house in the evening, Phil had everything ready. "You ready for the show?"

"Fire away, I hope you've got something interesting for me."

"We've got nothing like Martinez's girlfriend in her bikini. Nevertheless, there are some interesting things."

Phil showed Ralph the video. When they got to Jill coming out of the front door to get the paper, Ralph asked him to use slow motion. "I want to see if she has to use a code for a house alarm."

Phil set the video to slow motion and reviewed Jill's exit and entry a couple of times. "The angle's wrong, I don't think we can see if there is a house alarm," Phil said.

"You're right. Too bad."

They reverted to regular motion and kept watching. Phil fast forwarded through the dog walkers, the random kids riding bicycles, and Michael Miller's lawn mowing. After the first few days of the routine, he also fast forwarded through the cars coming and going, too. He did note the Monday evening routine for Ralph.

When the video finished, Ralph said, "There's not much there. These two seem like real stay at home folks. They act like an old married couple. Are they married?"

"No, they aren't. We actually learn quite a bit in the phone recordings."

"Great, let's hear them."

After several calls, Phil asked, "You want me to fast forward through Jill's discussions with her mother? They get repetitive after a while."

"No, let me hear them the first time. Part of me feels weird listening in to someone's life like this, but part of me kind of likes it."

When they finished listening to the phone calls, Phil said, "I think I can see how we can get him. We'll have to wait until Monday night."

~ 34 ~

ON MONDAY, PHIL PUT ON his disguise in a gas station restroom. Ralph had applied his fake tattoos in his apartment after turning the store over to Jim. Phil thought Ralph looked sort of ghoulish. The tattoos had vines running down one arm and up one side of his neck. It was OK for the tattoos to stand out according to Ralph. They were the only thing anyone would remember about him.

When they got close to Corning, Ralph used his cell phone to order a pizza at the place Miller used for his Monday night pizza. They duplicated Michael's order, peperoni and green peppers. Phil went in to pick up the pizza. They had it for a late lunch. The pizza was okay, nothing to write home about, but okay. Their next step was to go to grocery stores to pick up the same kind of peperoni. Because the peperoni slices were a little bigger than normal, it took a little searching to find an exact match. The green peppers were easy.

Late in the afternoon Ralph used the pay phone they'd located in a local shopping mall to order a cheese pizza from the same place. He gave them a phony name and arranged to pick the pizza up in twenty minutes. When he brought the pizza back to the car, he said, "The guy sure took a long look at my tats. He might remember them, but only them."

"I'm not worried about it. Let's get back. Here comes the tricky part."

When they got back to Michael Miller's neighborhood, Ralph let Phil off at the path behind the houses. Phil hoped it was dark enough as he bent over and ran along the path. When he got to the Miller house, he peeked through the slats. The coast was clear, so he placed the phone intercept device in place. The rest was up to Ralph.

Meanwhile, after he dropped Phil off, Ralph drove to the playground parking lot. First, he scrubbed off the distinctive tattoos. He didn't want Michael Miller to see them. Second, he plugged the heating element in the car. It was a small wand-like thing. He sure hoped it worked. Third, he double checked his notes to be sure he had the patter used by the pizza parlor down perfectly. Then he settled in for a wait.

About a half an hour later, like clockwork, he intercepted Michael Miller's call to the pizza place. Ralph thought he did a good job of mimicking the guy who took orders. Thank goodness, Michael Miller was a creature of habit. He ordered the same pizza, and Ralph told him it was going to cost the same amount it had on previous occasions.

Ralph then arranged the peperoni and the green peppers on the cheese pizza. He tried his best to make it look exactly like the pizza he and Phil had for lunch. He then used the heated wand to warm up the pizza. It took some time to get the peperoni edges crisp and the cheese melted. The final step was to lift two of the pieces of peperoni and an apply a smear of the poison under them. When he was finished, he slid the pizza into the box. It was time to make the delivery. He put on the ball cap and pulled it down.

Ralph pulled into the cul-de-sac and walked up to Miller's house with the pizza. Miller opened the door and said, "Where's Jack? He usually works Mondays."

Ralph was startled, but he recovered and said, "I don't know. They called me to see if I could deliver tonight. Anyway, here's your pizza."

"Thanks, here's fifteen dollars; that should cover it."

"Thanks," Ralph said as he turned to leave.

Ralph drove around to the path. Phil was there waiting. "I'm ready to get out of here," he said to Phil.

"Fine with me. I heard you pull up, so I grabbed the equipment."

"Good, I got a little nervous when it seemed like Miller wanted to talk. The regular delivery guy's named Jack. He asked me where Jack was. I mumbled something about not knowing, gave him his pizza, and left in a hurry."

"Good work. I bet he didn't see much more of you than a ball cap."

"I sure didn't look him in the eyes. I don't think he got a good look at me. Still, he could tell I wasn't Jack."

"If I remember the video, Jack is a big fat guy, so he wouldn't have to notice much to see you weren't Jack,"

"Yeah, you're right. I forgot we got a couple of looks at Jack."

~~~

Jill Humphreys got home a little early from her girl's night out. She went into the family room and greeted Michael. "How's the game going?"

"It's not a great game. Both teams are pretty lame. I'm still in it. Chicago has to keep it close for me to win."

"Pizza good?"

"Come to think of it, it seemed a little off tonight. It left an odd taste in my mouth. It was like my mouth was numb."

Jill looked over at the empty pizza box and said, "While it might have been a little off, it didn't seem to stop you."

"Yeah, it was good enough."

Jill took the empty pizza box to the recycling bin. As she came back by the door to the family room, she shouted, "I'm getting ready for bed."

"I'll be in soon. Chicago just scored. I think I have this one in the bag," Michael shouted back.

Jill was in bed reading when Michael got back to the bedroom. He seemed to be stumbling a bit as he walked.

"How many beers did you have with your pizza?" she asked with a laugh.

"Only two. I wanted to get the odd taste out of my mouth. It's not the beers. I think my feet fell asleep while I was sitting there. I'll be fine."

The next morning Jill wondered if Michael really was fine. He usually got out of bed and showered first. He always wanted to be at the dealership before the workers showed up. He didn't respond to his alarm. Finally, she shoved him and said, "Turn it off!"

"Okay, okay, stop bugging me."

Jill could tell Michael was trying to get out of bed. For some reason he was having trouble. "What's wrong, honey?" she asked.

"For some reason, I can't move my legs."

"What?"

"I said, I can't move my legs."

"Why?"

"For God's sake, how the hell do I know!"

Jill was concerned. She got out of her side of the bed and went around to his side. She pulled the covers off Michael. His legs looked fine. "You can't move your legs?"

"Yes," he replied, frustrated.

She poked him in the thigh. "Can you feel that?"

"Only a little."

She poked his foot and looked at him questioningly.

"Nope—nothing."

"I'm calling 911." Jill hurried around to her night stand where she kept her cell phone. "You need a doctor."

~ 35 ~

HALF AN HOUR BEFORE WEDNESDAY lunch, Phil did his first check of the Corning paper. He was startled to see a story titled, "Local Business Leader Stricken with Mystery Illness." The story was short because there wasn't much to report. It simply said Michael Miller of Miller Ford-Kia had been taken to the hospital on Tuesday. He had lost feeling below his waist, and the doctors didn't have any idea of the cause.

Phil sent a quick email to Ralph with a link to the story before he took off for Andy's. As he walked toward the restaurant, he puzzled over the story. It was published so quickly. It must have had something to do with Miller being a local business leader. Martinez had been new to Billington. Few people knew him. On the other hand, Miller had grown up in Corning. He was somebody, and when he got sick in a mysterious way, it was news in a small city.

~~~

Phil got to Andy's a little late, and everyone was already in the back room. His friends had taken the liberty of ordering for him. He was predictable.

After they had eaten most of their lunch, Bob said, "I've been thinking about our discussions about the split in the country, and I think religion plays a big role. We haven't included it in the discussion."

"Bob, I'm surprised," George said. "Aren't you the one who is so enamored of Sally's change idea? Come to think of it, I think religion fits."

"How so?" asked Bob.

"There are fundamentalists, fundamentalist Christians and fundamentalist Moslems. These guys don't like change. They believe every word in the Bible or the Koran is true and always has been. They don't like new interpretations. People with less fundamentalist views are more open to change. They don't think all truth comes from scriptures. I think differences based on religion fits into Sally's idea about resistance to change."

"Great," Bob said. "Another convert to Sally's change hypothesis."

"I think it's a bit too quick," William said. "I know people who I suspect you'd label as fundamentalist Christians, who are as wedded to their cell phones and other gadgets as anyone else. They don't seem to be afraid of change."

"Okay, but they aren't going along with lots of cultural changes," George answered. "I guess it's not change per se, only change challenging a literal interpretation of the scriptures. They think God wrote the scriptures and since God doesn't change, neither can his words."

"I could never figure out how people could believe in a literal interpretation of the Bible," Bert said. "I mean, which translation? Aren't there lots of different translations, and don't they say different things?"

"Even if there was only one translation, they'd still have a problem," Sally said. "People are going to interpret what you write. You can't stop them. And different people are going to have different interpretations of the same sentence or paragraph. Having only one translation doesn't clear up the problem."

"So, once again, resistance to change is part of the story," Phil said. "Not all of it. I still think Sally is on to something."

"Amen," Bob said, and they all laughed as they broke up to go back to work.

~~~

After lunch Phil wandered over to the campus. It was funny. He'd spent a great deal of his life on campus. Now he didn't miss it.

He saw Sherry Ahearn across the quad. She was walking briskly in his direction. Phil stopped and waited for her.

"I planned on calling you this evening," she said in greeting.

"Here I am," Phil replied with a smile.

"I wondered if you could join me for lunch this Saturday. There's someone I want you to meet."

"Sure, I'm game. Who is it?"

"Let's let it be my secret. Andy's at noon?"

"Andy's at noon works for me. I won't even need a menu."

"Yeah, I know. The Wednesday lunch group."

What is this strange lunch invitation all about? Whatever it was, he was happy about it. He liked the idea of spending more time with Sherry.

~ 36 ~

ON SATURDAY, PHIL PRIMPED A little more than usual and put on his favorite shirt. Then laughed at himself. This wasn't a date by any means. The mystery person was going to be there. Sherry had invited him to introduce the other person.

When he got to Andy's at noon on the dot, he could see Sherry sitting across from a man in one of the back booths. When he got to the booth, Sherry slid over offering Phil the seat next to her. She made the introduction. "Phil Philemon, my brother, Trick Ahearn."

Phil shook hands with Trick, and they exchanged greetings. Phil could see a strong resemblance between the brother and sister. Their coloring was similar, and they had the same eyes. Trick was much bigger and several years younger. It wasn't difficult to believe they were brother and sister.

"Phil was my history professor back in the dark ages. I ran into him at the football game a few weeks ago. It turns out he's a football fan. I thought it might be fun for him to meet a real-life football star," Sherry said.

Phil could tell Trick was blushing, so he filled the silence. "I certainly don't know what it's like to have a stadium full of people cheering for me. I was too little, too slow, and too uncoordinated to be any good at sports."

"Gee Sis, that's no way to introduce someone."

"It's okay," Phil said. He desperately wanted to talk sports—anything to avoid talking about Trick's current job. "No, I'm interested. Like I said, I never experienced it. Do you hear the fans cheering, or are you concentrating so much you block it out?"

"It's interesting, no one's ever asked before. In football you're far away from the fans, and it's a little hard to hear through the helmet. I don't think I remember any cheering... no, that's not right. I remember the huge cheer when we came out on to the field before the game started. During the games I was focused on not messing up the next play. As you said, I guess I blocked out the noise."

"Basketball must be different. Did you play basketball?" Phil asked.

"Yes, in high school. I wasn't very good. Still, our small school needed bodies, so I played. And you're right. There are no helmets in basketball, and the fans are right on top of you. There's no way you couldn't hear them. I don't remember hearing the fans while I was playing. A few times when we got on hot streaks, and, you know, the other team would call a time out to try to cool us down. Our fans went crazy. I remember fans cheering then. There was no way you couldn't hear it."

"No one cheers for history professors, do they Phil?" Sherry asked with a smile.

Before Phil could answer the waitress came for their orders. When she turned to Phil, she asked, "The regular?" and Phil nodded.

"Phil eats lunch here with a group of other faculty members every Wednesday, so he's a known quantity," Sherry told her brother.

"Must be nice," Trick said.

"It is. I think the same group of us has been eating Wednesday lunch for about fifteen years. Wednesday is right in the middle of the week. It splits things up nicely."

"I think they talk campus politics a lot," Sherry said.

"Usually we talk national and international politics. Actually, these TVs around here generate quite a few discussions."

"Huh," Trick said. "I wouldn't think college professors would like this channel."

"No, we don't. The conversation usually starts with 'You wouldn't believe what I saw on Andy's TVs.'"

"Okay, now I get it," Trick said. "Come to think of it, I have a similar lunch. All the police chiefs and the heads of the local security firms have a lunch every Friday. I haven't been going very long. I only recently got promoted to chief. My group likes this channel. I'll bet their take on the world is different from you professors."

"I bet it is. You know it baffles us. How can people living in the same country be so different? There's a widening political split in the country. We can't figure out what's driving it."

"Please tell us all if you ever find out," Sherry said with a laugh.

Their food arrived, and the conversation stopped for a while. As they were finishing, Sherry said, "I bet you talked to your Friday lunch group about your recent case, Trick. Why don't you tell Phil about it? I bet he'd find it interesting."

Phil started to get nervous. He couldn't help making a little jerk. Gamely he asked, "What's going on?"

"It's weird. I got a call from the local hospital about this guy, Dennis Martinez. The hospital called me because they thought he'd been poisoned. Though I know how it happened, I haven't got a clue who did it."

While Phil was still nervous, he was curious, too. "How'd it happen?"

"Someone broke into Martinez's house and planted a tack in one of his slippers. There was a little puncture wound. The poison left Martinez's right leg completely paralyzed."

"How'd they get into his house?" Phil asked.

"We aren't 100 percent sure. The house is new. It has a house alarm, but there was a problem with the back-door alarm. The alarm company was waiting for a part. I talked to them. They told me the front door alarm was tripped the day before Martinez stepped on the tack. When they responded to the alarm, they didn't see anything."

"Do you have any suspects?" Phil asked.

"We thought we had a suspect. Martinez has a girlfriend, one of his cleaning ladies. She's an illegal, so it was hard to find her. When we did, she didn't want to talk. It turned out she has an ironclad alibi for the day the poisoning must have happened. We got her to admit she had a date with Martinez when he discovered he couldn't feel his leg. She even made the 911 call."

"So, they're completely baffled," Sherry added. "And they don't know what the poison was."

"Yeah, I thought I sent them a good sample. The state lab hasn't been able to identify it yet. It must be exotic."

"I don't know anything about this kind of thing." Phil was relaxing. "Don't you look for a motive? Who'd want to harm this guy?"

"Yeah, we look for motives. Martinez was new to our neck of the woods. He moved in from Florida. Actually, he'd only lived there for two years. Originally, he came from Ohio. There was a scandal there right before he left. We're only starting to get the details. Maybe we can find someone who had it in for him."

"Would it be odd for a person from Ohio to come to South Carolina to do a poisoning?" Sherry asked.

"You're right, Sis. Interstate crime is unusual. Almost everything I've worked on involves locals. Most of the criminals I work with are stupid, and they keep being stupid. When things happen, I can give you a list of five guys and be almost sure one of them did it."

"You hear that about prisons," Phil said. "They're full of repeat offenders. As you say, stupid guys who keep being stupid."

"On that high note, Trick and I should leave," Sherry said. "It was hard enough prying him away from Mom for this lunch. I'd better get her son back before she gets upset. And I'll take the check. I was the one who set up this lunch."

"What you goin' to do with a modern woman?" Trick asked with a smile.

"Let her get the check," Phil said returning the smile.

After the check was taken care of, Phil got up so Sherry could slide out of the booth. He turned to Trick and shook his hand. "It was nice to meet you. Good luck with your mystery case."

~~~

Phil followed the brother and sister out of the restaurant and headed for Ralph's store. When he arrived, he paced around while Ralph dealt with a customer. When the customer left, he hustled Ralph into the back room. "You wouldn't believe who I just had lunch with," Phil blurted out.

"Sherry Ahearn; I already heard."

"Wow, this is a small town. Yes, Sherry Ahearn and her brother, too. You know, the police chief from South Carolina."

Ralph's eyes got big. "So, is he working on the Martinez case?"

"Yes, he is, and we talked about it. He doesn't have a clue who did it. They suspected the cleaning lady girlfriend, but she had an alibi. Now they're investigating Martinez's past in Ohio. The summary's clear. They don't have a clue. While it's frustrating Sherry's brother, it's fine with me."

"It's fine with me, too. Did you keep your cool during the conversation?"

"I think I did. I sure was nervous when we started talking about the Martinez business. I tried to stay calm. I think I succeeded."

"I hope you did. Anyway, combining this with what we learned about Michael Miller earlier in the week, things seem to be working fine. We're looking like a big success. Who's next?"

"Let me get back to you Monday. I'm not sure. Winter is setting in, and travel around here gets to be a little chancy. I've looked a little. I'm scheduled to work here Monday morning. I'll be ready to discuss it then."

~ 37 ~

PHIL CAME INTO RALPH'S STORE early on Monday. Ralph was busy in the back room with a computer repair he'd promised. While Ralph toiled away Phil helped three customers. He was proud he could deal with all three by himself.

At ten o'clock Ralph came out front lugging the fixed computer. "This is ready for the Murrays. They should be in at one. I replaced the power supply,"

"Things are calm out here."

"You want to make your report?" Ralph gestured toward the back room.

"Have you ever been to New Orleans?" Phil asked once they were seated.

"No, I hear it's an interesting place."

"I'm going to suggest Maynard Dennison, who lives close to New Orleans. The story on Dennison is a bit convoluted. Dennison was part of a very successful interior decorating business in New Orleans. He shot his business partner, Erica Robinson, when she was coming home from a party. He made it look like a mugging. The police were suspicious right away. The only clue was a shoe print in the mud by the scene of the crime. The shoe matched a pair of Reeboks Dennison owned. When the police confronted him, he confessed. In the long run, however, they couldn't use the confession in court. They hadn't given him his Miranda warning."

"How do we know all this?"

"The motive for the shooting was money. Dennison knew Erica was the key to their business success. She planned to marry this guy, Lewis Sherman, and move to New York City. Dennison was savvy enough to know the firm wouldn't be worth much without her. According to Sherman, the source of most of the back story, Dennison and Erica argued long and heatedly about the move. Erica stayed firm. They were planning to dissolve the partnership.

"Sherman is convinced Dennison was the one who shot Erica. The interior decorating business had taken out life insurance policies on the principals. As the sole surviving member of the partnership, Dennison would get the money. And there was more money involved. At the time of the shooting, the firm was about to receive a big payment. The job had been Erica's responsibility. The way the firm worked it, though the check went to the firm, Erica got eighty percent of the money. The agreement about the split of the money was informal. Nothing written down. With Erica's death, all the money, the life insurance and the big check for the recent job, went to Dennison."

"And, let me guess. Between the time they got the first confession they couldn't use in court and when they got back to Dennison, he got himself a lawyer who told him to clam up."

"You got it," Phil said. "The second time Dennison said he was so upset by the killing he didn't know what he was saying. What they took for a confession was his guilt. He said he killed her because he'd badgered her into going to the party. There were going to be high rollers there, the kind of people the decorating business needed to attract. When the police told him Erica had been shot, he was upset. He said he had killed her, because he was the reason she went out so late. The police made it sound like a confession when it wasn't."

Ralph interrupted. "How do we know about the Miranda warning and the shoes?"

"Like I said, Sherman was the source of the information. Apparently, he bugged the police so much they finally told him the story. Then he told it to a newspaper reporter. The reporter dug more, and the whole story got out. She even spoke to the officers who heard the first confession. While she couldn't use their names, she quoted them as saying it was a real confession, not Dennison's B. S.

"Since they didn't have a confession to use in court, the case against Dennison fell apart. Size ten Reeboks like Dennison's are common. And they never recovered a gun. They had motive enough, but no real evidence."

"There's one thing bothering me about this one," Ralph said.

"What?"

"This guy Sherman, Erica's fiancé. If we do our thing on Dennison, won't he be the instant suspect? There wasn't anyone like him in the other cases. He's obviously the person the police are going to go after. Won't it be a problem?"

"I don't think so. He lives in New York City. Erica was going to marry him and move there. I bet he'll be miles away when we do the deed. It should be easy for him to come up with an alibi."

"Oh, I forgot. Yeah sure, Dennison sounds like a great candidate. What have you found out about where he lives?"

"I haven't done any research yet," Phil said. "When I go home, I'll see what I can find."

"We're going to have to move in a hurry. The holidays are coming up, and things get very busy here, at least if I'm lucky."

"Okay, I guess I'll make the first trip to New Orleans by myself, and I'll get right on it. It's good for me to get away. New Orleans should be a nice place to spend a week during the dreary weather here. I'm going to the first basketball game. It's tomorrow night. I can leave the next day."

"I know you're a big fan. Is this going to be their year?"

"Hope springs eternal. Maybe this'll be the year."

~~~

Phil had arranged to meet Sherry at the basketball game. They sat several rows up at about center court. The turnout at the game was a little better than Phil remembered from previous years. Maybe the news about the big freshman had gotten out.

The game was sloppy. Lots of first games were sloppy. It was clear the competition wasn't very good. This made it difficult for Lackey to get into a smooth rhythm. Still, he could tell Nate Smith was going to be a very good player. He was big, and he could shoot. He hit two three pointers in the first half, and he seemed to have good moves around the basket. He was clearly the best player on the court.

Phil and Sherry enjoyed the game. At half time Sherry said, "You're really into this, aren't you?"

"Yes, basketball is a passion. I've been coming to Lackey games for a long time. They've broken my heart so many times. Each year I think they're going to turn the corner. Maybe this guy Smith will be the savior. He sure looks good."

"You have to consider the opponent."

"Not so good, huh."

"Their biggest player is six five, and what is Smith—six eight? He didn't have much trouble getting rebounds or making moves close to the basket."

"Okay, okay, I know I have to temper my enthusiasm. It's the first game, the opponents aren't very good. Still, six eight with two three pointers. Not many big men are going to be able to guard him away from the basket."

The rest of the game was a repeat. Smith ended up with twenty-seven points despite the fact he didn't play much in the second half.

After the game, Phil walked Sherry to her car. When she was about to get in, Phil said, "I'll be away for about a week. I'm going south to get away from the weather for a while. It should be nice in New Orleans this time of year."

"New Orleans is interesting. You'll have a good time. It's a little early to be worried about getting away from the weather, isn't it?"

"Yes, I guess it is. I felt like getting away for a while. No telling what I'll do when it gets really cold."

"Have fun," Sherry said as she got into her car.

~ 38 ~

BECAUSE HIS STOMACH DROPPED EVERY time he thought about flying using the false name, Phil decided to use his own name for this trip. Lots of people went to New Orleans, His trip wouldn't seem unusual. When he did his snooping around, he'd use a disguise.

Phil chose a little hotel close to the French quarter. When he got to his room, he wasn't impressed with the small space that had an odd odor. He wandered around the French quarter in the evening. The entertainment options seemed to be aimed at fraternity boys.

The next morning, he walked by Maynard Dennison's interior decorating studio. When he got to the right street address, he saw a sign saying the business was closed. The sign had a phone number. Phil recognized it as one of Dennison's numbers.

As he continued to walk around, he could see why people thought the city was charming. The buildings were interesting. The garish feel of Bourbon Street wasn't the whole story. Still, here and there things looked a little run down. The New Orleans climate made it important for homeowners to pay attention to maintenance. Clearly a few hadn't.

After he returned to the hotel, he got out the detailed map of New Orleans and reviewed the route to Maynard Dennison's house. The house was an old plantation fronting a river or canal. The back of the house faced the road. He was going to drive by to figure where he could put the surveillance equipment. If he was lucky, he could put the equipment up in daylight.

The drive out of downtown New Orleans was not easy. Phil realized how much he was a small-town guy. Though he'd driven through a few cities, he hadn't dealt with city driving very often. New Orleans didn't seem to be organized around a grid. He made it to the outskirts of the city and found the highway he needed. He slowed as he turned onto the little road behind Dennison's house. His internet information told him there were eight houses along the road. They all fronted on the water. It seemed odd to be driving along, looking at people's backyards.

The houses sat on large plots. The big trees lining the road and driveways were impressive. He slowed down even more as he approached Dennison's house. It was a little smaller than its neighbors and quite a bit closer to the road. It had two stories. A screened porch ran along the back. It would be easy enough to put a camera and maybe even a phone intercept device on one of the trees beside the driveway. Phil wondered why a chain-link fence went across the driveway maybe fifteen feet in front of the house. As he was trying to figure it out, he realized a pickup truck was coming up behind him, so he sped up. The pickup turned into the driveway for the house two down from Dennison's.

Phil continued to the next intersection. He knew it dead ended to the left, so he turned left. It wouldn't be odd to make a U-turn at the dead end. When he got back to Dennison's street, he retraced his route the other direction. First, he was looking for a place where he could park his car. Second, he wanted to figure out what the deal was with the chain-link fence across the driveway.

He checked his rearview mirror and paused right across from the Dennison driveway. After a minute or two, he figured out the reason for the fence. A guard dog patrolled the yard. As Phil surveyed the scene, the dog seemed to be taking an interest in Phil's car. This was not good. Phil could see a gate in the part of the fence spanning the driveway. Apparently, Dennison and his car went in and out through the gate. *The dog must be trained to not worry about his car.* When the fence was closed, the dog ranged between the house and anyone who wanted to get in.

He did find a very nice secluded parking place about a hundred yards past Dennison's property line. It would be easy to park there and make it back to Dennison's driveway. While his car wouldn't be completely hidden, it would be out of the way.

Phil sighed with discouragement as he drove back to New Orleans. The dog was going to make this very difficult. Before he could mount his equipment close to the house, he had to determine when the house was likely to be empty. If he got close to the house, the dog would likely make a lot of noise.

Phil developed a plan. Unfortunately, it would involve an extra couple of trips down the road behind Dennison's house. There wasn't any way around it. Tonight, he'd mount one of the cameras across the street. Two nights later, he'd retrieve the camera to see when cars went in and out of the driveway. He would have to rent a laptop. When he knew what kind of car Dennison drove and found out when he came and went, he'd know when he could mount equipment closer to the house.

Planting the camera was not difficult. When Phil turned onto the street, he took a chance and drove with his lights off. It was dark on the street, no streetlights. He coasted to a stop in front of the tree he'd chosen and placed the camera on a branch about six feet above the ground. The camera's wide-angle lens would easily cover Dennison's driveway.

He decided to collect images for two days to be sure he caught Dennison coming and going. The two days gave him a chance to play tourist. Seeing the tourist spots would be good for his cover story.

Phil studied the brochures in his hotel lobby and plotted his two tourist days. The first morning he signed up for a New Orleans Segway tour. He'd never ridden a Segway before, but it looked like fun. Phil was happy other beginners were on his tour. After about ten minutes of practice, he could ride the thing quite easily. He wasn't very good at going backwards, and he found standing still a little hard. Still, he was confident he wouldn't fall off when it came time for the tour itself. The hour and a half tour went by very quickly.

In the afternoon he took a tour to Oak Alley Plantation. The plantation was a little ways out of town, so the tour started on a bus. The bus was almost completely full, and he had the extra discomfort of being squeezed in next to an overweight, sweaty man. Phil did not like this kind of touring. The plantation itself was amazing. Phil knew the work building such a fabulous place was all done by slaves. That diminished the experience for him.

Phil spent his next day in museums. As a historian, Phil liked museums, so he had no trouble filling a day. In the evening, he drove out to retrieve the camera. This trip went smoothly. It was good Dennison lived off such a quiet straight street.

When he got back to his room, he fired up the laptop he'd rented. Though he thought he remembered how to get the video, he didn't. He had to call Ralph to walk him through the steps. After a brief conversation about the dog, Phil got to work reviewing the video. The street was quiet as Phil had suspected. Maynard Dennison left at about nine both mornings. He drove a red BMW sports car of recent vintage. Only one car ever used the driveway. Dennison didn't return until three the first day and seven the second day.

Phil saw several cars go by, and one woman walked her dog at three o'clock both afternoons. The dog walker got Dennison's guard dog very excited. It ran beside the fence wagging its tail vigorously and barking. As Phil suspected, Dennison's dog went crazy when the mailman made his deliveries. The afternoon Dennison came home early, Phil could see him in the distance running around with the dog. The same thing might have happened the second day. It was dark, so he couldn't see.

If the two-day sample was good, Phil had a quite a big window to mount his equipment. Dennison seemed to leave around nine and the dog walker didn't appear until three. Of course, cars passed by all day long. Phil ran the video again and counted the times cars came by. There was a burst of traffic early in the morning. Dennison, with his nine o'clock departure, was one of the late ones. Later in the mornings, traffic was light. There was even an hour the second day, from ten to eleven, when no cars came by. And there'd only been one car during that time slot the day before. Phil planned to mount his equipment at ten-fifteen.

The next morning, he drove to a diner at the intersection of Dennison's street and the highway. It was small, seven booths and about twelve stools at the counter. The breakfast rush seemed to be over, so a booth at the end was available. The booth had a good view of Dennison's street. The clientele of the diner were interesting—a mix of working men and business types in suits. Lots of people seemed to know each other. And the waitress seemed to know everybody.

Phil ordered his breakfast—the special: eggs and pancakes. He buried himself in a newspaper, so he wouldn't be easy to see. About five minutes after he sat down, he saw Dennison's red sports car at the intersection. Much to Phil's surprise, Dennison pulled into the diner.

When Dennison came in, the waitress greeted him. "Maynard, I see you're running a little early today."

"Oh, I guess so. Charley's not here yet. I don't beat him many mornings."

Dennison sat down two booths in front of Phil. A couple of minutes later another man joined him, apparently Charley. They seemed to be dressed for golf, polyester pants and rain-proof pullovers.

The waitress came over with a plastic pitcher of coffee and said, "Coffee for Charley. None for Maynard, right?"

"You know it, Jess. I couldn't see straight to drive over here without my morning brew. I don't need any of the nasty stuff you got in them pitchers."

"It ain't nasty. Charley, tell him it ain't nasty."

"The coffee's okay here," Charley said.

Phil overheard more banter between Dennison and Charley and the waitress, Jess. It was clear the two men were regulars. Apparently, they came in almost every morning before their golf game. Phil finished his breakfast quickly. He didn't want to hang out close to Dennison for very long. He had his wig and mustache disguise on. Still, he hadn't been this close to either of the other two guys. He settled up with Jess and

~ *39* ~

BY THE TIME RALPH GOT to Phil's house, Phil had reviewed the videos and phone recordings from Dennison's house. "Let me show you the highlights," he said to Ralph after they'd greeted each other.

"Sure, it's a lot easier than looking at everything."

Phil showed him a little of the video taken from across the street. It showed the whole house, though it was partly hidden behind trees. Ralph agreed the fence with its gate in the middle of the driveway was strange. Phil then switched to the closer video. His first selection showed Dennison coming out of the house with a coffee cup in one hand and a bag of dog food in the other. With the dog dancing excitedly around him, he went over to a fenced-in area with a dog house and dog bowls. He loaded up one bowl with the food and, using a hose, filled the other one with water. Phil said, "I think he pens up the dog if he's having company. Otherwise the dog is free to roam inside the bigger fence."

"It's a big dog. What is it, a Doberman?"

"I think you're right, and it's clearly trained as a guard dog. You should have heard the racket it made when I planted the equipment. If it hadn't been behind the fence, it would've torn me limb from limb."

"If we are going to have to get anywhere near the house, we're going to have to figure out how to deal with it."

"Here's my plan. You climb over the fence. While the dog is taking care of you, I'll get into the house."

"Very funny. Let's think of a plan B."

"Plan B it is. This next video is interesting," Phil said.

Phil zoomed in on the house for the next video. Through the screened porch it showed Dennison filling his coffee cup at a coffee maker in the kitchen. "Wow, the camera activated on the motion of him on the porch, and you can see through the windows into the kitchen. Amazing," Ralph said.

"Yes, I think it works because he turns on all the lights. Watch what happens when he gets back." Phil fast forwarded to Dennison's return from feeding the dog. He rinsed his coffee cup and put it beside the coffee maker. Then he poured out the unused coffee, rinsed the pitcher, and put it back on the coffee maker.

After this footage, Phil said, "He does the same thing every morning. He just rinses the cup and the pitcher. I suppose he washes them on occasion, but I didn't catch him doing it."

"So that's his vulnerability?"

"Yes, and he doesn't even lock his back door. Watch the next video. It shows him leaving." When the video finished, Phil added, "The red car's nice; it's easy to spot."

"Looks like a sweet ride. You're right, he doesn't even lock his door. He's relying on the dog. Frankly, it seems like a good plan."

"You're right, we're going to have to deal with the dog. Otherwise, it might be easy. Dennison is a real creature of habit. His morning routine is identical every day. He makes himself coffee, rinses the cup and pitcher, and then heads out to have breakfast at a diner."

"How do you know where he eats breakfast?"

"It was an accident. The day I wanted to plant the closer cameras, I had to be sure his car was gone, so I killed time hiding behind a newspaper at the diner. It had a good view of his street. After I'd been there for a few minutes, he drove up and walked in. He's a regular there. He meets a guy named Charley. And the last morning, I saw his car leave the diner at nine forty-five. I don't think he does much cooking. The diner served a good breakfast, and one evening he came home with a pizza box."

"Okay, did we learn anything from the phone intercepts?"

"Not much, he doesn't get many calls. Like Miller, I'm pretty sure he has a bookie. He bets on college football, not the pros like Miller. There is a long call on Thursday night in which he is placing a series of bets on college games."

"This is easy. We know where to plant the poison, and he leaves the house unlocked. We have one big problem: the dog."

"You got it. Let's think about it for a while. There has to be a way to get around the dog."

~~~

Phil went to the Lackey basketball game on Tuesday night. He met Sherry again. The game was a little more competitive than the first game. The freshman star, Nate Smith, played most of the game, and he made the difference in a close win.

As they walked back to the parking lot, Sherry said, "I think Nate Smith is the real deal. When's the last time Lackey had anyone as good as Smith? As I remember it, they were pretty bad during my student days."

"I don't think we've ever had anyone like Smith. He's an unusual case. He grew so much after he agreed to come to Lackey. I think he'd be at a big-time school if he'd grown a year earlier. Now we have to hope he doesn't transfer."

"He wouldn't transfer, would he?"

"Big time college basketball is sleazy. I wouldn't it put it past a big-time school to try to raid a guy like Smith."

"Let's hope it doesn't happen," Sherry said as they got to her car. She leaned over and kissed Phil on the cheek. "It was nice to watch the game with you." She opened her car door and got in.

Phil was surprised by the kiss but pleased nevertheless. As he walked home, he wondered where he and Sherry were headed. As it had in the past, this kind of thought made him feel disloyal to Mary Jane. While he didn't think she'd want him to mope around all the rest of his life, wasn't this a little too quick?

~~~

As Sherry drove home, she wondered why she'd kissed Phil on the cheek. She liked Phil. He was only one she'd clicked with since she returned to Lackey. He was easy to talk to, and they had things in common. She'd had a large group of friends in State College but hadn't developed friends here yet. Part of it was because she lived out on the farm with her mother. And it was strange with Phil. She was being the aggressor. All her life she'd had to fend off the advances of men. She didn't have much experience being the one pushing. And she'd better be careful. Though he hid it well, she knew Phil was still grieving.

~ 40 ~

TO FIT IN THE TRIP before Ralph's store got busy, Phil and Ralph took an early afternoon flight on Friday. When they got to their hotel, Ralph went out to see the sights. Phil had work to do. He drove to a Walmart Supercenter in a suburb across the Mississippi River. The Walmart was not very busy on Friday night. It took a little while to find the dart gun and darts on Ralph's list.

On the drive back to the hotel, Phil wondered if their plan would work. Ralph had acquired liquid tranquilizer to coat the darts. He told Phil his sources claimed the tranquilizer could take down an elephant. It ought to work on a dog. Ralph even found dosages for various animals. They planned to shoot the dog and hide in the woods until the tranquilizer took effect. When the dog was down, Ralph would go retrieve the dart. At the same time, Phil would plant the poison on the coffee cup and pitcher. It seemed like a simple plan.

The dart gun was a pistol. Phil and Ralph had talked about how difficult it was to aim a pistol. "In the Army, we once shot pistols," Phil said. "The targets were big, and they were close, maybe fifteen or twenty feet. I fired several times and was sure I hit the target. When I went to look, it was unmarked."

Ralph replied, "I've shot pistols in my time. I think I could hit a big dog from close range."

Phil was glad Ralph would be shooting. He didn't want to hurt the dog. It was odd. While he had no compunction about poisoning Dennison, he didn't want to be the one who shot the dog. Maybe it was because he was convinced Dennison deserved his fate. The dog didn't. Or maybe he was squeamish about inflicting pain. Anyway, he was happy with their plan.

Phil got back to the hotel before Ralph. He was in bed when Ralph knocked on his door. Ralph had enjoyed his tour through the French Quarter, but he wasn't happy with Bourbon Street. At one of the strip shows, he'd run into the two-drink minimum. He complained the drinks were watered down, and the girls weren't very pretty. Phil was tired and not very sympathetic. He figured Ralph had learned a valuable lesson, the kind of lesson experience can teach better than any instructor.

The next morning, they decided to go to the diner, so they'd be sure Dennison wasn't spending the morning at home. When they got there, Dennison's car was in the parking lot. They found a line of people waiting to get in. Apparently, Saturday breakfast at the diner was a popular pastime.

The people in the line were the same mix Phil had seen before. On Saturday there were fewer suits and ties. Lots of the talk centered on the LSU football game. A group of four in front of them all decked out in purple and yellow were leaving for Baton Rouge right after breakfast. Others said they'd be glued to their TV sets.

After they'd been in line for about fifteen minutes and made it to the front, Dennison and his friend Charley came out. They overheard Charley saying, "See you at the course." Dennison got into his car and followed Charley out of the parking lot. Phil and Ralph were glad he wasn't headed home.

When Jess the waitress poked her head out the door, they went in the diner. They were shown to a booth, probably the one vacated by Dennison and Charley. They'd talked about it, and Phil didn't think there was any risk. He had his gray hair and beard get up on, not the black hair and mustache. And besides, he had a companion this time.

The false tattoos Ralph had selected, big dragons on his right arm, were probably the most memorable thing about the two of them.

After breakfast, they hoped traffic on Dennison's street had calmed down. They didn't want anyone at the diner to see them going down Dennison's street, so Phil entered from the other end and parked in the hiding place he'd found on his earlier trip. Phil and Ralph kept to the trees as they approached the house. When they got across from Dennison's property, the dog had already sensed them and came right up to the fence across from them.

Phil and Ralph went a little further back into the forest. It looked like it was going to turn into a swamp if they went too far. After putting on his latex gloves, Ralph took out a dart and coated it with the tranquilizer. While the pistol was only a single shot, he doctored two darts just in case. After a moment, he was ready. "Here goes nothing."

"I'm hoping for more than nothing."

As Ralph walked across the road, the dog started barking and jumping up against the fence. Phil was impressed to see Ralph walk right up to the fence with the barking and snarling dog on the other side. Ralph took his shot. The dog kept right on barking and jumping against the fence. Ralph reloaded the pistol. For his next shot he got even closer. As the dog jumped, Ralph put the pistol through the fence and fired again. This time the dog yelped in pain and started barking even louder.

"What happened?" Phil asked when Ralph rejoined him.

"You wouldn't believe it; the first shot hit the fence and ricocheted off to the left. It missed the dog completely. I stuck the pistol through the fence the next time. I got him then."

"You think you can find the first dart?"

"I don't know. I'll try. It might be hard to find. And the dog is going to have a fair-sized wound from the dart. If anyone sees him up close, they might guess what happened."

"Still, it would be better to retrieve both darts."

"No question about it."

The noise from the dog had calmed down, so they went to look. The information about the tranquilizer said it took from five to ten minutes to take effect. Of course, they had no way to be certain they had the dosage right. As they got to the edge of the road, the barking started up again.

"He still seems very much awake," Ralph said.

"I'll say. Let's move back." The dog stopped barking as they entered the woods.

They waited another five minutes and made their way to the edge of the road again. They were surprised. They couldn't see the dog.

"Where is he?" asked Phil.

"I can't see him. Let's go. If we approach the house and he doesn't come over, the tranquilizer must have taken effect. I'll find him and retrieve the dart. Then I'll search for the other dart. You do your business. I'll meet you at the car."

When they entered Dennison's driveway the dog didn't come. They opened the gate, and Phil walked to the house while Ralph went off in search of the dog.

Phil opened the door to the kitchen area and found the coffee mug and pitcher right where he expected. Dennison was surely consistent. They were both still wet from their morning rinse. He got out his poison and coated the inside of the mug and for good measure, he put a smear on the lip of the pitcher. Tomorrow morning, Dennison's coffee would dilute the poison. From what he'd read, Phil was pretty sure it would still do the trick. He placed the mug and pitcher exactly where he'd found them and went back out the door. Over by the dog's fenced in area, he saw Ralph bent over what must be the dog. He hustled through the gate and down the driveway.

Phil had been in the car for what seemed like an eternity when Ralph finally showed up. "Did you find the first dart?" he asked as he started the car.

"Yep, it was in a little tree. We were smart to buy the darts with the red—what are they? They aren't feathers."

"And is the dog going to be okay?"

"I sure hope so. He was still breathing, but let me tell you he's fast asleep. I had to roll him over to get at the dart buried in his skin. It took

"Damn, what's happened to you?"

"How the hell do I know! All of a sudden, I lost feeling in my legs. Get an ambulance out here!"

"They're not letting no ambulance out here. It'd tear up the course." Charley looked around. "There's a threesome waiting on the tee now. I'll flag them down, and they can help me get you in our cart."

~~~

On Monday, Phil read the *New Orleans Times Picayune*. It had nothing about Dennison. It was okay. He didn't expect anything for a while.

He worked mornings at Ralph's store. He was getting used to the rhythms there. He could do most routine things. He had to call Ralph out when a customer brought in a computer with a difficult problem. At eleven on Tuesday, Ralph came out from the back saying he was all caught up on repairs.

"I can't remember when I've been in this good shape. I'm waiting on parts, so I haven't completed everything. Otherwise I'm caught up."

"So, I may be doing some good around here?" said Phil.

"Fishing for a compliment, are we?"

"No... or maybe yes."

"Well, I'll give you one. It's been good to have you here. I didn't realize how many times I used to get interrupted with trivial things."

"Trivial things?"

"Don't be upset. You know what I mean. People come in here all the time to buy mousepads, memory sticks, printer ink, and small stuff. If I'd had enough money to hire a clerk, I'd have done it long ago. Now I have a rich friend with time on his hands. It's been absolutely great for me."

"You're right. I can't do any of the complicated stuff, but I'm getting better."

"That you are, my friend."

~~~

On Tuesday night Phil went to the Terrell's house for dinner. He'd turned down two previous invitations because of his trips. There was no way to avoid this one. Jeremy and Linda had been best friends with

Phil and Mary Jane. He'd dreaded going. He wasn't looking forward to the "what are you doing?" question. He'd been very busy, but he couldn't talk about it. He and Jeremy had always kicked around ideas about classes and research projects. There was no way he could share the results of his current activities.

The Terrell's house was nice, bigger and newer than Phil's. Jeremy and Linda both came from well-to-do backgrounds, and about five years ago, their parents helped them build a new house. Linda and Mary Jane had spent several Saturdays hunting for antique furniture to fill the grand house.

With his recent windfall, Phil realized he too could build a new house. He could afford it. Still, he didn't need it. He also recognized he shouldn't be competing with Jeremy. He shouldn't make comparisons. Maybe someone in the psychology department could explain to him why he, like everyone else, seemed to make comparisons all the time. He had what he needed. It shouldn't matter that other people had more.

Jeremy and Linda greeted him warmly, and he accepted the proffered glass of red wine. They had a fire going in the fireplace, and, as always, the house looked immaculate. When they were seated in front of the fire, Jeremy asked, "Where have you been? You missed a Wednesday lunch."

"Oh, didn't I tell everyone? I decided to get away from the winter for a while. I went to New Orleans. I'd only been there once before at a conference, and I was mostly cooped up in a hotel then. I wanted to see more of the city."

"What did you think of it?" Linda asked.

"It's interesting. Part of it is cheesy—Bourbon Street and the touristy part of the French Quarter. Much of it is so different. I did a Segway tour and went through some very nice parts of the city."

"A Segway tour?" Jeremy interrupted.

"Yeah, it's a lot of fun. It's not hard to ride those things. They start you off with a training course. It was my first time. By the time the actual tour started I was comfortable."

"Didn't it spook you? Lots of the city is below the level of the river," Linda asked.

"No, it didn't bother me. I wouldn't like to be there in a rain storm, though. And I saw quite a bit of evidence of hurricane damage. The low-lying areas took it hard."

"Did you stay for the week?" Jeremy asked.

"No, cities are not for me. After a few days I took a drive. I went to Biloxi, Mobile, and Baton Rouge. I took the back roads. Interstates tend to look pretty much the same anywhere. While I drove on the smaller roads, I thought a lot about the split in the country we talk about at lunch. Those folks in Louisiana, Mississippi, and Alabama aren't on our side of the split."

"Did you learn anything?" Jeremy asked.

"No, not much. Most of the conversations I overheard were about college football. It's different down there. Almost every vehicle has a bumper sticker or two with college names on them. In Alabama, you're either an Auburn person or an Alabama person. In Mississippi, it's either Mississippi State or Ole Miss. In Louisiana, it's mostly LSU. For all my trying to listen to people, it's the big difference I saw."

Linda, who'd stepped into the kitchen while the guys were talking, brought a dish to the table. "Dinner's ready."

Phil enjoyed the dinner. When he finished, he said, "Linda, dinner was superb. Lately, I've taken to heating up things from the frozen food section. A true home-cooked meal is a real treat."

"Mary Jane was a good cook. She said you helped. Don't you know how to cook even a little?" Linda asked.

"No. When we cooked together, I followed directions. I guess I assumed Mary Jane would always be there to direct the show." Despite himself, Phil choked up a little. He recovered quickly. "I never learned much."

"So, you are like me, huh," Jeremy said with a smile.

"Sounds like it," Linda said. "Let's take our wine out to the living room. Leave the dishes, Jeremy and I'll get them later."

When they sat down in the living room, Linda started the conversation. "Phil, everyone is too chicken to ask, not me. What's going on between you and Sherry Ahearn?"

Phil was a little taken aback by the direct question. He should have expected it from Linda. "Well, you know she was a student of mine, actually ours. She took one of your classes, didn't she Jeremy?"

"Yes, I think she did," Jeremy said.

"And she was different from all the other students. She was older. She had an ill-considered marriage right out of high school. She came to college after the divorce. And she was very bright. I remember trying to get her to think about graduate school. She didn't. She went off to New York City and a high-powered job in the business world."

"Phil, there you go, evading the point," Linda said. "She was good looking, wasn't she? And she still is. And you two have been seen around town together."

"You're right. She was, and is, very good looking. I don't know what to say. She was older than the other students, not much younger than the young faculty like Jeremy and me. I remember a few of our colleagues wanted to date her, but dating students was strictly forbidden."

"What about now?"

"Honestly, I don't know."

"You must have an inkling," Sherry prodded.

"I guess I'd say we're friends," Phil continued. "At lunch I heard she was in town. Later, at the library, I greeted her. I was surprised she remembered me. We got together one afternoon at Andy's and exchanged life stories. She had a tough time in New York City. At first, she loved it and was very successful. Then she fell for her boss. He turned out to be no good and sort of ran her out of the company. Afterwards she kept getting propositioned by job recruiters and had bad experiences on jobs. We worry about sexual harassment at the college. Sherry's experience suggests maybe it's a bigger problem in business. She tried an MBA and had problems there too. Finally, she took her savings and went to library school. She worked at Penn State for a long time and then came here to be with her elderly mother."

"You've been seen with her more than once," Linda said.

"Yeah, you're right. We ran into each other at a football game, and we've sat together at couple of basketball games so far. She's a knowledgeable sports fan. And I have to say I enjoy being with her."

"And at Andy's again with another person."

"Oh yes, the other person was her brother, Trick Ahearn. He was a big high school football star around here. We'd talked about him at the football game. When he came to visit, Sherry arranged for me to meet him. A knee injury finished his football career. He's a police chief in South Carolina now."

"I remember hearing about him when he was in high school. He was a big star, and there was a to do when he didn't go to a local college, right?" Jeremy said.

"You've got a good memory. He went to the University of South Carolina. And he wound up there."

"So, you're just friends who run into each other every once in a while?" Linda asked.

"At this point, that's about it," Phil said. "Boy, this is a small town. Though we haven't even been on what you'd call a date, people are sure keeping track of us."

Linda responded, "Phil, we're not keeping track of you. We care about you. You're in a vulnerable position. Mary Jane hasn't even been gone for a year yet. We don't want you to rush into anything."

Phil became defensive. "Don't worry about me rushing into anything. And I think, after her failed first marriage and her terrible experience in New York City, Sherry isn't about to rush into anything either. We're friends. She's easy to talk to, and we both like sports. End of story." Phil wasn't about to tell them about the kiss on the cheek after the last basketball game.

"Linda doesn't mean to be grilling you," Jeremy said. "What you said about it being a small town is true. Several people have asked me about you and Sherry."

"I suppose I shouldn't be surprised. The guys at Wednesday lunch seemed to be excited about her showing up on campus. Come to think of it, good looking, unattached females are fairly scarce around Lackey."

~ 42 ~

THREE DAYS AFTER HIS DINNER with the Terrells, Phil came across a story about Maynard Dennison. It reminded him of the story about Dennis Martinez. The hospital had called the police. Mr. Dennison was paralyzed from the waist down, and the doctors couldn't find any reason for it. All the tests came up negative, so they suspected poison. Dennison couldn't think of any way he could have been poisoned.

The story went on to describe the police's search of Dennison's house. One of Dennison's friends, maybe Charley, corralled the dog. They didn't find anything out of place. On their way out, one of the policemen saw a mark on the dog's chest and called in a vet. The vet thought the mark was probably caused by a pellet or dart and guessed the wound was less than a week old. At this point, the police suspected the dog was shot with a tranquilizer dart to gain entry to the house. After that, they were at a dead end. They couldn't find any way a poison had been administered.

Phil went to Ralph's store early with the url for the newspaper story. Ralph went to the back room to read the story. When he came out front, Phil was alone. "Three for three," he said as he gave Phil a high five.

Phil looked around nervously. "Yes, we have been successful so far. I think we've been lucky. The back-door alarm wasn't armed at Martinez's house. Miller ordered a pizza every Monday night. And Dennison didn't even lock his door or wash his coffee cup. People aren't very careful."

"People are creatures of habit. We do a week, or even less this last time, of surveillance, and we know how they are going to behave. Going in I thought it would be more difficult. I didn't think people were so scheduled."

"I don't know if it's schedules exactly," Phil said. "It's more like they have patterns they repeat. A schedule suggests they're compelled to do things at certain times."

"There you are going all professor on me. Okay, they follow patterns not schedules."

"Sorry. Old habits die hard, I guess. I think we agreed not to take any trips until the first of the year. I checked my list of people, and we can make our January trip to Arizona. The weather should be nice."

"Sounds interesting. Southern Arizona I hope?"

"Yes, around Tucson, if my memory is right. I don't have the details on my fingertips now. I'll get them for you tomorrow."

"Good, because here comes a customer," Ralph said.

The rest of the day was surprisingly busy at the store, and Phil was happy to have his shift end at noon. After lunch he went back to his files to be sure the woman from Arizona was a good target.

Phil found the story from the Bloomington, Indiana paper, the *Herald Times*. Sandra Turner was the wife of a very successful business man, Joseph Turner. They lived in a small town near Bloomington. According to the story, Joe and Sandra's marriage was in bad shape. Joe had discovered Sandra was having an affair. Although Joe had visited a lawyer to discuss divorce, he hadn't done anything formal. Two days after his visit to the lawyer, Joe was shot leaving his office.

Given the position of the body, and the report of one witness, the police determined the shot had come from an abandoned office building a hundred yards from Joe's office. Sandra was the logical suspect. On top of being the spouse, she was a well-known expert markswoman. She'd won several shooting medals and was a frequent visitor to a local shooting range.

When the police got to Sandra's house, her garage door was open. They went inside and saw scrapes on her front bumper. One of the officers took a picture of the damage. The police felt sure the paint scrape on Sandra's car matched the color and position of paint they'd found on a post near the exit of the lot behind the building from which the shot was fired.

When the police knocked on the door, Sandra answered. She was very upset. There were tears streaming down her face. According to her, she'd just got home before they arrived. She'd only recently finished listening to an almost incoherent phone message from Joe's secretary saying Joe'd been shot. The police filled in the details. When they finished, they asked her where she'd been. She said she'd been out at the shooting range. The police asked to search her house. Sandra refused. She was offended they'd ask to search the house of someone who'd just learned about her husband's death. And didn't they need a warrant to search a house?

When the police came back the next day with a warrant, the paint scrape had been repaired. The police were sure the paint on the parking lot post was an exact match to Sandra's car. There was no way to determine if the mud-spattered bumper had been repaired recently. Sandra said she'd taken a drive out in the country the night before.

Phil thought this was odd. Wouldn't a recently repaired and repainted bumper be easy to detect? The only time he'd had body work done, the car smelled funny for a while. There was nothing in the story about the police being able to detect recent body work.

The police went to the shooting range to check out her alibi. The owner said Sandra had been at the range. She stored her rifle there. He showed the police Sandra's gun. The caliber of the rifle matched the caliber of the bullet they'd recovered from the crime scene. Unfortunately, the bullet was so mangled they couldn't match it with a specific rifle.

The owner of the rifle range couldn't recall exactly when Sandra was at the range. After a little thought, he volunteered a way of determining the information. The range had a time stamp for targets showing the time and date. He suggested the police ask Sandra to give them her most recent targets.

The police made sure they had a warrant when they went back to Sandra's house. She was happy to hand over the targets. She told the officers she should have thought about them herself. The time stamps showed she had been at the shooting range when her husband was shot.

Jill Owens, the police officer who'd found the scrapes on the car, told the reporter later it all seemed too easy for Sandra. On a hunch, she went back to the shooting range to look at the time stamp machine. It seemed as if it might have been tampered with. She then asked to see the time stamps on targets a shooter had just finished with. She found the time stamp was off by thirty minutes, showing the shooter there thirty minutes prior to the actual time. When another shooter finished, she looked at his time stamps. They showed him shooting fifteen minutes after he made the shots. She concluded the time stamp machine wasn't at all reliable.

At Sandra's trial, the district attorney couldn't use his best evidence, the paint scrapes on the parking lot post and the matching scrapes on Sandra's car. Sandra's lawyer got the evidence quashed. The police hadn't had a warrant. Though the police had gone to every body shop in a fifty-mile radius, they couldn't find anyone who did work on Sandra's car on the night in question. The evidence from the time stamps was inconclusive. On cross examination, Officer Owens had to admit the time stamps could have been right as well as wrong. Because the only evidence placing her at the scene of the crime was inadmissible, Sandra got off.

No one else was ever connected to the crime. And as Jill Owens told the reporter, she'd never seen another car the color of Sandra Turner's in the town. She was convinced Sandra Turner had killed her husband, but they couldn't use the best evidence they had.

The story ended by saying Sandra Turner had sold her husband's business and moved out of town. Rumor had it she had moved to Tucson, Arizona.

It took Phil a while to find Sandra in Arizona. There were several jurisdictions to search. He had to look over a couple of years of records.

Finally, he found her. The photos from the listing of the house she'd purchased were still up. The house was nice, a typical Southern Arizona house—one-story, beige stucco with a red tile roof, and a big swimming pool. It was located on the edge of a relatively new neighborhood and backed up to a desert park.

Phil collected the urls for the newspaper story and the real estate information to show Ralph the next day. As he did this, he wondered how Ralph would react to the notion of poisoning a woman. It didn't bother him.

He looked at his watch and realized he'd have to hustle to make it to the Lackey basketball game. He'd told Sherry he'd meet her there. With their winning streak, it would've been better if he'd left ten minutes ago.

~~~

When he got to the game, he had to excuse himself as he shuffled his way toward the seat Sherry saved for him. "Cutting it a little close, aren't you, Phil?"

"Sorry, I got involved in something. Time got away from me."

Gesturing to her left, Sherry said, "Isn't that your friend Ralph over there? Who's the girl he's with?"

Phil looked over where Sherry had indicated, "Yes, it's Ralph all right. The girl is Beth Watson. She's a nurse at the hospital. She was a friend of my wife's. I think she and Ralph have been going together for a while."

"She looks pretty."

"You think so? I always thought she was a little heavy." After a pause he continued, "Now that I've said it, it sounds bad. You know what I mean."

"Maybe. I think she looks fine."

Phil looked over at Ralph and Beth. "I'm trying to dig myself out of a hole here. I guess I agree. She's lost weight. She looks good."

The opposing coach had clearly scouted Lackey, and they double teamed Nate Smith every time he got the ball. After a timeout, Lackey adjusted. Smith became a passer more than a scorer. His teammates made several good cuts to the basket resulting in layups. Lackey was ahead by ten points at the half.

During half time, as Phil and Sherry talked about the game, Phil couldn't help himself from looking at where Ralph and Beth were sitting.

"Checking up on your friend?" Sherry asked.

"Um... yes, I guess. Ralph's a really good guy, and he hasn't had many girlfriends as far as I know. This town isn't full of females his age. The college girls are too young, and most of the females his age are already married. I hope this works out with Beth."

"It's sweet of you Phil. It looks to me as if they're getting along. She's leaning pretty close to him."

"I've got my fingers crossed."

After the game, an easy Lackey victory, Sherry and Phil walked to her car. Phil was a little on edge after the kiss on the cheek after the last game. When they got to the car, Sherry took the initiative, kissed Phil briefly on the lips, and smiled at him. "Goodbye."

Phil stood in the parking lot for a moment, somewhat dazed. Then he smiled and started walking home. Whatever it was, he thought he liked it. He hadn't had much experience with women. He didn't have a high school sweetheart back in Arizona. He'd dated a little in college, not much. Then there was Mary Jane. He chuckled, thinking he might have to change what he'd told Linda Terrell.

~ 43 ~

THE NEXT MORNING, PHIL GOT to Ralph's store early. He handed Ralph a card with the urls for the newspaper story and the property listing. Ralph said, "There are a couple of things I have to do in the back; then I'll take a look at these."

About three quarters of an hour later, Ralph poked his head out and motioned for Phil to join him. When they were seated, Ralph said, "A woman this time. Are you comfortable?"

"Yes. Look, I'm a firm believer in treating people equally. I see no problem targeting a woman. She's just as guilty as the men."

"Okay, I wanted to check. It doesn't bother me either. I wonder how those scrapes on her car got fixed so fast. And if they were repaired, how could the police not detect it?"

"It bothered me too," Phil said. "The only time I had body work done, it smelled funny."

"And if her car was such an unusual color, a body shop wouldn't be likely to have the paint."

"Maybe it wasn't unusual, just red. We don't know about this town. Lots of people avoid having a red car because they think they'll get more tickets. You're right though; the bit about the car and how she got it repaired so fast is weird."

"Still, I have to agree with Officer Owens. She did it. She had all the motive in the world, and she's a person who could have made the shot. If they could've used the photo she took of the paint scrapes, they'd have nailed her. Another search without a warrant."

"Good," Phil said. "We've got our next target. Did you look at the other url?"

"Not yet."

"It shows the house. It's on the outskirts of Tucson. The first difficulty I see is the lack of trees. We've usually used trees to mount our surveillance equipment."

"Aren't there cactus? Couldn't you use a cactus?"

"Yes, there are cacti, particularly in the back of the house. It backs up on a desert park. That doesn't get us a look at the front. As you'll see, houses in Arizona are different. They're out in the open. Lots of them have desert yards without any trees. Trees take water, and they don't have much water. And this is a new development, so the few trees aren't very big. They won't be any help to us."

"I see the problem. The openness makes it hard to surveil."

"I'll do more investigation on the internet. This one might be tricky." Phil got up and went back out front to mind the store.

~~~

December went by very quickly. Phil worked most days in Ralph's store, because, as anticipated, the Christmas season was busy. Also, Ralph gave Jim lots of time off during finals. Then Jim went home for the holidays. Despite being busy at the store, Phil didn't like the break in activity on his project. Doubts started to creep in. He'd poisoned three people causing them grievous harm. He'd been convinced they deserved it. Still, was he absolutely sure? He didn't like having doubts.

The Lackey basketball team won two away games before it took its break for finals. For the first time in a long time they took the break as an undefeated team. As a long-time fan, Phil was thrilled. The success of the basketball team was even the subject of discussion at one of his Wednesday lunches. Phil gave the lunch group a hard time for being fair weather fans.

Phil met Sherry for lunch at Andy's on a Friday the last day of exams. She was taking her mother down to South Carolina to visit her brother. The library closed during most of the winter break, so she was staying in South Carolina for three weeks.

Sherry was excited about her trip. "I think this is going to be the longest vacation I've taken in years. At Penn State the library hardly ever closed, only Christmas Day and New Year's Day. Now I've got three weeks off."

"What are you going to do in South Carolina?"

"I don't know. I'll be paying a lot of attention to Mom. It's going to be her longest vacation, too. She might have trouble at Trick's house. It'll be fairly crowded."

"I hope you have a good time. I'll be up north wishing I was in a warmer place. Actually, I'm going to take a trip to Arizona in early January."

"Sounds nice. It'll be my turn to envy you then."

Phil missed Sherry at the three home basketball games the team played after finals. It was too bad to have so many games when the students were away. Given the team's recent success, the games were much better attended than they'd been in other years. They won two of the three games, so their undefeated streak was broken. Nate Smith continued to be the team leader. At one of the games, Phil sat with the Terrells who made a rare appearance. Linda teased him. "I'm not a good substitute for Sherry Ahearn."

Phil tried not to blush and said, "No problem, the librarians get the break off. She's gone to South Carolina for the holidays with her family."

~ 44 ~

STARTING IN PENNSYLVANIA AND WINDING up in Arizona always struck Phil as odd. The background color changed completely. Pennsylvania was white and gray in January. When the plane got a little altitude, it looked nice and tidy. Over southern Arizona, the predominant color changed to reddish brown. In its own way Arizona was beautiful. The vistas were spectacular. And he loved the warm weather.

After he got settled in his motel, he scouted Sandra Turner's house, which was in a typical upscale Arizona subdivision. The builder bought several acres, put in streets and utilities, and then built the houses. The houses came in about five models with maybe three different fronts. You could spot identical houses. This neighborhood was better than many. The builder used a mix of colors and finishes on the fronts.

Sandra's house sat on the edge of the neighborhood. Phil paid attention to her neighbors. As he'd suspected, it wasn't going to be easy to set up the cameras and phone intercept equipment. The only trees were still short, and they were planted close to the houses. The people had dreams of shade trees in the future. And lots of yards had desert landscapes.

The easiest way to mount his equipment was to climb the mountain in the park behind Turner's house. There were trees there and several large cacti. Phil consulted a map. The entrance to the park was in another neighborhood. On his way out of Turner's neighborhood, he drove by her house slowly but saw nothing.

Phil found the park entrance after a couple of wrong turns. At the edge of the parking lot, a bulletin board had a map showing several hiking trails. Phil picked the trail leading to the small mountain behind Turner's house.

The mountain looked close. As he walked, he realized distances were deceiving. By the time he got to the mountain and started to climb, he recognized he'd made a mistake. He didn't bring water. His watch read five-thirty. It should cool down soon. He thought he could probably climb the mountain without doing himself any serious harm.

It took him fifteen minutes to make it to the top of the mountain which had a spectacular view of Turner's neighborhood. He could see right into the swimming pool in her backyard. In fact, there was a person in the pool. It was probably Sandra Turner; he thought she lived alone.

Down the hill toward Turner's house Phil saw where he could plant the surveillance equipment. A wash with small trees on the side ran along the side of the mountain facing her house. Usually completely dry, it was no doubt full during the rains. A concrete diversion ditch had been built to funnel rain away.

When Phil made it down from the mountain and back to the parking lot, it was getting dark. He was incredibly thirsty. He stopped at the first fast-food restaurant he saw and ordered a drink. Except for forgetting to bring water, he felt good about the day. He had no way of getting a camera mounted on the front of her house, but the mountain provided a good view of the back.

After he finished his drink, he pulled out his list of Tucson Mexican restaurants. He was hungry. While it was only seven-thirty in Tucson, it was much later back in Pennsylvania. He enjoyed his meal. Back at the motel, he set an alarm for six-thirty.

Early the next morning, carrying a bottle of water, two cameras, and the phone gear, he set off for the park. There were already hikers on the trail when Phil parked. He hoped he wouldn't run into any of them while mounting his equipment. The mountain seemed a little closer this time and not as steep. Taking a drink when he reached the top of the mountain, he wondered why the hike today had been so easy. Perhaps, even though he'd been sitting most of the time, plane travel tired him. Whatever the reason, he felt much fresher this morning.

As he surveyed the scene in front of him, a group of hikers entered the park through a fence at the back of Turners neighborhood. The gate was behind a house only a couple over from Turner's. The gate might come in handy later. Now, however, the possibility of people entering from below complicated things. He could be spotted, if anyone entered the park through the gate.

Before heading down, Phil made sure no one from the parking lot was on the path to the mountain and no one from the neighborhood was about to come through the gate. He hurried, but he had to be cautious. There was no path, and the footing wasn't always firm. He didn't want to fall onto a cactus. He mounted his first camera on a small pile of rocks near the wash. This camera should show the streets in Turner's neighborhood. Further down the mountain, he mounted another camera on a small tree, a paloverde, he thought. *This second camera should give a good view of Turner's back yard.* Finally, closer to Turner's house, he mounted the phone intercept equipment in a hole in a saguaro cactus.

All things considered Phil enjoyed the next three days in Tucson. He visited the sights: the San Xavier del Bac Mission, the Saguaro National Monument, and the Arizona Sonora Desert Museum. And he made quite a bit of progress on his list of Mexican restaurants. On his fourth day in Arizona, he took off his disguise in the restroom of a gas station on the way to Apadoca.

It was odd to be back in Apadoca. Phil hadn't been back since his mother died twelve years ago. He drove by his old house. It didn't look like the new owners were taking very good care of it. A car rested on blocks in the side yard. There were probably lots of places as bad or worse in Pennsylvania. Back home similar houses would be hidden behind trees. In Apadoca, people's messes were there for all to see.

He went to Zorro's for lunch. It had been his family's favorite and the place he'd learned to like Mexican food. The restaurant looked the same. He'd gone to high school with Linda Mendez, one of the owner's daughters. He thought Linda's little brother had seated him. Phil ordered chili rellenos, his favorite at Zorro's. His food came quickly and, as always, the plate was hot. The food, however, wasn't up to the standard of the food he'd enjoyed in Tucson. As he walked out, Phil was disappointed the great memories of Zorro's had been ruined. Perhaps it was best not to go back.

He wandered around downtown Apadoca for a while. A few of the stores were the same. More of them were different. There were empty store fronts too. While the people were different too, many more Hispanics and fewer blacks, Apadoca reminded Phil of the small towns he visited in Mississippi and Alabama. He saw the same franchises: Subway, Dollar Store, and CVS, and the same lack of hustle and bustle. The town seemed dead.

Phil drove to the parking lot overlooking the open pit copper mine. He was sure the mine must have grown. It was difficult to be sure how much. It had always seemed so big. It was an amazing sight. At the bottom, dump trucks moved around. From his vantage point the trucks looked tiny. Phil knew the tires on those trucks were massive, fifteen or twenty feet high. Those huge trucks could haul a lot of rock.

As he drove back to Tucson, he wondered whether he'd ever go back to Apadoca. He hadn't liked the place. It wasn't a great place to grow up. Then again, it had been interesting to take Mary Jane there. She had been amazed at the vastness of the mine, and she'd loved the food at Zorro's. Arizona was so different from Iowa or anywhere else she'd been. She loved the mountains and the vistas. It had been a great trip. Mary Jane was gone now. Thinking about it put Phil in a funk.

Two days later he went to retrieve his equipment. The whole process was going very smoothly. He found everything, and it didn't look like it had been touched. When he started climbing back up the mountain, a person stood on the summit—a park ranger. Phil ran his sweat-drenched hands through his hair. He decided to be friendly, so he said, "Hi."

"Don't you know you're only supposed to hike on the paths?"

"What? There's a rule? I'm from out of town."

"Didn't you see it on the sign at the entrance? It's written in great big letters—stay on the trails."

"I'm sorry, I must have missed it."

"This desert landscape is fragile. It won't last long if people tramp all over it. One person won't make a big difference. Many days we get a couple of hundred people. If all of them roamed around, it would be ruined. That's why we made the trails."

"I see. I'll stay on the trails from now on. It's beautiful here. I wouldn't want to ruin it."

"Okay, have a good day."

Phil was happy to get away from the ranger. His shirt was damp from sweat. If the ranger had asked him what he was doing on the side of the mountain, or what was in his backpack, he didn't know how he'd have handled it. If the ranger had arrived at the top of the mountain two or three minutes earlier, he certainly would have asked those questions. He'd dodged a bullet. Everything had gone smoothly setting up the surveillance equipment in the other locations. Here it was almost a disaster.

~ 45 ~

STARTING IN THE MOUNTAIN TIME zone and flying to the Eastern time zone made Phil arrive home late. After breakfast the next morning, Phil downloaded the video. First, he looked at the long-range footage. It was tedious, since every time a car drove by, he saw it. Even on the edge of Turner's neighborhood, there was quite a bit of traffic. Also, every time people entered the park from the gate near Turner's house, they activated the camera. What he thought was a path behind the houses was actually an alley. Large garbage cans were behind each house. He saw several people putting garbage bags in the cans, and on Thursday, a truck came by.

He did learn a few important things. For one, Sandra Turner drove a white BMW 3 series. Apparently, she'd gotten rid of the red car. She seemed to leave the house at nine-thirty every morning. She wasn't consistent about when she came back. One day she came back about an hour after leaving and stayed in the whole day. Another day she didn't come back until three. And on another day, she was in and out several times. She stayed in most evenings. One day she went out and didn't come back till quite late. Phil didn't like it. People who followed more consistent patterns were easier.

Next, Phil looked at the footage from the camera focused on her back yard. This camera wasn't activated nearly as often. It did show a pattern. Every afternoon between four and five Turner came out for a swim. Phil could tell she had a heated pool because mist rose off the water. Turner was a serious swimmer. Each day she did laps of her pool. The second day, Phil counted and got twenty. The next day she did another twenty laps. Each night after her laps, she took off her swimming cap, dried off, and sat in one of the lounge chairs with some kind of a drink. His guess was gin and tonic. After the drink, Turner put her cap back on and did a few more laps. These laps were clearly not a serious as the others. There was no consistent count. After the second set of laps, she went back inside presumably to fix dinner.

Phil only intercepted six phone calls. Turner made five of them: one to make a haircut appointment, one to her gardener to complain about how he trimmed the front-yard bushes, one to a female friend back in Indiana, one to make flight reservations for a one-week trip to San Francisco, and one to confirm her reservations with the Indiana friend. The two of them were going to meet in San Francisco and tour the wine country. The only call Turner received was from a guy named Robert, who confirmed a date. He wanted to pick Turner up, but she insisted on driving. This explained the one evening she didn't return until late.

~~~

Phil showed Ralph everything. There wasn't any need to edit it. Phil simply fast forwarded through the repetitive parts. When they finished the video, Ralph exclaimed, "I don't know how people can stand to live there. It's so stark; everything looks so new. And there are almost no trees."

"It's different all right. Still, it has its charms. Wouldn't you like to have a swimming pool in your back yard?"

"No, there'd only be a couple of months I could use the thing."

"Turner's pool's heated. She can use it even in the winter, not that they have much winter in Arizona."

"Did we pick up anything on the phone intercept?" Ralph asked.

"Not much, she doesn't use her phone often. She had one date, and the first week in March she's taking a trip with a friend from Indiana.

They're going to California—San Francisco and the wine country."

"So, she's probably staying put until then?"

"I think so."

Ralph looked perplexed. "I don't see it. I don't see any way of getting at her. Her house is so out in the open. And she isn't a creature of habit like the other ones. Dennison always drank his coffee, Martinez always got his morning paper in his slippers, and Miller always ordered his Monday night pizza. As far as we know, the only thing she does on schedule is swim her laps in the evening."

"She does something every morning. It takes her out of the house at nine-thirty."

"Yeah, but we don't know what it is."

"I think we might be able to use the swimming. Let me tell you my idea," Phil said. After Phil told Ralph his plan, they went out to eat.

~ 46 ~

ON WEDNESDAY PHIL WENT TO his lunch group. Everyone was busy getting ready for the second semester. There were rhythms to the academic year. He'd always liked semesters. When he was a student, he got a whole new set of courses. As a faculty member, he liked it for a similar reason. He got a whole new set of students. While he thought he might miss it, he didn't.

The discussion around the table contained typical complaints. Syllabi weren't quite finished and research projects were not as far along as planned. Phil broke in and told them about his Arizona trip, particularly his visit to Apadoca. Everyone agreed. It was odd to go back to the places where they'd grown up.

After a brief lull Phil offered, "How about the basketball team? They won two games while I was away. They're eight and one. And there's a game this Saturday night."

"So, what's different?" Bob asked.

"The big deal's this freshman, Nate Smith," Phil said. "According to Coach McSweeny, he was a good catch out of high school. He's a six two guard who can really shoot. Then he showed up on campus, and he'd grown six inches. Jeremy and Linda came to a game with me. They enjoyed it."

Jeremy said, "I've always thought Phil was crazy going to all those basketball games. Our teams have defined mediocre for so long. He's right. This guy Smith is seriously good, and they're winning. The atmosphere on Saturday should be great. The students will be back." After the basketball discussion, the lunch group broke up. Phil didn't think he'd see many of them at the game.

~~~

On Saturday night, Phil sat with Sherry. She was full of news about her trip to South Carolina. Her mother had done well despite being uncomfortable on long car rides. They'd stopped in a motel in Virginia to break up the ride. Trick and his family had been great with her mother. Sherry had gotten time to lie on a lounge chair in the back yard and read. The weather had been great.

Phil didn't ask her if her brother had made any progress on his interesting case, and he was glad she hadn't volunteered anything. Right before the game started, he looked around the packed arena. He could see Ralph and Beth, Jeremy and Linda, and even George and his wife Helen. He might have missed others in such a big crowd. Maybe his talk on Wednesday had an effect.

The first half was interesting. Nate Smith had an off night. He missed several shots he usually made. He did get a few rebounds and made some very nice passes, but he only had six points in the first half. Lackey was behind by eight.

At half time Sherry asked about his trip to Arizona. Phil gave her the same spiel he'd given the lunch group. She said it was different in her case because she now lived where she grew up. Also, Phil told her about Zorro's and finding the food he'd thought was wonderful didn't stack up well.

Smith came out on fire in the second half. He hit two three-pointers in the first two minutes. Lackey erased the deficit and went on to win by twelve points. "Wow, we outscored them twenty points in the second half," Phil said at the buzzer.

"Yes, it helps when your star makes baskets."

"For sure. He wasn't himself in the first half."

They nodded to several people on their way out of the arena. When they got to Sherry's car, they stopped. Phil was a little nervous. He got up his courage. "Look," he said. "The theater department's big production, *Noises Off*, is Saturday after next. Do you want to go?"

"*Noises Off*, a comedy, right?"

"Yes, you know it?"

"I think I saw the movie several years ago. And yes, I'd love to go with you."

"Great, it's a date."

"Yes, it's a date," Sherry said as she leaned over and gave Phil a kiss. This one was not a brief peck, and Phil enjoyed it very much.

"Good night." Sherry broke away and got into her car with a smile.

As Sherry drove away, Jeremy and Linda Terrell walked up to Phil. "Only a friend, huh," Linda said.

Phil blushed. "Yep. Friends. What'd you think of the game?"

"It wasn't nearly as interesting as the goings on in the parking lot afterwards," Linda said.

"Leave the guy alone, Linda," Jeremy said.

"Yes, leave the guy alone," Phil said as the Terrells got to their car.

~ 47 ~

PHIL AND RALPH FLEW INTO Phoenix three days later. It was only a three-hour drive to Tucson, and they didn't want to be connected to Tucson. They figured the less time spent there the better.

Part way through the drive, Ralph exclaimed, "This is different. There's so much sky. Are those actually mountains in the distance? It looks like a movie set. I always thought those mountains were painted in."

"No, they're real. You can see for a long way around here. Back east we're hemmed in by trees. Often people from out here feel claustrophobic back east."

"I'd miss the green."

"Me too," Phil said. "Still you have to admit, in its own way the scenery here is spectacular. See the mountain coming up on the right? It's Picacho Peak. You're not going to see anything like that in Pennsylvania."

"You're right, for sure."

They reached Tucson by late afternoon. Phil took Ralph on a drive by Sandra Turner's house. After they saw the front, they climbed the mountain behind the house. Their scouting trip didn't tell them anything they didn't already know, so they went to dinner. Phil chose his favorite Mexican place from his previous trip.

The next morning, they drove to Mount Lemmon on the other side of the city. The views were spectacular. The change from desert and cactus to pine trees surprised Ralph. They came down from the mountain in plenty of time to get what they needed.

On the way to Turner's part of town they stopped in a florist shop and bought a bouquet of cut flowers. Ralph dropped Phil off at the entrance to the park, and Phil made his way to the trail behind Turner's neighborhood. The park was quiet. At three-fifty, he positioned himself behind Turner's trash can. He couldn't see anything in her back yard. Twenty minutes later he heard her come out the back door. A few minutes later he heard the splash as she started her laps. He looked at his watch and started to time her workout. They'd checked before. Her twenty laps took about fifteen minutes.

Meanwhile, Ralph sat in the car with the flowers. He'd parked a couple of blocks away from Turner's house in front of a house under construction.

The swimming noises stopped right when his watch hit fifteen minutes. Phil sent the text message he'd queued up on his cell phone.

When his cell phone vibrated, Ralph waited a minute then started the car and drove to Turner's house. Pulling down his cap and adjusting his sun glasses, Ralph got out with the flowers in his hand. He ran up to the door and rang the doorbell.

Phil heard the doorbell and moved in position by the gate in Turner's fence. When he heard Turner go through the back door, he reached over the gate and undid the latch. He opened the gate as carefully as he could. Not more than five steps in front of him was Turner's drink. He got out the Q-tip he'd loaded with poison and stirred it into the drink. After he thought enough of the poison had dissolved, he retreated as quickly and quietly as possible.

When Turner opened the door, Ralph said, "Flower delivery. Are you Sandra Turner?"

Turner looked surprised. "Yes, I am."

Ralph held out the flowers. "They're for you."

"Yes, I can see from the tag. They're very pretty." Ralph held the flowers, because he could see through the house. Phil was still stirring the drink. When Turner reached out for the flowers, Ralph let half of them drop.

"Oh, I'm so sorry," he said as he bent down to retrieve the flowers. "I'm so clumsy." When he got up with the flowers, he could no longer see Phil in the backyard. He handed the flowers to Turner. "Sorry about that," he said as he hurried to the car.

Ralph replayed the scene at the front door after he picked Phil up. Phil complimented him. "Dropping the flowers was a master stroke. I moved as fast as I could. I had to be quiet, and I wanted the poison dissolved."

"Anyway, I think it worked. Now the waiting comes."

"Yes, we should be miles away before there's any evidence of our handiwork."

~ 48 ~

PHIL AND SHERRY ARRANGED TO meet at the campus parking lot before the play. Phil decided to wear a coat and tie. He'd laughed at himself for being so worried about his appearance. When they got to the theater and took off their coats, he could tell Sherry was a little more dressed up, too. Their tickets were in the fourth row on the right side of the small theater. As Phil had suspected, lots of his college friends were there.

When Phil went to the Lackey plays, he was always a little nervous for the students and the theater department. They worked hard, but the talent pool could be thin at a school like Lackey. At least *Noises Off* wasn't a musical. Musicals often suffered from a lack of vocal talent.

When the play started, Phil's concerns disappeared. The cast handled the demanding play extremely well. They had the timing down, and they made the slapstick comedy work. On several occasions, Phil and Sherry joined in as the audience roared with laughter.

At the first intermission, Sherry said, "I don't know when I've laughed so hard."

Phil nodded. "Me too. It's been a long time since I've laughed like this."

"Oh, I'm sorry. What was I thinking... your wife. I guess you haven't had much to laugh about," Sherry said with a concerned look on her face.

"No, it's okay. I don't think I'll ever be completely over it. Still, I need to laugh. It's good to laugh." Then he looked Sherry in the eyes, and added, "And it's good to be with you sharing the laughs."

"Thanks."

When they sat down after the intermission, Sherry reached over and held Phil's hand. They enjoyed the rest of the play. It got more and more farcical as things progressed. The audience loved it. At the end they joined in the standing ovation. They got into their coats, gloves, and hats and walked slowly back toward Sherry's car. They'd dawdled a little, so the parking lot was almost empty. The goodbye kiss was even longer than the last one.

Before Sherry got into her car, Phil said, "We should do this again."

"Angling for another kiss?"

"No... not that I mind. But I mean go somewhere together."

"I'd like that," Sherry said, and she gave Phil a short kiss before getting in her car.

As Phil walked home, he recognized he was happier than he had been in a long time.

<center>~~~</center>

During the ensuing week he became a little concerned. His daily search through the *Arizona Daily Star* hadn't come up with any mention of Sandra Turner. He guessed he shouldn't be surprised. Turner was a recent transplant to Tucson. She didn't have any standing in the community, so there was no reason for her trip to the hospital, if there had been such a trip, to make the news. He might have to take another Arizona trip later to see if the poison had worked.

When there was a pause at the store on Monday, Phil said to Ralph, "Let's move on to the next person. We can go back to Sandra Turner later if we need to. We've only got enough of the poison for one more. I've reviewed the files and narrowed it down to two people. If you can come by tonight, I'll let you choose."

"Sorry, tonight won't work. I've got a commitment."

"Commitment?"

"Okay, a date—a date with Beth... satisfied?"

"I didn't mean to pry. You guys have been together quite a bit. I hope it's going well."

"I think it is. We hang out together a lot, and it's fun."

"Where do you think it's going?"

"I don't know. We're both sort of wary. This is the first serious relationship either of us has had." Ralph blushed. "And the physical part of it is good. I don't know what the next step will be."

"My nephew Andrew and his girlfriend are living together. Are you thinking of cohabitating?"

"Maybe. You and I have to finish our project first. I can't be taking off all over the country with you if I have a live-in girlfriend."

"Okay, we need to get this last one figured out and finished. If Monday night doesn't work, how about Tuesday?"

"Tuesday will work."

~ *49* ~

ON MONDAY AFTERNOON PHIL LOOKED closely at two possible people. After his investigation, he decided he had no reason to have to bring Ralph in on the decision. He was convinced Jonathan Royal was the best choice. Phil's source was a story written in the *Saint Louis Post-Dispatch* a year ago about the brutal murder of two teenage girls. Royal lived in a small town in Missouri. He was thirty-six years old and came from a wealthy family. He had no known employment. According to neighbors, the two girls had been seen at Royal's house several times. One of the neighbors suspected Royal had been supplying the girls with drugs. The two girls' bodies were found in a shallow grave five miles from Royal's house. They'd been bludgeoned by a blunt object; the police couldn't tell what. The story had details about the girls and their families. The girls seemed a little out of control to Phil.

When the police got to Royal's house to question him, they didn't find any drugs. They did find a shovel with what looked like dried blood on it. A policeman took a sample of the blood. The next day the police recognized they didn't have a proper warrant for the search, so they came back. The shovel wasn't there anymore. The policeman who cooperated with the reporter also said Royal's car smelled suspiciously of cleaning fluid. The second search came up with nothing to link Royal to the crimes. Despite being the result of an improper search, the police sent the blood sample to the crime lab. It matched the DNA of one of the two girls.

Phil thought Jonathan Royal was a great choice. Like the others, he'd committed murder. He would have easily been convicted if the damning evidence had been admissible. On top of it, he did not come across as very nice. If the neighbor was right and he was supplying the girls with drugs, surely another strike against him. Phil felt thoroughly justified in choosing Royal.

Phil found an address for Jonathan Royal on the internet. Then he looked at his house on Google Street Views. This didn't turn out to be much help. Royal lived down a long driveway off a main road. The house wasn't visible from the road. The overhead view showed only trees. Royal's house sat on a big parcel of land bordering a small river or stream.

~~~

On Tuesday evening, Ralph quickly agreed. Jonathan Royal was a good choice. "He seems like a real scumbag."

"Yes, I don't think I'd like him if I met him. The bit about supplying drugs to teenage girls bothers me. And even if he wasn't supplying them with drugs, what was he doing hanging around with teenage girls? He's thirty-six years old. He sounds like a pervert."

"Maybe so. I think I have the same concern I had about Dennison. Remember I was worried his partner's fiancé would be the obvious suspect. I have the same worry in spades in this case. The girls' family members would be obvious suspects. Some of them sound like they might be hotheads."

"I don't think it'll be a problem. He's our last victim. When we follow through, everyone will know we poisoned Royal. Any suspicion will fall away from locals."

"Good. If you want to use the tree cover, we are going to have to wait till spring."

"Fair enough, I want this all to be over. But you're right, we've got to wait."

~ *50* ~

AT WEDNESDAY LUNCH A WEEK later, George started the conversation. "We haven't talked about the split in the country for a while. So, what do you think about this summary: conservatives care about property rights and liberals care about human rights?"

"It doesn't work all the time," William said. "What about charity? Lots of deeply conservative people give to charities. Think about religious conservatives. They are willing to give up their property to feed hungry people and cure sick people. They're more concerned with human rights than property rights."

"Fair enough, but when we are doing things through government, those charitably inclined conservatives tend to object," Bob said. "They object to the government compelling people to pay taxes to support welfare."

"You've put your finger on it, Bob," Sally said. "They don't like the government telling them what to do."

"Where does that come from?" George asked. "Doesn't it come from being concerned with property rights? They want control their property."

"And isn't it difficult to know what human rights are?" Phil asked. "Is it a human right to have a job, or a house, or three meals a day? And even if we agree those are human rights, what kind of job, or house, or meals?"

"Good question. In Denmark, where I still have relatives, the government makes lots of things, a few nice things, available to everyone," Bert said. "Our welfare system isn't nearly as generous."

"I think the conservatives would say you've put your finger on the problem with Denmark and most of Europe," George said. "They give too much away. And if you're sure things are going to be given to you, why work hard?"

"There is a grain of truth there," William said. "Economics is all about people responding to incentives. A great number of people will not be inclined to work if they don't think working will improve their situation."

"I have a problem with most economic analysis," Jeremy said. "Don't you always assume a rational actor's in charge—a person who can weigh the cost and benefits of choices?"

"It's a very useful assumption," William answered.

"What about the children?" Jeremy said. "So, the father thinks going to the race track is the path to riches. He's weighed his personal costs and benefits. The race track is the rational choice. It turns out he's an idiot, and he loses all his money. The way I see it, we all have an interest in his kids. We want them to grow up to be healthy, contributing citizens. We don't want them ending up in jail costing us lots of money. I can't put my faith in a rational economic man."

"I think Jeremy's nailed it," Phil said. "And it explains what George is talking about. Like the economic models, the conservative wants those in power to make decisions passing their cost benefit test. They are concerned with their property rights. Liberals on the other hand, are concerned with those not in power—the children in Jeremy's example. They want every human to have a chance. They're concerned with human rights."

"That can't be it entirely," Bob said. "I still think Sally's notion about how you deal with change is important. And what about the urban rural split, and the North South split, racial bias, and the splits based on education and religion? I don't think it's as simple as property rights versus human rights."

"Often those splits don't come down on traditional liberal conservative lines," Jeremy said. "I think there is more to it than political attitudes."

"And making it a stark dichotomy may be wrong," Sally said. "Doesn't there have to be a balance? We can't completely abandon property rights. The fall of communism should have taught us that. At the same time, we can't have robber baron capitalism either."

"Ah, Goldilocks raises her blonde head again," George said. "Not too much, not too little, just right. You're right, Sally. Your view recognizes compromise is critical. And compromise is becoming a dirty word in many political circles. I think the media's making it worse. We need more Goldilocks and less extremism."

"It's satisfying to have us solve all of the world's problems over lunch," Bert said. "If everyone could only listen to us. Work calls. See you in a week."

~~~

Phil and Sherry met at the basketball game on Saturday afternoon. The arena was packed. It seemed like the entire student body was there and quite a few townspeople as well. By the time the game started, all the seats were taken.

Phil looked around. "Who would have thunk it? We might have to have reserved seating. I know there are row and seat numbers on the bleachers. It's always been general admission."

"Winning is a great tonic. It's nice to see the students so excited. Sports can bring a community together."

The game itself was boring. The opponent was from the bottom of the conference, and Lackey dominated. Nate Smith played brilliantly. Lackey was ahead so much he sat for much of the second half. Many of the second and third string players got in good minutes. This thrilled the students. At a place like Lackey, lots of the students knew the players. They went crazy when the seldom-used players scored.

On the way to the parking lot, Sherry asked Phil if he could come over to her house for dinner. After a little discussion they settled on the next Thursday night. Her mother had almost demanded it. "She wants to meet you."

"Sure," Phil said. "I have a quick trip planned. I'll be back by Thursday. I'm looking forward to it."

~~~

While Phil didn't like the idea of flying to Arizona again, nothing had appeared in the Tucson paper. On Sunday afternoon he flew to Tucson.

The next morning, he drove by Sandra Turner's house. He wasn't sure what he was looking for. However, it was right there staring him in the face—a ramp to the front door. It had to be there to accommodate a wheelchair. To be doubly sure, he climbed the mountain behind her house in the early afternoon. There wasn't any action at the house during the hour and a half he spent watching.

Of course, it would be better to know for certain. Still, Phil thought the signs looked good. He couldn't drive by the house too often without arousing suspicion. He made three trips by the house the next day and watched from the mountain top again in the afternoon. There were no signs of Turner. She didn't swim her laps. Everything pointed in the right direction. The other cases had been easier. For one reason or another there had been newspaper stories confirming their success.

~ 51 ~

PHIL WAS TIRED WHEN HE returned from Arizona Wednesday evening, so he slept in on Thursday. He arrived at Sherry's farmhouse promptly at six. The farm was about twelve miles from Lackey on the outskirts of a little village.

The farm house was big, maybe four bedrooms. There was a large red barn behind the house. The fields around the house looked abandoned.

Sherry open the door as Phil raised his hand to knock. She greeted him with a little hug and took his coat. Then she ushered him into the living room and introduced him to her mother.

"Mother, this is Phil Philemon, the professor I've been talking about. Phil, this is my mother, Gladys Ahearn."

Phil shook Sherry's mother's hand. She was a frail looking gray-haired woman. Phil could tell by her bright eyes she was very much alert.

Gladys said, "I remember you from when Sherry graduated up at the college. You had thicker hair then, didn't you?"

"I guess I did. Did you come to the department reception after graduation?"

"Yes, we did. It was a big deal for us. Sherry was the first person in the family to graduate college. Also, we wanted to see the professor she had a crush on."

"Oh Mother, please," Sherry pleaded.

Phil filled the awkward silence. "It was a long time ago. Now you have two children with college degrees. I met your son Trick a few months ago. I understand you visited him in South Carolina."

"Yes, we did. It was a wonderful trip. I don't get to see my grandchildren very often. It was wonderful, just wonderful."

Sherry went out into the kitchen, and Phil continued his conversation with her mother. He found it was easy to talk to Mrs. Ahearn. She was full of news about her grandchildren. She did complain about being too old to really play with them. As she explained, Sherry, their oldest hadn't produced any grandchildren, and Trick was born when she was in her mid-forties. On top of that, he had his kids late.

Sherry interrupted, calling them to dinner. The dinner was the traditional thing one would expect on a farm in Pennsylvania: baked chicken, mashed potatoes, and green beans. Phil complimented Sherry. "Everything tastes great. I don't get home cooked meals often. I don't know what I'm doing in the kitchen and mostly heat things up."

"Oh, how terrible of me," Gladys said. "I forgot to tell you how sorry I was to hear your wife died."

"It's all right. It happened a while ago. Thanks for thinking about it."

"Phil and I have been going to the basketball games together, Mom," Sherry said. "And the team is good this year."

"Basketball is fine," Gladys said. "I liked football better. Our Trick was a real good football player."

"I know," Phil said. "What did you think about him going away to play his college football? It must have been hard on you."

"Oh, what a mess. When Trick was a senior, those college coaches were calling him all the time. He liked the attention. A bunch of the coaches came to the house and tried to sell me and my husband on their schools."

"Didn't you want him to stay close to home?" Phil asked.

"I tell you what, professor," Gladys said. "We couldn't tell Trick anything. He was so full of himself. We tried. We told him we wanted to be able to come to his games. You know, I'm not sure it didn't drive him away."

"Teenagers aren't easy."

"Mom's right, Trick had a pretty big head back then," Sherry said. "Everyone complimented him all the time. I'm not sure he listened to anyone in the family. The coach from South Carolina was a charmer, and in the end, maybe Trick was right to get away from here."

"When he got injured, I think he grew up," Gladys said. "It was real hard on him. It turned his life upside down, but he came through it. He's a chief of police now."

"Yes, like I said, I met him when he was here," Phil said. "I think you have two very successful children."

"Yes, yes, I do, thanks for saying so," Gladys said. "I wouldn't have given you a nickel for Sherry's chances of turning out good. She wasn't much for taking advice as a teenager, either. She started going steady with Joel Watkins when she was a sophomore and he was a senior. It was all we could do to get her through high school before she married the jerk."

"I'll clear the dishes," Sherry said. "I've heard this all before."

"I met Sherry after her divorce," Phil said. "She seemed like she had a good head on her shoulders then. She was a great student."

"We all learn from our mistakes, and Sherry's no different. My husband and I knew Joel was a mistake. He was a no good. You know girls are at times attracted to the bad boy types. Anyway, we couldn't talk to Sherry back then. She did what she wanted to do."

"Look at her now. She's got a master's degree and a good job. I'd say you should be proud of both your children. They turned out fine."

Sherry interrupted them with dessert—apple pie with ice cream.

Phil stayed another hour talking to Sherry and her mother over coffee in the living room. When he excused himself, Sherry got his coat and things. They both stepped out on the porch.

"Your mom said she went to the graduation reception to see the professor you had a crush on."

"Oh, you be quiet, it was a long time ago, and my mom has a wild imagination." Sherry leaned in and gave Phil a kiss. "Thanks for coming."

"I enjoyed it a lot," Phil said, and he walked to his car.

~~~

Sherry went back inside and asked her mother, "So, what do you think?"

"I like him, Sherry. He seems like a real gentleman. You'd better be careful. His wife died not too long ago. I think he's still in a confused state. There's something bothering him. I don't know what it is."

"I don't understand what you're talking about, mom," Sherry said. "Can you describe it?"

"It's probably nothing. I can't give you an example. Only a feeling, nothing concrete. It's like he's got a big secret or something."

~ 52 ~

THE LACKEY BASKETBALL TEAM CONTINUED its success and wound up winning twenty-three games in the regular season. Phil and Sherry went to all the home games. They were part of the large crowd at Andy's watching the conference tournament. The semi-final game was against a team Lackey had beaten twice. It was not their night. Nate Smith got in early foul trouble and had to sit for most of the first half. He then got another foul a minute into the second half and had to sit again. It was too late when he got back in. Lackey ended up losing by five.

Everyone was sad as they talked about the game. Phil was not. "Look," he said. "They won twenty-three games—a school record. And the team is young; Smith's only a freshman. Winning like this should make it easier to get good players. If I was a good high school player, I'd love to play with Smith; he can really pass."

As Sherry and Phil walked to Sherry's car, she said, "What you said was nice. You're a glass half full kind of person. I like that."

"Thanks, I've been a fan for a long time. Twenty-three wins is great. We've never done it before. The people in there were all down about tonight's loss. The big picture is bright."

"I like your attitude," Sherry said.

~~~

After the conference tournament, Phil and Sherry started having lunch together at Andy's every Friday. And they went out to dinner at the Mexican restaurant in Henderson one evening.

At the restaurant, Sherry told Phil she'd gotten an interesting phone call from her brother Trick.

"Does he call often?" Phil asked.

"Yes, he's a faithful caller. Mom really looks forward to the calls."

"So, what's so interesting?"

"You know the case he talked to us about—the guy who'd been poisoned? They finally identified the poison."

Phil started fidgeting, playing with his napkin before putting it down. "I remember. What kind of poison was it?"

"It was from a frog, a poison dart frog, if I'm not mistaken. It comes from Central and South America."

"Strange. I guess it shoots your brother's idea about the criminals being locals."

"Not exactly, with all the immigration, legal and otherwise, there could be locals with South American connections. Trick says it's the strangest case he's ever seen. They made progress by finding out the kind of poison used. Still, it didn't lead anywhere."

Their food arrived, and to Phil's relief the conversation moved on to other topics.

~~~

After Phil dropped her off, Sherry was puzzled. Phil had reacted strangely when she brought up the bit about the poison. *That's odd, but the whole thing with Phil is a little odd.* She liked him a lot, and he seemed to like her. It was frustrating. They'd had lots of good night kisses, but nothing else. She knew his wife died several months ago. It was hard living with her mother. She couldn't invite Phil in at the end of one of their dates. They might have gotten past a good night kiss if she had her own place. Still, Phil had a house, and he hadn't thought to use it. She guessed she'd have to be patient as much as she didn't want to.

She still couldn't see what her mother had seen in Phil. Maybe she couldn't see it because she liked him so much. Then again, her mother wasn't always right about things either. Yet, she thought about Phil's many short trips about which he had so little to say. Maybe he was keeping something from her.

~ 53 ~

IN THE MIDDLE OF APRIL, Phil flew to St. Louis. After picking up a rental car, he drove to Jonathan Royal's property. He could only see a little corner of the house up the driveway. Though the trees had leafed out more than those back in Pennsylvania, they still had growing to do. This was okay with Phil. There was a tradeoff. Thicker foliage made it easier to get close to the house unobserved. At the same time, thicker foliage made it more difficult to get useful video. He scouted around the local roads trying to find an inconspicuous parking place. He found a good spot. The little road bordering Royal's property had a bridge over the stream at the back of the property. There were several worn spots on the edge of the road, probably used by fishermen. No one would think twice about a car parked there. He could get a fishing rod to add to his disguise.

He found an out-of-the-way motel. They didn't have any problem with him paying in cash. At a Dick's Sporting Goods, he bought a cheap collapsible fishing pole and a small tackle box. The next morning, Phil drove to the parking spot. His was the only car there. Getting out his new fishing gear, he went down toward the stream. The fence along Royal's property was easy to get around. A little path suggested people had frequently circumvented the fence.

As he walked along the bank, the valley in which the stream ran became narrower and steeper. There was only a little path beside the water at one point. Then the valley became wider, particularly on Royal's side. The wide spot was obviously used quite a bit; and it had a picnic table and a fire pit. Also, stairs had been built to help make it up and down the steep slope. This must be Jonathan Royal's fishing and picnicking spot.

Phil continued following the stream. Soon the valley narrowed again. He was not able to get to the other side of Royal's land. This failure wasn't very important. He retraced his steps, ditched his fishing stuff behind a large tree, and climbed up the slope of the little valley. He stayed in the woods at the edge of Royal's wide spot. While the stairs would have been easier, he didn't want to run into Royal coming the other direction.

He went as quietly as he could through the woods until he had a view of the back of Royal's house. He mounted the first camera on a tree and the phone intercept equipment on another. He placed a little bit of green tape on each tree. In the woods like this, he might need these markers to find his equipment. He gave the house a wide berth and made his way to a tree with a view of the front of the house. He mounted his second camera, put on his marker and walked away from the house.

After a long hike, he found his fishing gear and made it back to the car. He was glad there didn't seem to be any other fishermen parked near him. Back at his motel he checked out. He returned his rental car and got a bus into town. At the bus terminal, he took a cab to the boat docks on the Mississippi River. After killing a couple of hours with lunch and looking at the river, he got on the big paddle-wheeler for his river cruise. He'd booked it because it seemed better than trying to find a week's worth of things to do in St. Louis.

The boat tried hard to make passengers feel as if Mark Twain traveled with them. Looking at the other passengers, Phil figured he brought down the average age by quite a bit. The first stop was Hannibal, Missouri, which fit the Mark Twain theme.

Phil had several books to read, and he spent considerable time in his cabin reading. He also spent time watching the scenery as it passed. They stopped in Davenport and Dubuque in Iowa, La Crosse, Wisconsin, Red Wing, Minnesota, and finished in St. Paul. It rained the day they were in La Crosse, and Phil didn't get off the boat. On the whole, he found the experience very relaxing.

It took him a full day to drive from St. Paul back to St. Louis. He found another motel on the edge of town not too far from Jonathan Royal's property. The next morning, he retraced his steps to pick up his surveillance equipment. While it was only a little over a week later, the trees had leafed out more. Things didn't quite look the same. Phil was happy he'd used the green tape marks. He retrieved his equipment with no difficulty.

~~~

He got back to Lackey late, so he didn't download the cameras until the next morning. The camera focused on the front of the house revealed very little. Royal's car was a Jeep. Phil saw it leave several times in midmorning and return most days in the afternoon. Only on one day did Royal get in late at night. One other car came on the Saturday. No one came or went via the front door.

The camera focused on the back of the house revealed more. Early on Tuesday, Wednesday, and Friday mornings, Royal left via the back door with fishing gear. Phil figured he took the path down to the stream. A few hours later, Royal came back. On two of the days he cleaned fish at a table in the backyard. There must not have been any keepers the other day.

On Saturday, a group of teenagers came to Royal's back door. They must have come in the other car. Royal let them in. A little while later the whole group came out and went down Royal's path. They came back two hours later. Except for a deer walking in front of the camera, there was nothing.

The phone intercept provided a little more information. Royal called several friends to arrange a poker game. This accounted for the one evening he arrived home late. He made several calls to a woman, Cindy, who sounded quite young, and they discussed lots of insignificant things. Royal seemed to be able to get the girl to open up about her problems with her parents. A couple of these calls ended with see you on Saturday, so she must have been one of the teenage girls Phil saw. There were no calls to teenage boys, but there were a couple in the group who'd visited Royal.

When he showed Ralph his information, Ralph said, "This doesn't look good. The only pattern is his fishing."

"Don't you think he has a thing for teenage girls?" asked Phil.

"Yes, I think you're right. I don't think I could put up with all the nonsense on the phone. Is it any help?"

"No, not much. It is consistent with the story in the paper. He liked to hang around teenage girls."

"How are we going to get him?" asked Ralph.

"I think I have a plan. It's sort of risky."

"Let's hear it."

~ 54 ~

THE NEXT SUNDAY AFTERNOON SHERRY Ahearn returned from a conference in Denver. As she filed off her plane in the Pittsburgh airport, she saw Ralph in line to board a plane. She almost shouted at him, but she stopped. Ralph was talking to the person in front of him. Sherry stepped closer to get a better look. The other guy was Phil. Before she could say anything, Phil and Ralph disappeared down the jet bridge. She went over to check and found their flight was headed to St. Louis. The whole thing seemed very odd. Phil had recently come back from St. Louis. His Mississippi River trip started there. He'd stopped by the library on Tuesday and told her all about it. *Why was he going back? What was Ralph doing with him?*

~~~

In St. Louis, Phil and Ralph found a motel and went out shopping. They got fishing poles and another dart gun—a rifle this time. They took their purchases to a secluded spot in a park, and Ralph did target practice. After a half an hour, Ralph felt confident.

Early Monday morning, they parked the car and walked along the stream. When they got to Royal's wide spot, Ralph went up the stairs and planted a camera on a tree. It would give a good view of anyone coming down the path. Next Ralph set up the rest of his equipment.

Meanwhile, Phil searched for a hiding place. Ralph had to have an unobstructed view for his shot, and they needed to be hidden from Royal. He found a large tree with thick bushes at the bottom. Ralph returned from his setup and approved of Phil's choice.

They settled in to wait. The picture on Ralph's little computer was very clear. They could see anyone coming on the path. They couldn't be sure Royal would come to fish. All they could do was wait. A fishing trip became less and less likely after a light rain started. They were under the cover of the tree, so it wasn't a bother. When the rain intensified, it was a different matter. They decided to scrap their effort. They left Ralph's equipment in place and headed for the car. They were soaked by the time they got there. Tomorrow they'd bring rain gear.

The next day they had rain parkas in their backpacks and a small tarp to sit on. Though the rain had let up in the evening, the ground in their hiding place would be soaked. When they arrived, Ralph checked his set up and came back to tell Phil nothing had been disturbed. The camera worked fine.

About half an hour after they settled in, the computer screen showed Royal coming down the path, fishing pole in one hand and tackle box in the other. Ralph grabbed the gun and settled into firing position. Phil and Ralph stayed as quiet as they could as Royal came down the stairs. Royal walked over to the stream bank and started to fiddle with his tackle box.

Ralph held his breath as he had during target practice and squeezed the trigger. It was a close shot, only about thirty feet, and the dart went right where he aimed it, striking Royal on the back of the neck. Ralph was surprised when Royal fell over.

On his knees, Royal swiped his hand and grabbed the dart from his neck. "What the hell?" he shouted as he threw the dart down. He looked around, searching for where the shot came from. "Who are you?" he yelled.

When there was no response, he got up and ran down the river bank looking into the woods. Luckily for Ralph and Phil, he ran away from them. When he came back their way, they were able to shift behind the tree. When they heard him walking back to his original spot, Phil peered around the tree. Royal got his cell phone from the tackle box. Phil looked back at Ralph and made a phone gesture. Ralph nodded.

When Royal dialed his phone, Ralph and Phil could hear he only got static. They exchanged a smile. Royal tried another number with the same result. Next, he dialed only three numbers, no doubt 911. It didn't work either. They could tell Royal was frustrated. He picked up his fishing pole and tackle box and headed for the stairs. Ralph pushed a button, and they heard a small pop. Royal heard it too. He ducked and wildly swiveled his head from side to side trying to figure out what was going on.

When he didn't see anything, Royal charged forward toward the stairs. When he got to the third step, he tripped over the fishing line strung across the stairs. Phil and Ralph smiled at each other. This was the chanciest part of their plan. From the noise Royal made, they could tell it had been a success. The fall would delay Royal and get his blood pumping extra hard. This should help spread the tranquilizer in his system. Royal got up, rubbing his knees and elbows where they'd landed on the stairs. He looked around and didn't see anything. After a minute, he went back down the stairs to retrieve his tackle box. He then started back up at a much slower pace.

Ralph checked his computer. After a moment, they saw Royal on the path back to his house. He wasn't walking steadily. The tranquilizer was starting to take effect. Royal only made it maybe twenty yards further before they saw him stumble and fall. He got up. Two steps later he fell again sprawling on his right side.

On their way to Royal, Phil and Ralph picked up their gear: the trip wire, the mechanism to spring it, and the camera. When they got to Royal, they checked his pulse. It was strong. Phil took a needle out of his vest pocket and carefully covered it with the last of the poison. He shoved the needle into Royal's left buttocks.

When they first talked about their plan, Ralph wanted to shoot Royal with a dart covered with the poison. Phil nixed the idea. He was worried Ralph might miss. He didn't want any chance of wasting the poison.

They only had enough for one more poisoning.

Phil knew their plan was risky. Now he was incredibly happy everything had worked. They left Royal laying in the path and retraced their steps to make sure they left no evidence of their visit. They retrieved the tarp, spent time fluffing up the leaves in their hiding place, and picked up the first dart. When they were satisfied they'd left no traces, they grabbed their fishing poles and headed back to their car. As they approached, they could see a group of fishermen getting out of a car parked behind theirs.

"Quitting early, guys?" one of the fishermen called out to them as they approached.

"Yeah, his work just called," Phil said gesturing toward Ralph. "He screwed up, he's got tomorrow off."

"Keeping track of days can be tough," one of them said with a laugh.

Phil and Ralph didn't continue the discussion. They packed up and left in a hurry. On the drive back to the motel Ralph said, "I didn't like this one. I didn't like actually touching him. All the others were more remote. We left the poison, and they took it."

"I agree, I was nervous. What if the tranquilizer hadn't worked in time? And I didn't like shoving in the needle. I'm glad it's our last one."

"Yes, no offense, but now I can get my life organized."

"How so?" Phil asked. "What do you mean?"

"All these trips are hard to explain. Beth and I are getting close. I've had to invent lots of odd explanations for these trips. I don't like lying to her."

"I'm sorry I put you in a bind. Come to think of it, I wonder what my friends think about all my short trips. I'm retired now. Still, my travel patterns are odd. I tried to have explanations for most of the trips. I guess it's another reason to be glad it's over."

~~~

Phil didn't have to wait long before the *St. Louis Post Dispatch* ran a story about Jonathan Royal's poisoning. The story appeared two days after he got back and had lots of detail. Royal reported he'd awakened on the path behind his house at three in the afternoon unable to walk.

His left leg was completely useless, so he called 911. The police got to his house at the same time as the ambulance. Royal told the police about the dart in his neck. He hadn't been able to see who'd shot him. He'd tried to call 911 then. For some reason his phone didn't work. The hospital found traces of a powerful tranquilizer in Royal's blood. It would cause temporary effects. There was no explanation for the paralysis in Royal's left leg.

Phil told Ralph about the story when he got to the store in the morning. Ralph said, "Yes, I checked, and I saw it. The poison worked quickly this time."

"I guess the needle got it into his system quickly, and maybe the dosage was bigger. I finished off the poison on him."

"So, are we clear on the next step?"

"Yes, I have a copy of the email on this thumb drive. I want you to look at it."

"Okay."

As Ralph had explained, Phil had to take one more trip to complete the project. Apparently, it was a hassle to conceal the origins of an email. The next Monday Phil drove to Buffalo, New York, to send it. He put on his disguise, gray hair and a beard, and found a computer at the Buffalo public library. It was easy to copy the message from the thumb drive to the email program. Everything went smoothly. He was in and out of the library in fifteen minutes and back home late in the evening.

~ 55 ~

NORMAN HOAGLAND DIDN'T LIKE GOING through his email twice a day. He knew it was a necessity. As a crime reporter for the *New York Times,* he got lots of crank emails. There were important ones, too. Fortunately for Norm he had an intern who did the first sort. The spring intern, Cathy Sims from the Columbia School of Journalism, was good at this task.

When Cathy got the email with nine urls she didn't quite know what to make of it. She figured she'd better check it out. The first url led her to the story from the *Cleveland Plain Dealer* about Dennis Martinez. Cathy skimmed the story and then looked at the second url. It was a story from the Savannah paper about the strange poisoning of Dennis Martinez. Cathy started to get excited. The third url led her to the story about Michael Miller from *The Leader* in Corning, New York, and the fourth was from the same paper telling of Miller's poisoning. Cathy started taking notes. When she finished, she rushed over to Norm's desk.

"This email with the urls. I think it may be important," she said when she got Norm's attention.

"Urls?" said Norm.

"You know, web addresses," she said.

"What about it?"

"So, there are nine urls, and the message is simply signed V. Here's a printout." She handed the paper to Norm. "And the urls are in pairs. For example, the first two are about this guy who murdered his wife three years ago. He got away with it because the evidence was gathered without a warrant. The matching url is about the same guy being poisoned last year. The rest of the urls follow the same pattern."

"You said there were nine?"

"Yes, one of the urls is about, let's see..." Cathy looked at her notes. "Sandra Turner from Indiana. There is a story about her getting off on a technicality, but no story about her being poisoned."

"Where are these stories from?" Norm asked.

"It's weird, they're from all over. This guy Martinez was from Ohio, and the poisoning happened in South Carolina. One pair of stories is from Corning, New York, another is from Louisiana, another is from Missouri, and like I said, Turner was from Indiana."

"Where was the email from?" asked Norm.

"I have no idea; there was no information other than the V signature."

"Here, let me get the email up on my computer," said Norm. After a brief search he said, "This is it, right?"

"Yes."

"So, if I hit reply, what happens?" asked Norm.

"Try it and see."

Norm hit reply and typed in *Who are you?* "We'll have to see if we get any reply. I bet we don't. I bet this V wants us to carry the ball for him."

"So, should we?"

"We sure should. This is news, this is really news. Somebody's going all over the country poisoning people. See if you can find out if anything's happened to this Sandra Turner. I'm going to read through all the stories."

"I'll get on it," Cathy said. "I wonder if other reporters got this email."

"Maybe they did," Norm said. "That's all the more reason to move quickly. Get cracking!"

An hour later, Cathy came back to Norm's desk. "I finally got information on Sandra Turner. She lives in Tucson, Arizona now. I called her, and sure enough she is paralyzed from the waist down, and no one knows how it happened. Nothing was written about it in the Tucson paper because it was only a mystery illness. It wasn't news."

"Great work, Cathy. I've been on the phone to people I know in New Orleans and St. Louis. My New Orleans contact had to look up the stories on the guy, Maynard Dennison. He remembered it after he found the stories. The police there have no clues about what happened to him. The St. Louis case was more recent. According to my source, the police have run into a blank wall there, too. I'm in the middle of writing my story right now. The information about Turner will be useful. I'll fit it in. I've got another hour before the deadline."

"Should I go alert the front-page people?"

"Great idea. See if you can get a minute with the editor. You've met him, right?"

"Yes, he won't know me. I know Roger, his intern, and Roger might be able to get me a minute."

"I'll make a quick call. It should help too."

~ 56 ~

PHIL WAS SHOCKED AT HOW quickly the *New York Times* ran the story about the email from the mysterious V. He'd sent the email on Monday, and the story appeared on Tuesday. The story ran on the front page and continued for a full page in the inside. Phil read it all the way through twice. It was thorough. The urls had supplied a great deal of the information, and the *Times* reporter had done some digging, too. Sandra Turner in Tucson was paralyzed as Phil suspected. And the New Orleans and St Louis police weren't making any progress. All in all, he was incredibly pleased.

Phil took a hard copy of the paper over to Ralph's store. Ralph was alarmed when he saw what Phil had. "Get the paper out of here, Phil," Ralph said. "We don't want to be associated with it at all."

"Gosh, you're right. What was I thinking? I'll put it in the back and throw it away on my way home. I was just so excited."

When Phil returned to the front, Ralph was calmer. "Our job now, Phil, is to be flies on the wall. We only want to observe. If the chatter I saw on the internet about this story is any indication, it's going to be a big deal for a while."

"Chatter on the internet?"

"Yes, I'll write down places for you to look. There are lots of sites people use to spout off about what's happening in the world. This story got a lot of them going. Some people want this guy V to run for president. Other people want him found and executed. It's weird."

A customer came in the store interrupting their discussion. After a busy day, Phil ditched his newspaper in a dumpster behind the drug store. When he got home, he went to his computer and entered one of the urls Ralph had given him. He was astounded. On one site there were over a thousand comments about the *New York Times* story. He'd never paid much attention to comments on the internet. As a rule, he didn't think it was sensible to read things people wouldn't put their names on. It was certainly not anything academic historians did.

He couldn't read all the comments, so he decided to look at every tenth one. They varied widely. A few people clearly thought V had done a wonderful thing. There were several diatribes against lawyers. These people seemed very pleased V had gotten back at the legal profession. The lawyers had gotten guilty people off and made money to boot. There were several lengthy comments full of details about trials in which lawyers had done devious things according to the writers. Phil wasn't sure the comments were all on target. Maybe it helped these people to vent.

He also found strings of comments like conversations. One of them started out with a thorough-going condemnation of V. The writer didn't like vigilante justice. The legal system was there to protect us, and we should abide by its decisions. Several people leaped all over him. According to this group, V's victims were people who'd taken advantage of the legal system. The system had not dispensed justice in their cases. They had gotten off on technicalities. This group also had several contributors who thought all the restrictions on police were the problem. If there weren't so many technicalities, guilty people couldn't get off. The person who'd initiated the discussion by arguing V was wrong tried to defend his position. Finally, he appeared to give up as more and more commenters jumped in on the other side.

After Phil read through about three hundred comments including the back and forth, he found he had sympathy with the guy defending the legal system. The people on the other side seemed to be ganging up on him. They didn't take his argument seriously, and they were nasty. Their language bothered Phil.

Throughout his academic career Phil believed there were almost always two sides to issues. In many cases, reasonable people could disagree. The exchanges over the internet suggested the participants didn't share this view. They went after each other ruthlessly. The person with a different view was apparently the scum of the earth.

He didn't know what to think as he got ready for bed. He was surprised he'd been so sympathetic to the person who didn't like vigilante justice. Partly he was bothered by the way the other people were so vicious. Still, the guy had a point. This bothered Phil. He wanted the people on his side to be the ones with reasonable arguments. Why didn't they argue for a middle ground? Couldn't there be situations in which technical matters could be waived? Phil understood the reason for search warrants. He did not want to live in a totalitarian state where the police could search anyone they pleased any time they pleased. Nevertheless, shouldn't it be possible to waive the requirement for a warrant in some cases? Jake McMahan's situation was one obvious instance.

Phil felt better after he had thought this all out. He didn't really believe in vigilante justice. He wanted a middle ground. He didn't want to throw out the legal system like V's defenders. He simply thought there were clear cases in which what was legal wasn't just. And, in those cases, justice should prevail. His acts, V's acts, were designed to point that out.

Even with justifications, Phil argued with himself. *Who am I trying to kid? Wasn't this project an act of vengeance? Didn't I want revenge? I couldn't do it directly. Didn't I want to terrorize Jake by making him think he could be next?* Wasn't his reason for becoming V visceral not cerebral? Wasn't he rationalizing?

He finally got to sleep. He wasn't in a better mood when he got up. This was supposed to be one of his victory lap days. When he got the copy of his first book, he'd taken it to the office to show everyone in the department. He and Mary Jane had gone out for a celebratory dinner. Finishing this project wasn't the same. He couldn't do a public celebration. And at least based on what he'd read in the comments yesterday, he didn't feel good about the people who liked what he'd done.

~ *57* ~

THE NEXT MORNING, HE WENT to the store and explained his reaction to Ralph. "I don't like some of the people who approve of V," he said.

Ralph replied, "I had a similar reaction. Quite a few of V's fans are downright nasty. The internet allows you to be anonymous. It's not always good. There are weird dudes out there."

"Yes, many of them should shut up. And who has time to write comments all the time? A few of the comments were two or three paragraphs. Don't these people have a life?"

"I bet they don't. Most of what you get over the internet is the unvarnished gut reaction of the people. And V struck a nerve with a lot of people. I looked this morning; a whole bunch more comments were posted last night and earlier today. One guy has even set up a site where people can nominate victims for V."

"What?"

"Yes, this guy set up a site and asked people to nominate people who got off on a technicality. He's going to publish the list. He seems to think he can help V out."

"Wow, I didn't know all this would happen so fast. The rhythm is all off. I mean, normally we do the poisoning. Then we wait around for the newspaper story. At times, like with Turner, it doesn't come. There was no waiting this time. I sent the email on Monday, the *Times* ran the story on Tuesday, and it's all over the internet the same day."

"So, what about the list? Should I nominate Jake McMahan?"

"What?" Phil said, confused.

"Should I give Jake McMahan's details to the guy who's setting up the list for V?"

"I understand. Yes, sure. I didn't see it; it's perfect. If my idea was to terrorize Jake by making him think he might be next, this is perfect. I thought the newspaper story would do it. This could be better. Sure, do it."

"No problem," Ralph said with a smile.

~~~

When Phil got to his lunch group Bert and Andy were looking at the TVs. "Ah Phil," said Andy. "What do you think of this V business? As usual, we have a disagreement going. Bert doesn't like it. I say it's fine."

"You're just parroting what your TVs are telling you. They like it, so you like it," Bert interrupted.

"Is that right Andy?" Phil asked. "Do the right-wing commentators endorse vigilante acts?"

"Yes, in this case, they do," Andy said. "As I tried to tell your friend here, this guy V isn't randomly picking out people and poisoning them. He targets miscarriages of justice. Who's in favor of miscarriages of justice?"

"How many times have I said this over the years?" Bert asked. "Andy, it's not that simple."

"I think it is," Andy responded.

Phil broke in and stopped the argument. "You two aren't going to agree on this one. Come on Bert, let's get to the back room."

When the others joined Phil and Bert, the discussion still centered on the V story. Bert started, "Andy and I got into it again on this V thing. The commentators on his TVs were defending... heck, they were praising this vigilante. I couldn't believe it."

"Come on, Bert, I'm surprised the guys on Andy's TVs still have the power to surprise you," William said.

"Yes, I know. This one seems so simple," Bert responded.

"How so?" Phil asked. He was stung by the notion the right-wing commentators were supporting V.

"It's about the rule of law," Bert said. "How can we have a civilized country without the rule of law?"

"I don't think it's simple at all," Jeremy responded. "Don't people have an innate sense of justice? And don't the cases involved violate people's sense of justice?"

"I hope it doesn't bother you, Phil," George said. "Your experience with Jake McMahan seems useful. It's a concrete example. The guy was guilty of a crime, everyone knew it. He got off on a technicality. It's the kind of case involved with this guy V."

"It's okay to use it as an example," Phil said still reeling a bit.

"Everyone who was at the meeting with the district attorney went away thinking justice hadn't been served," Jeremy said. "I was really steamed at the time. I know why it's important to get search warrants. We don't want the police to do searches on a whim. We should have checks on police power. Still, we all thought McMahan's case wasn't one where a warrant should have been needed."

"Still, you can't take the law into your own hands," Sally said. "It's what's wrong with this guy V. He took it on himself to punish these people. We can't have people taking the law into their own hands. Bert's right, the rule of law is important. Not simply the police dotting all the i's and crossing all the t's. It's letting the system punish people, not an outraged citizen."

"Your editorial position?" Bob asked.

"Yes, unless you can convince me I'm wrong,"

"I can see your point," Jeremy said. "Can you see the power of the other side's argument? People want justice, and in these kinds of cases, they aren't getting it."

"Councilman Terrell, I'm surprised at you. You have to have rules to run a society, you can't have people making their own rules," Sally said.

"I suppose you're right," Jeremy said. "I still remember feeling the

Jake McMahan thing was so wrong. Couldn't we bend the rules in the right situations?"

"Jeremy, you know who'd bend the rules," Bert said. "The rich and well connected. And they already bend the rules enough. I understand our system lets a few guilty people go free. It's a price we have to pay to live in a civilization."

The conversation had given Phil a chance to collect himself. He said, "Is this one of those issues with the same split as other issues? I think it is. Bert couldn't believe Andy's right-wing friends were praising V. And the table seems to have come out against him, or her, I guess. Once again, liberals and conservatives come out on different sides of an issue."

"Why would you predict that?" William asked.

"As Sally and Bert said, society needs laws. I think Jeremy's point was people want justice. So, if you think about society as a whole, like a liberal, you can't have guys like V. If you think more about individual liberty like the conservatives, it doesn't bother you so much. You might even like it."

"Doesn't everyone want law and justice?" Bert interrupted.

"Yes, Bert, and usually they get it," Jeremy said. "The cases here show there can be a conflict. It's what we're talking about. I like Phil's summary—society needs laws; individuals want justice. It's nice."

"We did it again; if more people could come to our lunches, the world would be a saner place," George said.

"I agree with Jeremy," Sally said. "Phil, your summary is a good one. Is it okay if it makes its way into my editorial?"

"Sure, Sally. Permission granted." Phil said, relieved.

~~~

Phil went back to the store after lunch. He filled Ralph in on the lunch discussion and his discomfort with the right-wing commentators on Andy's TVs praising V. Ralph assured him what he eventually said was okay. It sounded very even-handed and professorial. He gave Phil more urls to look at.

Phil walked home and spent another afternoon looking at op-eds and comments. There was no doubt V had started a national conversation.

Whether it was a good one was less certain. Still, if it got Jake McMahan worried, it would be good. And maybe people would think seriously about the difference between the requirements of the law and the requirements of justice.

~ 58 ~

ON FRIDAY PHIL WENT TO lunch with Sherry. When she got to the table, she was very excited. "My brother got quoted in the *New York Times.* There was a write up about him," she said.

Phil already knew. "About what?"

"His poisoning case. It's part of the V deal. His case is one of the cases in the original *Times* story. Trick was the only one who found out it was a frog poison. Remember, I told you. The *Times* sent a reporter to Hilton Head to interview him. I think he came off sounding very efficient, very on top of things."

"Great. Did you save a copy of the article to show your mother? She'll be thrilled."

"Yes, it's back behind the reference desk. I heard you have a very intelligent view on the whole V controversy. I want to hear it."

"Who're you talking to?"

"Jeremy Terrell—he's a font of information about you."

"Well, here goes. I don't think it's very insightful. This V guy is looking for justice. He doesn't think the legal system dispensed justice in these cases. Quite a few people think he, or she, has done a terrible thing. They think it's a mistake to take the law into your own hands. His supporters are concerned with seeing justice done, and his detractors argue we must follow laws to be civilized. I think my summary line was this—society needs laws; people want justice."

"I think I see it. Aren't laws the way society gets justice?" Sherry asked.

"Yes, most of the time. I guess V would tell you, not all the time."

"Sure, but who appointed him the decider? How did this guy get to be the one who decides when justice wasn't served by the legal system?"

"Great point, and if they ever find V, they'll throw the book at him. It's the 'society wants laws' part of the story. I think V's supporters would be upset, because they think what he's done is just. The 'people want justice' part of the story."

"I guess I'm with the society needs laws people," Sherry said. "I know justice isn't always done. Still, we have to have laws. I don't want to live in a country ruled by vigilante justice. Do you think V stands for vigilante?"

"I have no idea what V stands for. It might be vigilante," Phil replied. "I guess it's hard for me to come down on one side or the other. Do you know the details about my wife's death and what happened to the guy who ran into her?"

"Gee, I never thought about it. Jake McMahan got off on a technicality like the cases in the V story."

"Yes, and I hate to admit it. Right after the trial, I was very inclined toward vigilante justice myself."

"I see, sure... it must have been very hard to see McMahan get off with no punishment. I bet you wanted to exact revenge."

"What could I do?" Phil asked. "I wasn't going to go out and kill him. Still, my experience gives me sympathy for the notion that justice should be done by another means when the legal system fails."

"Shouldn't the legal system be fixed when the legal system fails? We can't live in a country where people take the law into their own hands. It's about who gets to decide, and it's not right to let any old body decide."

"You're right. And I didn't say I thought V was right. But I have sympathy for where he's coming from."

"Sure, I can see," Sherry said. "And I can tell your experience is still raw. I'm sorry this whole thing dragged it up again."

"It's okay. The McMahan business came up at Wednesday lunch too," Phil said. "While my situation is not exactly like the ones in the V deal, it's close."

~ *59* ~

IN THE EVENING SHERRY REVIEWED the lunch discussion. Phil's take on V had a personal dimension. It made him get a little uptight. He wasn't quite as relaxed as usual. Come to think of it she'd seen him get nervous a couple of other times. The first was when she introduced him to Trick at the lunch at Andy's. It wasn't during the sports talk. He kind of tensed up when Trick started talking about the mysterious poisoning case. At the time Sherry hadn't thought much about it. And the second time was at the restaurant in Henderson when she told him about Trick finding out what the poison was. It was the same thing; Phil tensed up. Not many people would have noticed it, but Sherry was tuned into Phil.

Sherry got out her laptop and found the original V story on the *New York Times* website. She got out a pad of paper and wrote down the locations and the dates for the poisonings. The first one was the one Trick worked on in South Carolina. Then came Corning, New York, New Orleans, Tucson, and St. Louis. St. Louis hit Sherry hard. She'd seen Phil and Ralph boarding a plane to St. Louis a couple of days before the poisoning. At the time Sherry had thought it was odd. Phil just got back from a trip to St. Louis. Why was he going back, and how did Ralph fit in?

Sherry remembered Phil had taken a trip to Arizona around the time of the Tucson poisoning. She ran and got her diary out of its hiding place and checked the dates. Phil's trip to Arizona was the week before the poisoning. She paged back to what she'd written about Trick meeting Phil at Andy's. She found her account of Phil reacting oddly. Also, she had an entry about Phil and Ralph taking a trip to South Carolina. It was to Spartanburg and Charleston not Savannah. But the dates might have linked up with the poisoning Trick was investigating.

Could Phil be V? She didn't think so. Still, with a little investigation, she'd placed him in the right locations at roughly the right time for three of the poisonings. Then she remembered the first time she'd seen Phil at the library with the book *Poisons of the World*. She remembered thinking it was odd. Phil taught American history. Wait, the poison Trick's people identified came from a Central or South American frog. Another piece fell into place for Sherry. Phil took a trip to Panama and Costa Rica before all this started. They probably had poison frogs there too. She checked on the internet. Yep, there were poison dart frogs in Costa Rica.

Sherry closed her laptop. This was too weird to even think about. She liked Phil, maybe even loved him. They were getting close, no doubt about it. And now she was making the case he was a criminal mastermind. She told herself it was all circumstantial evidence. She didn't have hard facts. Maybe she wasn't right about the times he tensed up. Lots of people probably were in St. Louis, Arizona, and South Carolina at those times. Had those same people taken Central American trips before their travels in the US? No, Sherry's notions of how probabilities worked told her there wouldn't be too many of those people.

It was like a math problem. Suppose a tenth of the people in the US went to St. Louis during the year, and a tenth of the people in the US went to South Carolina in a year, then one in a hundred were in both St. Louis and South Carolina. Adding Arizona to the mix, would bring the probability of all three places down by a factor of 10. And factoring in the Central American trip made the probability of all four things tiny. Her original tenth was probably way too big, too.

Phil couldn't be V. Sherry didn't think he could poison anyone. He was kind and considerate. Her mother had called him a real gentleman, and Sherry had thought it was a good description. Then again, her mother thought Phil was hiding something. If he was V, she was surely right.

~ 60 ~

AT HIS STORE, RALPH SHOWED Phil the website taking nominations for V's next victim. The list was long. In fact, it was much longer than reasonable. It included people he'd rejected. And it included people who weren't like V's victims at all. Apparently, a few nominators didn't understand what it meant to get off on a technicality. Most importantly, it included Jake McMahan. The website listed the url for a short story Sally had run on the court hearing and the reason for the small fine. Phil remembered her saying Jake's father had been incredibly mad at her for the story.

"Scroll down to the comments," Ralph said.

Phil found the comments. There were about fifty of them for the Jake McMahan nomination. They read like internet comments. Some were calm and sensible. Others were over the top and nasty. When he finished, Phil said, "This is wonderful. These people think Jake deserves to be punished. There is a clear theme. This guy's a no good who got away with a crime."

"And I think the guy who runs this website is going to finish up with a contest. He's going to ask people to vote for the nominee they think is most deserving of punishment."

"So, we should stuff the ballot box for Jake, right?"

"No, we are a fly on the wall, remember," Ralph said. "There'll be no ballot box stuffing. Look, this is already working better than we ever expected. And remember those comments. I've read the comments on the other cases. They're more mixed. Jake's leaving the scene, a crime itself, allowed him to get off. The whole thing bothers people. I think he'll do well in the vote without any ballot box stuffing."

"So, we're having our fifteen minutes of fame. At the same time, we can't tell anyone about it."

"Exactly right, except maybe it's a whole half hour. If you google V, you get an incredible number of hits. This is big. Op-ed writers from most of the major newspapers are starting to write about it. There are even commentaries about it in a few European papers."

"I had no idea it'd be so big," Phil said. "I guess I didn't factor in all the websites covering things like this."

"It strikes a chord with lots of people. And it gets people going on both sides. That's what's so interesting to me. People are split on V. People love him, and other people hate him."

"I know. Sherry and I had a talk about it. She's a V hater. She thinks the V stands for vigilante, and she doesn't want to live in a world with vigilante justice."

"How did you respond?"

"I guess I came off like a professor," Phil answered. "I tried to get her to see the other side. I told her because of what had happened with Jake, I could empathize with those who supported V. In the end, I sided with those who didn't think guys like V should be out there."

"Sounds tame enough. You professors are good at seeing both sides of issues."

"Has it come up with Beth?"

"Yes, and you can put her on the side of those who are not fans of V. And since I'm not a professor, I agreed with her."

"Good thinking."

~ 61 ~

ON HER BREAK AT THE library, Sherry looked at *Poisons of the World*. Sure enough, there was a write up on poison dart frogs. It didn't say whether anyone could purchase the poison. Sherry went back to her desk and searched the internet for poison dart frogs. Most of the recent stories were related to the V story, including the *Times* story with Trick's interview. The rest of the stories were either for biologists or for people who wanted to have the frogs as pets in their terrariums. She didn't learn anything useful.

Sherry decided to do more investigation. She placed a call to Beth Watson, Ralph's girlfriend. Since Beth had an evening shift, they agreed to meet at a break room at the hospital.

Sherry hadn't been in the local hospital. The receptionist gave her directions to the break room. Beth waited for her there.

"It's nice to meet you," Sherry said as they shook hands.

"You too. I feel like we have a connection. Ralph thinks Phil is really taken with you."

"And Phil has mentioned similar things about you and Ralph. He's happy his friend found someone."

"While I'm not supposed to tell anyone, we're going to move in together next month. Actually, I guess next month starts next week."

"Wow, how exciting," Sherry said. "It's a big step."

"We think we're ready. I hope we're right."

"I have a few questions I want to ask. I hope you don't mind," Sherry said.

"Okay." Beth had a quizzical look on her face.

"I know Phil and Ralph have been taking short trips together. I wonder if you know about any of them."

"Sure. The first one was to South Carolina. I was just getting to know Ralph before we were dating, I think. Anyway, I sure heard a lot about the BMW plant down there. I thought it was nice of Phil to arrange the trip. Ralph's store is a big responsibility. I think the South Carolina trip was Ralph's first vacation in a long time."

"Do you know of any other trips?"

"Ralph doesn't talk about the other trips. I think there have been at least a couple more. They've been short. I do know he went with Phil to New Orleans in the fall. He brought me back Mardi Gras beads."

Sherry got very excited. "Do you remember the dates for the New Orleans trip?"

"Not off the top of my head, but I could find out. I keep a diary. I'd have the dates there."

"Thanks, here's my card. You can leave a message with the dates at this number. I would really appreciate it."

"Why are you so interested?"

"I'd rather not say at this minute. And please don't tell Ralph about my questions. I don't want Phil to think I'm checking up on him or anything."

"You are, aren't you?"

Sherry paused. "Yes, I guess I am, and I'm sorry I can't tell you why. Look, I'll make you a promise. If anything comes of this investigation of mine, you'll be the first person I'll tell."

"Is Ralph in trouble?"

"No, no trouble. In fact, it's probably nothing at all. I'm just curious. Phil and I might be getting serious. I want to know more about him."

"I knew his wife very well. She was super. He's lonely now. He's been great helping out at Ralph's store. Still, I can tell he's lonely."

"Yes, and I think he's a great guy. I haven't had very good luck with men, and I want to be sure."

Walking away from her meeting with Beth, Sherry thought about her math problem. She'd forgotten Phil's trip to New Orleans. If the dates from Beth fit, and she was almost sure they would, the likelihood a person who went to Central America and then was in South Carolina, New Orleans, Arizona and St. Louis around the time of the poisonings was tiny. She doubted anyone other than Phil Philemon would fit all those requirements. Phil was V. She was almost sure of it now. And Corning was a short drive away. Phil could have gone there a bunch of times. There'd be no way of checking.

As she drove home from the hospital, she wondered what she should do with her information. If she was sure about what she said about vigilantes, it was clear. She should call her brother and give him her information. It would make Trick famous. How did knowing Phil was V make her feel about her anti-vigilante stance? She really liked him. It was hard to square V with the man she knew. He was one of the gentlest people she'd ever encountered. He was always considerate, always polite, and had friends who cared for him deeply. Most men were such creeps. Phil wasn't a creep at all.

~~~

When Sherry got to the library the next morning, she picked up her phone and retrieved her messages. As she had expected, the dates Beth gave her for the New Orleans trip were right when the poisoning happened. And Beth added dates for a short trip Ralph and Phil had taken to Arizona in January. Two other shoes had clearly fallen. She knew they were in St. Louis, New Orleans, and Arizona exactly when the poisonings had happened. And they were in South Carolina when the poisoning happened. They said Charleston, not Savannah or Hilton Head, but things weren't far apart in South Carolina. She knew nothing about Corning. His weird reaction to the early discussion of the South Carolina poisoning made the case stronger.

Sherry decided to wait a week before she did anything. This was too big to simply blurt out. And she might need at least a week to figure out what to do with her information. It would be weird to see Phil at their Friday lunch.

~ *62* ~

PHIL AND RALPH GATHERED REGULARLY in the back of the store to check the reactions to V. As with all other stories, V got shoved off the front pages. It came back when a guy in Idaho came forward claiming to be V. The story faded fast when it was discovered he'd turned himself in several other times for sensational crimes. Also, a guy from Nebraska was stopped when he tried to buy dart-frog poison in Brazil. It wasn't close to Costa Rica, so Phil was relieved. There would probably be other attempts by copycats. It came with the territory. They couldn't do anything about it.

They had the most fun watching the results of the voting on the site with the nominations for V's next victim. Much to their delight, Jake McMahan did very well. He ended up second when the voting stopped. They thought about mentioning this site to Sally, but it wasn't the kind of thing a fly on the wall would do. They hoped Jake knew about his popularity.

A few days after the voting stopped, Ralph told Phil he was sure Jake knew about it. "We have several Facebook friends in common, and his coming in second in the poll is all over their posts. Jake didn't take too kindly to this. He got mad at one of the guys. The guy seemed to think it's a joke. Jake didn't take it that way. It looks like we got under his skin."

"Hallelujah," Phil said. "I knew I liked the internet. It's made historical research much easier. This social media is another whole thing. It's working to our advantage."

"Yes, it is. People all over the country, including all his so-called friends, know Jake got off on a technicality. And lots of them think he deserves to be punished. If nothing else, this should make him very nervous."

"I wanted to get back at Jake when I started this, terrorize him. Somewhere along the line it changed. It became something bigger. I think every one of our victims deserved what they got. I sort of liked being a vigilante. Now it's out of my system. I'm done."

"Good, because you've lost your sidekick. Beth and I are moving in together this weekend. I'm not about to go all around the country poisoning people. I want to stay home and enjoy life."

"Wow, this weekend. Do you need help moving?" Phil asked.

"No, a bunch of friends have already volunteered. I'm actually moving into Beth's apartment, and I don't have much—at least much worth moving. I've been throwing out stuff for the last month. I'm giving away my pots and pans. There's no reason to duplicate what she's already got. And most of her things are better than mine."

~~~

At lunch on Friday with Sherry, Phil learned she and Beth had cooked up a plan. On Monday evening, Phil and Sherry were going to pick up pizza so they could be Ralph and Beth's first house guests.

"I didn't know you knew Beth," Phil said.

"We've gotten acquainted recently. She seems very nice, and she is beyond thrilled to have Ralph moving into her place."

"He's looking forward to it, too. He only announced the move to me a couple of days ago."

"Beth said the plans have been in the works for a while. I think she was more eager to finalize things than him. Eventually he came around."

"He said he got rid of a lot of stuff. By their age, you collect a lot. I think he's lived in the same apartment for close to ten years."

"How long have you lived in your house?" Sherry asked.

"Gosh, it's been more than twenty-five years. We got our house the second year I taught here. I'd hate to think how long it would take me to pack up."

"Well, I travel light. I moved around a lot in New York City. I did have a place in State College. I got rid of lots of my belongings when I moved in with Mom. Her house is jammed full, so there wasn't much room for me to bring anything."

~ 63 ~

ON MONDAY EVENING, PHIL PICKED up the pizzas at Andy's and then got Sherry. When they arrived at Beth's apartment, Ralph greeted them at the door. Phil and Sherry took the tour. It was a surprisingly spacious two-bedroom place. One of the bedrooms was still full of boxes. Ralph told them it was going to be an office/computer room. The other bedroom didn't look as if it had been changed much by Ralph's arrival. Phil and Sherry complimented Beth on how nice the apartment looked.

Beth had four places set at the table. Sherry had brought a bottle of wine, and Beth produced both a corkscrew and four wine glasses.

Ralph said, "It's a good thing I moved in here; we'd have been out of luck for wine glasses at my old place."

"We'd have brought beer to your old place," Phil said.

"Beer would've worked," Ralph replied.

"Eat your pizza and drink out of a glass. You're getting civilized now," Beth said with a laugh.

After they finished eating, Sherry, who'd been silent throughout the meal, got up and opened her briefcase. Phil thought, *That's odd. I've never seen her with one before.*

"Take a seat over in the living room everyone. I have a little presentation for you."

Ralph looked at Beth. "Did you know about this?"

"Listen to the lady, Ralph; take a seat. In fact, why don't you and Phil sit on the couch. I'll take the chair."

Sherry handed them each a sheet of paper titled "Phil and Ralph's Adventures." It listed destinations and dates for trips either Phil or both of them had taken this last year. It started with Phil's Central American trip and ended with their joint trip to St. Louis. The trips were listed on the left side of the paper. They were not evenly spaced on the page, but they were in chronological order.

Sherry looked at Beth. "It turns out you both are involved with women who write in their diaries almost every night. Are the dates right?"

Phil and Ralph looked at each other and nodded. "Yes, I don't remember the exact dates. These are close enough," Phil said.

Sherry took out another bunch of papers from her briefcase and took off the paper clip. She handed out these papers.

Phil gasped when he saw a list of V's poisonings on the other paper. This list was down the left-hand half of the paper too.

"Hold the two pages side-by-side," Sherry said.

Phil and Ralph did as they were told. The two pages lined up nicely. The entry for Michael Miller, Corning, New York lined up with a blank space on the Phil and Ralph's Adventures sheet. Otherwise the names and places lined up with the trips. Phil and Ralph were stunned. They stared at the pages and didn't look up.

Sherry finally got impatient. "So, what do you have to say for yourselves? Phil, tell me I'm wrong."

Phil took a moment to compose himself. He finally looked up. "I can't."

"I've got all sorts of questions," Sherry said. "To start out, I want to know how, and then I want to know why. Phil, tell me how."

"All right. First, I got the poison in Costa Rica. I guess you figured that."

"Right."

"Each time we targeted a victim, we made two trips. Your sheet with the trips leaves a couple out. First, I would go and plant our surveillance equipment. I'd put cameras around the target's house. Most times I also planted a device to intercept phone calls. We needed to get a sense of what was happening—when the victim came and went. We'd leave the equipment up for a week or more. Does that answer the how question?"

"Yes, before you go on, where did you get this equipment?"

"Procuring equipment was Ralph's department," Phil said.

"It's all readily available on the internet. Lots of houses have surveillance cameras. They're meant to be aimed away from the house. We ordered the smallest ones and turned them around. Aimed them at the house. They'll sell them to anyone," Ralph said.

"Go on, what did you do next?"

"After we retrieved our equipment, looked at our video, and listened to their phone calls, we found these people have habits, patterns of behavior making them very vulnerable to someone like us. They ordered pizza every Monday night, went swimming every afternoon, or went to their fishing hole almost every day. On the second trip we planted the poison, and then we left. Most of the time, we were miles away when they actually came into contact with the poison."

"You broke into people's homes, and you even shot one of them with a tranquilizer gun," Sherry said.

"Yes," Phil said. "We broke all kinds of laws."

"If it makes any difference, we didn't like shooting the guy with the tranquilizer. We had to," Ralph said.

"Had to?" Beth said. "I don't see how you had to do any of this."

Ralph hung his head. An awkward silence followed.

After a few minutes Phil asked, "You said you had lots of questions. What's next?"

"I think I know the answer for this. How did you pick your targets? You didn't know any of these people, did you?"

"I searched the internet, mostly in newspaper archives. You can use key words like 'got off on a technicality' or 'search without a warrant.' It took a lot of time. It wasn't a problem. I've spent a lot of hours in libraries and archives in my time."

"So, it was like a research project for you?" Sherry asked.

"Yes, the first few weeks after Mary Jane was killed, I didn't know what to do, and then after the trial I completely lost it. When I finally started to function, I knew I needed a project. I needed a focus. I got fascinated with cases where people evaded justice because of legal technicalities."

"Fascinated I understand, but you poisoned these people. You caused them serious harm."

"We didn't target just anyone. Every one of our victims was a murderer. These were bad people. They killed someone. They deserved to face justice."

"Let's turn to the why," Sherry said. "Why did you think you were appointed to be the ones to see justice was done?"

"Like I said, it starts with the Jake McMahan trial. I was devastated. I couldn't do anything. I don't know if you know I was out of control in the court room. I shouted, and I threatened Jake right in front of the crowded court room. I don't know what I would have said or done if Ralph and Jeremy hadn't hustled me out of there."

"I've heard the story. It didn't seem like you at all," Sherry said.

"You're right, it wasn't like me. Anyway, I couldn't directly get at Jake. I would be the prime suspect. But I could get at people like him. Actually, like I said, we picked people who were worse than Jake. Our victims were cold-blooded murderers who got away with it. My original idea was to terrorize Jake by making him think he might be the next one poisoned."

"And it worked, too," Ralph said. "I don't know if you know about the site collecting nominations for V's next victims. Jake got nominated, and he was very high on the vote for the next victim. The chatter on Facebook shows he's upset, and maybe even a little afraid."

"So, you're proud of yourselves," Beth said.

"Yes, a little, I guess," Ralph said. "We had a project, and we finished it. I know Phil was really into the Jake revenge thing—for me it was two things. First, I wanted to help Phil. He was in terrible shape. I would have climbed Mount Everest with him if he wanted to. Second, I thought all our targets were real scumbags. They murdered people, and they got off. They deserved what we did to them."

"Why you?"

Phil responded, "I don't know. How does anyone know how they get an idea? I wondered if Jake getting off on a technicality was unusual. I found it wasn't. I felt people like that should be punished. So why not me?"

"So why not you, huh." Sherry turned and paced around the apartment. When she got back in front of the couch, she said, "So why V?"

"It was a last-minute decision. The idea was to catch the attention of the *New York Times* reporter. I thought an unsigned list of urls might not work. I gave him a name."

"What does V stand for?"

"Actually nothing. There are five victims, so it could be the Roman numeral for five. When we talked about it before you thought it was vigilante, but it could even be for vengeance, or even victory. I simply like V," Phil said.

"Victory?"

"Yes, victory. Our project is complete. It's over, and we thought we'd won."

"So, you thought you got away with it?" Sherry asked.

Phil looked up at her. "Yes, we thought we got away with it."

Sherry turned and walked toward the table, pivoted and walked back toward the two men shaking on the couch. It was eerily quiet in the apartment.

Finally, Phil said, "What happens now?"

Sherry did another walk around the room. When she came back in front of the couch, she said, "What happens now? What happens now is I want to use you two guys. I've got a project for you."

Turn the page for an exciting preview of the next book in the series...

Guilty Until Proven Innocent

Chapter One

At 11:00 p.m., Phil Philemon and Ralph Williams collected the camera they'd installed the night before. Back in their hotel room, they were pleased with the clear picture of the front of the brownstone housing the Smith, Banbridge, and Sites law firm.

"Can you fast forward to see if there's a night watchman?" Phil asked.

"We didn't use a motion-activated camera because of the traffic. I'll have to do it manually." Ralph stopped fast forwarding at the point where they could see a security firm's car pull up.

"Back it to when he gets there," Phil said.

"Okay, okay, I'm on it. There's not much light on the street. I almost didn't see the car."

"Sorry, I don't know why I'm so nervous. We haven't actually done anything yet."

The security guy got out of his car and entered the building. He typed a code into the keypad to gain entry. They could see his flashlight passing by windows. Finally, he left.

"He got there at one-thirty, and left by one-fifty. Let's see if he comes back." Ralph switched to fast forward. The security guard didn't show again, so Ralph didn't slow the video until people started arriving for work. When the first person approached the building, he switched to slow motion. After watching the guy enter, they both shook their heads in disappointment.

"He's very security conscious," Phil said. "He cupped his hands around the keypad. There's no way we could see what he typed."

"Yeah, we'll have to hope everyone isn't as careful."

After three more disappointments, the fifth person came with a bundle under one arm so she couldn't mask what she entered.

"Bingo, I got it… three, seven, three, four," Ralph said.

"Yes, I got the same. Rewind it, I want to be absolutely sure."

"Okay, let's look at her again. Also, we better hope we get another shot. While I know it's unlikely, there might be different codes for different people."

There were only two other employees of Smith, Bainbridge and Sites who were sloppy about their use of the keypad. Phil and Ralph got three, seven, three, four each time.

"We have what we need." Phil walked away from the computer screen. "What do you want to do in Milwaukee? We've got most of tomorrow to kill."

"I looked on the web. I'm most interested in the Harley Davidson Museum. What about you?"

"I want to see the Frank Lloyd Wright houses. There's a whole block of houses he designed called the Burnham Block. They give tours."

"Houses don't do it for me. So, I guess we'll go our separate ways."

"All right, after breakfast tomorrow we'll split up."

The next morning Phil looked at himself in the mirror before breakfast. What he saw didn't entirely please him. He still had clear blue eyes, but at sixty, he sagged in places. Also, he didn't like his hair. Balding or graying were in a race, and he didn't think the in-between looked good. At least he'd been able to keep his weight down, so at a fraction under six feet he appeared thin. He shook his head. He remembered his mother saying, "Getting old isn't for sissies."

He got to the hotel's breakfast before Ralph, so he sat down and waited. When Ralph arrived, he took a good look at his friend as he walked toward the table. Clearly living with Beth had improved Ralph's appearance. They'd been exercising. As a result, Ralph had shed ten or fifteen pounds. Ralph measured only five nine, and Phil had always thought of him as pudgy. Not true anymore. Also, it appeared Beth had changed his wardrobe and hair. He had new clothes and a new haircut. His sandy-colored hair looked neater than Phil remembered. Phil recognized he'd be considered the dowdy looking one of the pair.

It didn't make him feel good.

After breakfast they went their separate ways. Phil got back to the hotel at four. He'd enjoyed the Frank Lloyd Wright houses. After eating at a nice sandwich shop for lunch, he'd wandered around the city. He'd grown up in a small town, and he always found cities fascinating. When he got back, he took an hour-long nap. He wanted to be well rested for the night's events.

At 11:30 that night, Phil and Ralph approached Smith, Banbridge, and Sites with their collapsible ladder in a carrying case. The case looked like a regular suitcase not like a ladder. Ralph entered the code in the keypad, and they got right in. They took the stairs to the third floor. While the building had some years on it, the interior had been upgraded, with lots of glass and chrome.

"Samuel Turbridge, right?" asked Ralph.

"Yep, he's the one."

They entered the first room in Turbridge's suite. "The secretary sits here," Phil said. "And his office is through the door."

Ralph turned on the flashlight on his phone and looked at the ceiling briefly. "Get the ladder; I think I see where we can plant the first camera."

Phil took the ladder out of its case, unfolded it, and handed it to Ralph. Ralph then put the ladder below the sprinkler in the middle of the ceiling. He climbed the ladder and mounted the tiny camera in the sprinkler. "It fits," Ralph explained. "Using the camera with sound recordings makes it a tight fit. No one will see it. People never look at sprinklers. They're part of the background."

"I hope you're right. Even in the dark, I can see the camera."

"You're looking for it," Ralph said. "I'm going to mount the other camera the same place in the inner office. Why don't you go check to see if anything is happening on the street?"

Phil headed back toward the stairwell. It had a window looking onto the street below. When he got to the window, Phil could see the security guard's car parked in front. The guard had just entered the code on the keypad. Phil ran back to Ralph. "The security guard's about to come in the building," he whispered.

"I'm done. There's no way we can get out of here."

About the Author

Robert Archibald was born in New Jersey and grew up in Oklahoma and Arizona. After receiving a BA from the University of Arizona, he was drafted and served in Viet Nam. He then earned an M.S. and Ph.D in economics from Purdue University. Bob had a 41-year career at the College of William and Mary. While he had several stints as an administrator, department chair, director of the public policy program, and interim dean of the faculty, Bob was always proud to be promoted back to the faculty. He lives with his wife of 47 years, Nancy, in Williamsburg, Virginia.

CPSIA information can be obtained
at www.ICGtesting.com
Printed in the USA
FFHW010022170819
54328071-60021FF